OBSESSION

USA TODAY BESTSELLING AUTHOR

T.K. LEIGH

OBSESSION

Published by Carpe Per Diem, Inc

Edited by Kim Young, Kim's Editing Services

Cover Design: Cat Head Biscuit, Inc., Santa Clarita, CA

Cover assets:

© Pugavica88

Used under license from Deposit Photos.

BOOKS BY T.K. LEIGH

ROMANTIC SUSPENSE

The Temptation Series

Temptation

Persuasion

Provocation

Obsession

The Inferno Saga

Part One: Spark

Part Two: Smoke

Part Three: Flame

Part Four: Burn

CONTEMPORARY ROMANCE

The Redemption Duet

Commitment

Redemption

The Possession Duet

Possession

Atonement

The Dating Games Series

Dating Games

Wicked Games

Mind Games

Dangerous Games

Royal Games

Tangled Games

For more information on any of these titles and upcoming releases, please visit T.K.'s website:

www.tkleighauthor.com

PROLOGUE
(END OF PROVOCATION)

Julia

"I'm going to kill him." Lachlan's voice was eerily calm as he stared into space. "But first, I'm going to make him suffer for every woman he hurt. For Piper. For Claire. For all of them. By the time I'm done with him, he's going to be begging me to put him out of his misery."

"Lachlan..."

When I placed my hand on his leg, his gaze shot to mine, snapping out of whatever trance he was in.

"It could be nothing, like Ethan said." I flashed Ethan a smile, begging him to help me talk Lachlan down from choosing a course of action he'd eventually come to regret. "There's nothing definitive here. So what? Daxton was born only seven months after his parents married. Nine months after his mother filed an incident report alleging sexual assault."

"Sexual assault that has your ex-husband's signature all over it," Lachlan snipped back.

"True." I inhaled a calming breath, attempting to be the voice of reason when it felt like all reason had officially left the room. "But that still doesn't mean—"

"And how about the fact he obviously knew Autumn Quinn?" he spat, nostrils flaring, spittle forming in the corners of his mouth. "Is that also a coincidence? Not to mention he just so happens to volunteer for a fucking prison program and has had access to your ex. Is *that* all a coincidence, too?"

Hearing footsteps padding on the second floor, I glanced over my shoulder at the stairs before refocusing my attention on Lachlan, lowering my voice. "Please keep it down. For Imogene. She can't know about this. Not yet."

He squeezed his eyes shut, digging his fingers through his hair. "I introduced them."

"Who?"

"Dax and Piper. And Claire." He laughed to himself. "I should have—"

"We still don't know anything for certain." I held his gaze for a moment before facing Ethan again.

"With this new...development, is that enough to involve the FBI? Or, at the very least, reopen the investigation into Claire's death? And perhaps Autumn's?" I gestured to her photo.

"I put a call into Agent Curran this morning and am waiting to hear back. I'm sure he'll be of the same mindset we are." Ethan glanced at Lachlan. "That it *is* suspicious."

"Damn straight it is," he growled.

"Still... Whatever we do, we need to be delicate about this."

Ethan looked toward the front windows as sirens blared in the distance. It was strange to hear them this far out in the suburbs. Then again, as I'd learned, bad shit could happen anywhere.

"Daxton isn't your run-of-the-mill criminal. If he *is* the one behind this, he's gotten away with it for five years now. And with his wealth, he has limitless resources that have probably helped him do that. Based on the profile I've put together over the months, I'm all but certain he's already several steps ahead of us. We need to be careful to not... poke the beast." He gave Lachlan a knowing look, eyebrow raised.

"What are you getting at?"

"You can't just go into his office and accuse him of being a goddamn serial killer. We need ironclad evidence. Need to try to...catch him in the act."

"Catch him in the act?" Lachlan shot back with a disbelieving laugh. "So... What? We're supposed to wait until October thirteenth and hope we know exactly when and where he plans on killing another innocent woman?"

"Without definitive evidence implicating him otherwise, I don't see any other option," Ethan argued as the sirens grew closer.

With each second that passed, my pulse increased. Hearing sirens wasn't an odd occurrence. Not in this city. There were areas of Atlanta that had pretty high crime rates. Still, I couldn't shake the premonition deep in my gut that something horrible was about to happen.

When the sirens came to a stop in front of my house, tires screeching, I knew it for certain.

"Mama!" Imogene shouted, darting down the stairs, eyes wide, panicked. "What's going on?"

"I don't know, baby." I wrapped her in my arms, a chill washing over me when an incessant knock sounded from my front door.

"Julia Prescott? Georgia State Patrol. I'm here to do a welfare check. It's important I speak with you immediately."

Heart in my throat, I swung my eyes to Lachlan's, both of us frozen in place.

"Please, ma'am. This is an emergency. I need to make sure both you and your daughter are okay."

Without waiting for me to give him permission, Lachlan strode toward the front door, while Ethan calmly collected his papers, returning them to his file. I kept my arm around Imogene, our steps slow as we walked into the foyer.

Lachlan pulled open the door, a large, Black man in a state trooper's uniform standing there. Recognition briefly flashed in his gaze when he saw Lachlan. Then he shifted his eyes to Imogene and me, a hint of relief within before his expression turned stoic once more.

Removing his hat, he squared his shoulders. "Ma'am, I'm Captain Patrick Dawson of the Georgia State Patrol."

I nodded slightly, not saying anything, fear snaking through me with every second that passed.

"I regret to be the one to inform you..." He glanced at Imogene before returning his gaze to mine, "but at approximately seven hundred hours this morning, the prison transport vehicle carrying Domenic Jaskulski crashed, resulting in several casualties."

I exhaled a tiny breath. "Nick's...dead?" Hope filled my voice, desperate to hear those words fall from his lips.

He slowly shook his head. "No, ma'am." He swallowed hard. "The prisoner... He wasn't found in the wreckage."

My breathing increased, heart racing as tremors overtook my body. Imogene tightened her hold on me, tears filling her eyes.

"What are you saying?"

"Your ex-husband has escaped custody and his whereabouts are currently unknown."

CHAPTER ONE

Nick

The constant sound of helicopters and sirens wailing in the distance settled over the suburban community, neighbors stopping neighbors in the grocery store parking lot to comment on how scary it was.

How they struggled to comprehend how something like this could happen.

How they planned to go home and pray "that horrible man" was found.

How they'd also pray for his wife's and daughter's safety.

Domenic Jaskulski never understood how someone could truly believe all they had to do was pray and everything would be resolved.

He'd tried that when he was younger.

But no amount of praying ever rectified his situation.

"Pray all you want," he muttered, laughing to himself as two women passed, looking his way and smiling. Yet they didn't recognize him. "It's not going to help."

The women walked to their separate cars, putting their groceries into the trunk before driving out of the lot. He briefly considered following the blonde with the obviously fake lips and augmented breasts, just to see the look on her face when he asked if she thought praying would help when he had her tied up, a knife marring her skin.

But she wasn't what Nick desired. He had very particular tastes. He either did this right or not at all.

That was another lesson he was forced to learn early in life.

Settling into the seat of the work truck, he resumed his search, listening to the morning news on the radio. As expected, the main story of the day was his escape.

And, as the media was prone to do, they reported it to death, telling the world of his supposed crimes, causing mass hysteria and panic in the immediate area surrounding where he'd escaped custody.

But the authorities could comb through those woods for hours. Days.

They wouldn't find anything.

Well, that wasn't entirely true.

They'd eventually find his prison jumpsuit, socks, and slippers.

Nick had made sure of it.

Then the trail would go cold.

He had made sure of that, too.

As the reporter went on to detail Nick's crimes of stalking, raping, and murdering women, the terminology Nick took issue with, he kept his attention focused on the parking lot, more and more people arriving to do their weekly shopping, mostly women, some with kids in tow.

Which was why Nick chose this location for his...surveillance.

And the work truck that had been waiting was the perfect cover vehicle. No one questioned seeing a work truck sitting in a parking lot. Over the years, Nick had learned most people were completely oblivious to their surroundings, too consumed by their own lives to open their eyes and look around.

It was this lack of awareness he often used for his own purposes.

Like he planned to do today.

As he analyzed every person coming and going from the grocery store, he kept a clipboard in front of him to make it appear as if he were writing up a report from his latest job. In a way, he was. Or he would be once he found what he was looking for. Although the longer he sat here, the more he worried he never would.

He was about to give up and try a different location, perhaps a gym or beauty salon, when he finally saw her.

Long, blonde hair. Mid-thirties. Face sporting a touch of makeup, but her natural beauty didn't require much. She was dressed in capri pants and a tight fitting tank top, giving the impression she'd just come from the gym.

Nick sat up, spine straight, slight smile curling his lips

when she stopped her cart by a dark SUV just a few spots down and across the aisle, allowing him the perfect view as she loaded her groceries into her car.

Once she was finished, she pushed her cart to one of the return areas, a rarity Nick had noticed over the past few hours. Most people just left them in the parking lot, too selfish to push their cart a few extra feet.

Not this woman, though.

Which confirmed that she was perfect.

Compassionate.

Agreeable.

Subservient.

Returning to her car, the woman jumped into the driver's seat and cranked the ignition, reversing out of her spot before making her way out of the parking lot.

Nick sat there a moment, not wanting to be obvious. But she was too perfect to let out of his sight for long. She even looked like Julia. Same eyes. Same smile. Same petite build. She'd have to do until he could get to the real thing.

A practice run, so to speak.

Slowly pulling out of his spot, he followed the SUV onto the busy, commercial street lined with shops, restaurants, and big-box stores.

Nick had only been in prison seven years, but he barely recognized the world around him anymore. Everyone seemed to be in a hurry. At every stop light, people immediately took out their phones to check their texts or social media. If they just looked up, perhaps they'd recognize him, since his face was plastered all over the news.

But they never did.

It truly was remarkable.

And it emboldened him to take more risks than he'd originally planned.

Like right now.

After a mile of doing his best to keep the SUV in sight through all the cars on the road, the area eventually gave way to condominiums. The woman slowed, turning into a subdivision.

Nick followed.

Without the luxury of heavy traffic to act as a buffer, he drove slower, keeping as much distance between his car and hers as he was comfortable with.

He followed her through a series of turns, the houses becoming larger the farther into the development they drove. Finally, she pulled into the driveway of a three-story brick building that screamed upper middle class.

It reminded him of the home he and Julia had shared in Charleston.

He had always worked hard to give her everything she needed. Everything she deserved.

How could she throw it all away?

How could she say it didn't matter?

How could she move on?

Because Nick hadn't moved on. Hadn't forgotten.

And he'd be damned if he'd allow Julia to move on.

They'd made promises to each other. "Till death do us

part." Nick had every intention of ensuring Julia fulfilled her end.

Not wanting to bring attention to himself, Nick drove past the woman's house, turning around at the dead end and parking down the street and on the opposite side. The woman disappeared into the house, leaving the garage door wide open, allowing him a brief glimpse into her life.

The space was surprisingly neat, built-in cabinets lining the rear and one side. On the other wall, a tool cabinet sat beside a gun safe and a refrigerator that had seen better days.

After several minutes, the woman emerged through the door connecting the garage to the house, a man wearing a UGA hat, shirt, and shorts following. He was a walking billboard for Georgia's beloved Bulldogs.

Nick was too far away to pick up on their conversation, but judging from the body language, it was obvious the man was upset with the woman. Probably berating her for asking him to help with the groceries when he'd hoped to sit on the couch all day, drink beer, and watch the game.

She deserved better.

Deserved to be free from what was obviously a miserable marriage.

And Nick would do exactly that...

Free her.

CHAPTER TWO

Julia

I stared straight ahead. Not blinking. Not breathing. Not moving.

This couldn't be happening.

Any minute, I'd wake up and learn this was just a dream.

Or, more appropriately, a nightmare.

Just like the other day when I dreamed of Nick strangling me. That was all this was, too. Right?

But when I felt Imogene's arms around me, I knew this wasn't a dream. This was real.

My ex-husband had managed to escape custody.

My serial stalker, rapist, and murdering ex-husband.

My serial stalker, rapist, and murdering ex-husband who would love nothing more than to add me to his list of victims.

He was currently free, his whereabouts unknown.

A dizzying sensation consumed me, but I did my best to keep it together. For Imogene's sake.

I had to be strong... For Imogene's sake.

Had to remain in control... For Imogene's sake.

"How is this possible?" I squeaked out. "How could he escape?"

"I understand how upsetting this must be," Captain Dawson offered, his voice deep and commanding, yet still filled with compassion. "Investigators are still scouring through the crash scene to figure out the details. What we do know is that this morning, Domenic Jaskulski was being transported from the prison in Trion down to the diagnostic prison in Jackson. According to the warden, the prisoner had been exhibiting certain...behaviors that made him believe he may benefit from reclassification to a more secure unit.

"Approximately fifty miles in, the van went off the road and down an embankment. As I mentioned, investigators are still on the scene, piecing together what happened. Search dogs are combing through the wooded area and attempting to pick up his trail. Right now, we have no reason to suspect foul play."

"Really?" Lachlan scoffed, vein in his neck throbbing. He glanced at Imogene, struggling to temper his remarks. "A prison transport van carrying that bastard just so happens to go off the road and crash. Miraculously, he's the only one who manages to escape with his life. Probably without so much as a scratch on him, since he hasn't been located. And you don't think that screams foul play?"

"Until we find physical evidence supporting that theory, we need to base our determination on what we *do* know. In addition to Jaskulski, there were two other prisoners in the van, all three men chained and shackled. Since Jaskulski was sitting the farthest back from the source of impact, we believe that was what saved him. The guard in the front and the driver most likely died the instant the van hit a tree at what investigators believe to be full speed. It's possible the impact of the crash dislodged the restraint bar the prisoner was shackled to, allowing him to escape."

"Great. Bloody great."

"I appreciate what a shock this is." Captain Dawson turned his eyes toward mine. "How uneasy you must feel. Atlanta PD is fully aware of the situation and has assigned twenty-four-hour surveillance over these premises in the event Jaskulski attempts to pay you a visit."

I opened my mouth to respond, but Lachlan interjected.

"You think that's a comfort?"

"I understand you don't have the best...history with some people in the department."

"You've got that right," he muttered.

"But I can assure you, they're treating Ms. Prescott's safety with the highest level of importance. As is the GBI."

"GBI?" I asked, brows furrowed.

"Georgia Bureau of Investigation. They've been called in on this matter, as has the FBI and US Marshals. We're utilizing every resource possible to find Jaskulski and return him to custody. Most convicts don't last more than twenty-four hours on the run, the majority found in less than four."

Lachlan parted his lips, about to argue once more. But before he could, I placed a hand on his bicep, giving him a look of warning.

"Thank you, Captain Dawson." I passed him a congenial smile. "I appreciate your concern. And everything you're all doing to keep us safe."

"Of course, ma'am," he replied with a nod. "With your permission, I'd like to send a small team in here to do a thorough search of your house and property. Make sure he's not hiding somewhere."

"You think he could already be here?" My voice rose in pitch, hair on the back of my neck standing up. I couldn't shake the feeling someone was watching me. It couldn't have been Nick, though.

Could it?

The prison was about ninety miles from here. If the crash happened fifty miles away, that was still forty miles. The only way he'd be able to make that distance in such a short amount of time was if he had a car.

God, I prayed he didn't have a car.

The only thing that gave me anything remotely resembling peace of mind was the fact he was on foot. That he probably wouldn't be able to outrun the authorities.

That all changed if he had transportation.

"This is simply a routine check. Particularly after the

warden informed us of your meeting with him yesterday and the threats he made. So we'd like to take a look around."

I hugged myself, trying to ward off the chills trickling down my spine. "Of course."

"Thank you, ma'am." He turned, signaling a handful of uniformed officers hovering outside to enter my home.

As they headed in every direction, weapons drawn, all I could do was try to wrap my mind around this new reality.

Nick had escaped prison.

He was on the loose.

He could be anywhere.

"I, uh... I should probably go," Ethan said, cutting through my anxiety.

I flung my eyes to his. I'd forgotten he was even here. Forgotten everything he'd come over to share. That he'd found evidence connecting Daxton, one of the team owners, to not only these recent murders, but also Nick.

Circumstantial evidence, but evidence nonetheless.

"It looks like you have your hands full here. Plus, I could really use some sleep." He ran a hand over his weary face. "You'll be okay? Keep me updated if you hear anything?"

"Of course."

"Good." He stepped toward me, hugging me. "Be safe," he whispered shakily.

"I will."

He held me a moment before releasing me and

saying his goodbyes to Lachlan, then Imogene. It didn't matter they'd never met. He knew who she was. Hopefully with everything else going on, Imogene wouldn't ask who he was and what he was doing here. I wasn't sure how I'd explain it. I still struggled to make sense of it myself. Still wondered if Nick's escape was purely a coincidence or if it were directly related to my visit yesterday.

I feared it was.

Once Ethan left, Lachlan spun toward me, eyes intense. Determined. Fierce.

"Here's what we're going to do. We're going to California today, like we'd planned." He looked at Imogene. "All of us." He refocused his attention on me. "After the game Monday, I'll fly you and Imogene to Hawaii before coming back for the first game of the playoffs. Provided we win these next few games. You two will be safe there."

I blinked, mouth slackening, slowly shaking my head. "You want me to...leave?"

"Why wouldn't you? It's safer than staying here."

I gaped at him, not believing my ears. Then I faced Imogene, gritting out a smile.

"Can you give us a minute, sweetie? Stay where I can see you. I just need to speak with Lachlan for a moment."

"This involves me, too." She placed a hand on her hip, holding her head high, exuding confidence and determination. "I should be a part of the conversation and decision."

I gave her a look. My "mom look", as she often called it.

But unlike when she was a little girl, she didn't back

down. If anything, she held her head higher, eyebrow raised.

I wanted to tell her she was only fourteen and didn't get to make decisions yet. At least not like this. But over the years, she'd proven herself to be a very levelheaded teenager. I should at least listen to her thoughts on the situation.

"Fine."

I turned back toward Lachlan, expelling a sigh. "I appreciate your concern, but I'm not going to allow Nick to force me out of my home. Away from my friends. Away from my family. Going to California, then hiding in Hawaii for God knows how long while they try to find him?" I shook my head. "I won't do it. Not to mention, Londyn's in her third trimester. Considering she was one of his earliest assault victims, there's no telling what kind of stress this is causing her right now. What kind of stress this could cause the baby. If anything happens, I need to be close by. Not a nine-hour flight away."

"But she has Wes to watch out for her. Who will watch out for both of you when I'm not here?" He glanced at Imogene before returning his worried eyes to mine.

"I managed just fine before you, Lachlan."

My words came out more biting than I intended, but I wasn't going to take them back.

I'd survived everything Nick threw at me for years without anyone coming to my aid. I could do the same now. I didn't need some knight in shining armor to protect me or Imogene. I could do that myself.

"That was before your goddamn psycho ex escaped a fucking prison transport!"

Before Imogene could call him out on it, he reached into the pocket of his gym shorts and pulled out a few twenties, handing them to her.

"Paying in advance?" I remarked, the mood lightening momentarily.

"She charges me a higher rate because of who I am." He crossed his arms in front of his chest, a ghost of a smile playing on his lips as he feigned annoyance. "Complete bullshite if you ask me."

"Like I said... You can afford it, Hale," she teased.

I smiled, grateful for the brief moment of levity, then blew out a long sigh.

"Lachlan..." I placed my hands on his chest, the mood becoming serious once more. "It means a lot that you'll go through all that to keep us safe. But look around you." I stepped back, gesturing at our surroundings, my house swarming with cops. "Nick would be an idiot if he tried to come here. His face is probably plastered on every television within the state. Hell, across the country. He won't get far. You heard what Captain Dawson said. Most escaped convicts are apprehended within the first twenty-four hours."

Lachlan widened his stance. "Most escaped convicts aren't bloody geniuses like your ex-husband."

"It'll be fine. I'm sure he'll be back in prison by this time tomorrow." I forced a smile, attempting to offer him some sort of assurance.

When he didn't say anything, I added, "Please, Lachlan. Let me make this decision for myself. For Imogene. Don't let him chase us out of our home."

He studied me a moment longer, then relaxed his stance, exhaling deeply. "How about a compromise? I won't push California and Hawaii if you agree to stay at my place instead."

"I just got done telling you I refuse to allow Nick to run me away from my home. I—"

"And he's not," he attempted to placate me, running his hands down my arms.

"But—"

"I don't want you to think of my place as just mine. I'd like you to feel as if it's your home, too, love." He gave me a shy smile that chipped away at my resolve.

God, why did he have to have such a sexy smile? It was impossible to say no to him when he peered at me that way.

"Plus, the entire perimeter of my property is gated, making access quite difficult. There's also a top-of-the-line security system, complete with cameras at each entry point, as well as several along the exterior. So even when I *am* gone, I won't have to worry about your safety being left in the hands of a bunch of cops I don't trust to guard a pile of garbage."

I chewed on my lower lip as I contemplated his offer. I did like his house, especially the kitchen.

"He does have a great pool," Imogene offered in

support of Lachlan's proposal. "And that theater room is to die for."

"See." He playfully waggled his brows. "Imogene likes my plan."

I glared at both of them before pushing out a sigh. "Fine. We'll stay at your place. But it's only temporary."

In a heartbeat, it was as if a giant weight had lifted off Lachlan's shoulders. He wrapped his arms around me, pulling me against his chest.

"Thank you." The relief in his voice nearly broke me.

Then he reached out for Imogene, pulling her into our embrace.

It was just a hug, something people did all the time. But as we held each other in the middle of my kitchen, it felt so much deeper and more powerful than a simple hug.

Like the bonds of our embrace would protect us from anything, as long as we had each other.

I could only pray it would protect us from what I feared in my heart the future held.

CHAPTER THREE

Lachlan

"Is she okay? Julia? Imogene? How are they?" Nikko asked frantically when I answered the phone later that morning, not even allowing me a chance to say anything in greeting. "How did this happen? I called the second I could. My god, bruh. What the fuck?"

"They're fine," I assured him, glancing toward the kitchen from where I sat on the couch in the living room. My heart warmed at the sight of Julia walking from the island to the oven, a tray of muffin in her hands.

It didn't take long for her and Imogene to settle into my place, making it feel like a home, not just somewhere I slept whenever I was in town.

Within minutes of arriving, Imogene claimed one of the guest rooms, immediately ditching the décor I paid an interior decorator an obscene amount of money to design in favor of some of the things from her home that brought her comfort. And, as expected, Julia took over the kitchen, stocking the pantry with everything she needed. I told her she didn't need to cook, but as I recalled from Hawaii, baking was her happy place. Her stress reliever.

And that was precisely what she'd spent most of the morning doing.

About an hour ago, Wes and Londyn had stopped by to make sure Julia was okay. And probably to get a break from the cops stationed to watch their house, as well. It was obvious the situation caused Londyn quite a bit of unease, as it did all of us. All we could do was hope we'd soon get a phone call informing us Nick had been caught. It gave us some comfort to know Agent Curran had been asked to assist in tracking him down. Besides Nikko, he was one of the few law enforcement officials I actually *did* trust. When he vowed to do everything in his power to find Nick and keep Julia and Imogene safe, it wasn't an empty assurance. He would gladly risk his life to protect them.

Just like I would.

Taking a sip of water, I shifted my eyes to the sliding glass doors, watching Imogene and Eli kick a soccer ball around.

"They're safe. I moved them all over to my place for the time being."

This caught Nikko's attention. "You're in Atlanta? But you're supposed to be in California."

"One second, cousin," I said, then met Julia's gaze in

the kitchen, Londyn sitting on one of the barstools, Wes beside her.

I knew they hadn't told Londyn a lot of what was going on regarding the possibility of a copycat mirroring Nick's kill cycle. Because of that, this wasn't a discussion I could have out here.

"I'm heading down the hall to talk to Nikko for a second. You okay?"

Julia smiled. "I'm fine. Just another Saturday," she tried to assure me, although it was anything but.

"Another Saturday," I repeated, walking toward her and kissing the top of her head. Giving Londyn and Wes a smile, I made my way down the hallway and into my office, closing the door behind me.

"Sorry. Didn't want to have this conversation in front of an audience."

"What's going on?" he pressed.

"A lot."

I sighed, falling into the chair. I didn't even know how to begin to explain the events of the past week. "Remember how I mentioned Agent Curran had learned Claire had visited Nick on several occasions in the weeks leading up to her death, including the day before?"

"Of course."

"Ethan had been trying to figure out what they'd discussed. Combed through her notes and files. Unfortunately, he came up empty. So Curran paid Nick a visit himself."

"And what did he say?"

"That he'd share what he and Claire discussed... But he wanted something from Curran first."

"Why do I have a feeling I'm not going to like what he asked for?"

"Because I think you already know what that is."

"Julia?"

"He wanted her to visit him. I was against it. As was Wes." I shook my head, rage bubbling inside me at the reminder of everything I learned about Nick and Julia's relationship this week. All the messed-up shite he did to her...

"But Julia wanted to do it, didn't she?"

"She thought it might help. I tried to get her to see it was just Nick trying to manipulate her again. We got into a pretty heated argument over it. Even broke up for a bit. At least I think we did. Suffice it to say, it was a rough few days. So when Wes called to tell me when Julia planned to visit Nick..." I pushed out a breath, running a hand over my face. "Part of me regretted the way I'd left things with her. I thought if she was willing to confront her demons, the least I could do was be there for her. So I hopped on a flight back here."

"And how did the visit go?"

"Terrible. We got nothing out of him, other than the fact Claire seemed to focus on Nick's early years. Before he and Julia first met. Or met for the second time, since they were at the same foster home as kids."

"That's something, though."

"Ethan thought so, too. Started looking through Claire's things again. See if anything stood out."

"And did it?"

"Actually, yes."

"What?"

I heaved a sigh, then proceeded to run Nikko through everything Ethan had shared with us this morning.

How he'd uncovered an incident report from when Nick was a PhD student at Brown.

How a woman named Lucy Ellis reported a sexual assault that fit Nick's MO — leaving a night out with friends early after not feeling well, making it to her apartment, then not remembering anything until she woke up the following morning, only to discover blood between her legs, sore in places that shouldn't have been sore.

How the complaint was never pursued or investigated.

How Lucy ended up pregnant.

How she married a man named Alton Shea, then gave birth to a boy seven months later, naming him Daxton.

"Just because this report fits what we know about Nick doesn't mean—"

"There's more. Ethan found proof that Daxton knew Autumn Quinn, the copycat's first victim. The Emory student who volunteered at Homes for the Homeless. In fact, it appears Dax and Autumn dated."

"Again, that's—"

"Dax also volunteers with a prison outreach ministry. The same one that has visited Nick."

"Is there proof Dax visited Nick?" Nikko asked.

"Ethan's working on that."

There was a brief pause before Nikko sighed. "I won't deny it's suspicious, but I doubt any judge would sign an arrest warrant based on this information. There's no smoking gun, so to speak."

"Ethan also mapped out the kills. Want to know what he found out?"

"What's that?"

"While a majority of the kills occurred within a 200-mile radius of Atlanta, all the kills that took place outside his comfort zone, with one exception, occurred on a date the team had away games in that particular city."

"And the exception?"

I lowered my voice. "You know what it is, Nikko."

"Of course." He paused, then asked, "As part owner, does Dax travel with the team to away games?"

"Not all of them, but he does go to quite a few. He's the only owner who does."

Another brief silence passed as I waited for Nikko to see how suspicious all of this was. Instead, he blew out a long breath.

Which he did whenever he was about to tell me something I didn't want to hear.

"I don't mean to burst your bubble, Lachlan, but none of this is an indicator of guilt. The fact Daxton Shea was born nine months after his mother reported being drugged and assaulted on campus doesn't mean anything. Unfortunately, rapes on college campuses aren't rare. They're pretty fucking common, as awful as that sounds. And the use of drugs to subdue a potential victim is just as common. Simply because one or two of Nick's other victims reported the same thing doesn't mean he was the perpetrator, even if he was attending the same college at the same time."

"Yes, but—"

"Even if it's true, even if Daxton *is* the result of Nick raping Lucy Shea, it doesn't mean jack shit. Becoming a serial killer isn't in your DNA. By that rationale, we should be suspicious of Imogene, as well. You need something more than just a few pieces of circumstantial evidence, especially in a murder investigation."

"So I'm just supposed to pretend I don't know any of this when I see Dax at my next game?" I asked incredulously, my frustration with the situation making it increasingly difficult to breathe.

"That's *exactly* what you're supposed to do. This guy is smart. Smart enough to kill and not raise any doubt as to the method of death being self-inflicted. I guarantee he's covered every track he could think of. If Daxton is involved and you accuse him of something like this, he'll erase any remaining tracks. Believe me, bruh. I want this guy to pay for what he's done. But I want to make sure we find the right guy this time. Not jump to conclusions."

I squeezed my eyes shut, pinching the bridge of my nose. Sometimes I hated how sensible Nikko could be. But Ethan had also insisted we needed more proof before accusing Dax of being a serial killer, especially considering who he was. It still didn't make it any easier to know everything I did and not be able to do anything.

"When do you go back to California? Isn't there a game tonight?"

"My original plan was to fly back today, but with everything going on, I'm delaying that since I'm not scheduled to pitch until Monday. But I have to leave tomorrow night. It's one thing to skip a game I'm not playing in, which they'll fine me heavily for, but I *can't* miss Monday. It's the last game of the regular season. And with the standings the way they are, it could be the game that decides if we go straight to the playoffs or have to fight for a wild card spot. I just don't know how I'm going to focus enough to pitch knowing Julia's here and that fucker's on the loose. Sure, her brother's close by and they've established a twenty-four-hour watch around my place, in addition to my regular security, but—"

"I'll come out," Nikko interrupted. "Once I heard the news, I was thinking about it anyway. I can catch a flight this afternoon and be there around seven tomorrow morning."

I blinked, surprised. "What about work?"

"I have more personal time coming than I know what to do with. I've been on the force nearly ten years now. The last time I took any time off was..." He trailed off. I didn't need him to spell it out. The last time he took time off was to mourn Piper's death.

"You'd really come all the way out here?"

"If it gives you peace of mind and helps keep your girl safe, you bet I will. You're *ohana*. And *ohana* takes care of each other. No matter what."

I closed my eyes, instantly feeling lighter.

Like I could breathe again.

All morning, this had weighed heavily on my mind. The concern I'd leave and my biggest fears would come true. That I'd lose Julia. Lose Imogene.

If I couldn't be here, there was no one I trusted more to keep them safe than Nikko.

"Send me what flight you want. I'll have my assistant book it for you."

"You don't have to. I—"

"You're willing to sit on a plane for nine, ten hours in order to keep my girls safe. The least I can do is pay for it. And make sure you're in first class instead of coach, since I know you're too cheap to splurge on it yourself."

"I'm a simple man."

I chuckled. "A simple man who would have to squeeze his massive frame into one of those economy seats. So send me the flight you want. I'll make it happen."

"Will do. *Mahalo.*"

"I should be the one thanking you. You have no idea what this means to me."

"I'm pretty sure I do. I'll see you tomorrow."

CHAPTER FOUR

Lachlan

I lifted the underside of the pancake, checking the color. Satisfied, I flipped the batch. Who knew I'd become an expert at making pancakes? Or at least more comfortable making them than I was during my first attempt all those months ago.

When I woke up this morning, the same tension that had permeated my house since yesterday was present. If anything, it was thicker, considering it had now been twenty-four hours and there hadn't been one viable lead as to Nick's whereabouts. I was beginning to worry he might never be found.

It didn't help that his escape was the headline news story across the nation. To make matters worse, some reporters even interviewed security consultants, asking how easy it would be for Nick to start life again under a new identity.

That wasn't something any of us wanted to consider.

So, in an effort to enjoy some sort of normalcy, I turned off the TV, telling Julia and Imogene there'd be no talk of Nick, his escape, or anything remotely related to it for the next hour. Instead, we'd enjoy a normal breakfast on a normal Sunday.

For the past half-hour, as Imogene helped me whip up the batter, Julia watching us work together, everything *was* normal.

And I desperately needed normal, especially if I was expected to get on a plane tonight and fly to the opposite side of the country.

Just as I finished flipping the pancakes, the doorbell rang. I opened the app on my phone to see Nikko's imposing frame standing on my front porch.

"Nikko?" Julia arched a single brow in question.

When I told her I'd taken him up on his offer to come keep an eye on things while I was away, I braced myself for an argument. Surprisingly, she thought it was a good idea. Even confessed she'd feel much better having Nikko here, too. I couldn't blame her. Nikko *was* an intimidating guy. Once aspired to be an MMA fighter...until his father died in the line of duty and he decided to follow in his legacy.

"Can you take over for a minute?" I asked her.

She took the spatula from me. "Of course."

After placing a kiss on her temple, I made my way to the foyer and opened the door.

"*Pohili*," Nikko greeted. He gave me a quick hug, our foreheads touching briefly before he pulled back. "*Howzit?* You all hanging in?"

"We are. Thanks for being here. It means a lot."

"Like I said... Anything for *ohana*. You need me here, I'm here. No questions."

I held his gaze, giving him an appreciative smile. I didn't realize how much I missed having him around. He'd always been a voice of reason. Always offered me advice when I needed it. Always kept me grounded, even as my star continued to rise.

And despite any length of time we went without speaking to or seeing each other, he'd always drop everything if I needed him.

Like now.

He sniffed the air, the aroma of vanilla, sugar, and maple surrounding us, a smile slowly forming on his face. "Is Julia baking?"

"Actually, I was just making pancakes."

He gave me a sideways glance, raising a brow. "You? Cooking? Since when?"

I shrugged. "Since Julia."

"Damn, bruh." He shook his head, patting my back. "Julia looks good on you."

I smiled slyly. "In more ways than one."

He squeezed my shoulder. "I'm happy for you. Truly. You deserve this."

"Thanks, cousin. Come on. I'll introduce you to Imogene."

I started toward the kitchen, Nikko following. The second we turned the corner, both Julia and Imogene looked up from where they stood, side by side, preparing breakfast.

In my kitchen.

Such a simple, innocent scene. But it made me want more of this. And not just because Julia's ex-husband had escaped prison. I wanted to walk into this kitchen every day and see the two most important women in my life.

It was a strange feeling, considering mere months ago, I shied away from anything remotely resembling a relationship. But Julia changed my mind about that.

She changed my mind about a lot of things.

"Nikko...," Julia exhaled, stepping into his embrace.

"Good to see you again, Julia. Just wish it were under happier circumstances."

"As do I. Hopefully next time it will be."

"I'm going to hold you to that." He smiled, his teeth blindingly white compared to his naturally tanned skin. Then he looked toward the stove.

"And you must be Imogene."

"I am...," Imogene drew out, wide eyes fixed on Nikko, mouth slightly agape.

I could only imagine what was going through her mind. At six-five and 280 pounds of pure muscle, Nikko's physique intimidated adults. To a teenager, he must have seemed larger than life.

Hell, he seemed larger than life to *me* at times, and I

was almost as tall. But while I had a decent build, it was nothing compared to Nikko's.

The man was enormous.

"I'm Nikko." He held out his hand. "Lachlan's cousin. He's told me a lot about you. I'm happy to finally meet you."

Imogene hesitantly placed her hand in his, shaking it as she peered at him quizzically. She glanced at me before returning her eyes to Nikko, nose scrunched.

"You're related? You don't look it."

Releasing his hold, he laughed. "Technically, we're not related."

"Our mums grew up together on Oahu before mine moved to Australia to be with my father," I explained. "When she brought my sister and me back to Hawaii during our breaks from school, I spent a lot of time with Nikko and his family. Once my mum moved back to the island after our father passed, they became like a second family to me. Blood doesn't make you family."

She met my eyes, giving me an understanding smile.

If anyone knew that, Imogene did. I hated that she was forced to learn that lesson early in life, and not in a good way. Even though she shared blood with Nick, he was never a true father to her. Nor would he ever be.

Hopefully she'd learn the positive side of it. That people who weren't related by blood could still care about her as if they were family.

Could still love her as if she were their own.

Because that was precisely how I felt about her. As if

she were my own, even if my blood didn't run through her veins.

"Would you like to join us for breakfast?" Julia asked. "Lachlan made pancakes. Or would you like something else? I'm positive my loco moco wouldn't be nearly as good as your mother's, but I can attempt it."

He waved her off. "No need to trouble yourself. Pancakes are fine." He hesitated, leaning toward Julia and lowering his voice. "Are you sure they're edible, though?" He playfully grimaced. "You did say Lachlan made them."

Julia laughed, the sound like music to my ears after the past twenty-four hours. Which further confirmed this was precisely what we needed. To live our lives as if everything were normal.

As much as I hated to admit it, Julia was right in refusing to come to California. Her life was here. While we couldn't completely ignore our reality, we didn't have to let Nick interfere with our lives.

Didn't have to allow him to *control* our lives.

"He's actually gotten quite good at them." Julia beamed at me. "He's even attempted a few different variations, too."

"A few weeks ago, he made macadamia nut pancakes." Imogene closed her eyes, pure bliss covering her expression. "So good."

"What's on today's menu?" Still somewhat skeptical, he glanced at the pancakes piled high on a serving platter.

"Maple bacon," I announced.

"Maple...bacon?"

"They're good, cousin." I nudged him with my elbow. "It was Julia's idea. She makes a maple bacon cupcake that's out of this world. If it works as a cupcake, it will work as a pancake."

He pinned Julia with a stare. "I'm going to trust you on this one."

"Come on." She pushed him toward the table, her petite body seeming even tinier next to Nikko's size. "I'm certified in first aid and CPR, just in case." She winked, gesturing to a chair as we all sat.

This entire scenario must have been a bit of a shock to Nikko. For the past several years, I'd paid a chef to prepare all my meals. Hell, before Julia, the only reason I stepped foot into my kitchen was to make coffee. Now here I was, making pancakes for my girlfriend and her teenage daughter.

"Here goes nothing." Fork in hand, he sliced through the large stack and brought it up to his mouth. "If I die, tell *Eme* I love her."

I rolled my eyes. "You can tell her yourself, you arse."

I immediately reached into my pocket, then slapped a five dollar bill down on the table in front of Imogene.

Nikko furrowed his brows, lowering his fork. "What's that for?"

"Swearing. You've got to watch your language around her. She'll charge you for each swear."

"Five dollars? That's kind of steep."

"It's usually only a buck," Imogene muttered around a mouthful of pancake.

"But because of who I am, the cheeky little thing charges me five. Complete bullshite if you ask me." I placed another bill in front of her, winking.

"I'll do my best to refrain from swearing then." Nikko smiled. "Cops don't make nearly as much as baseball players."

All eyes were trained on Nikko as he brought the fork back to his mouth and hesitantly took a bite. He chewed, seeming to draw out the motion, then closed his eyes, his appreciation evident.

"I'll tell you what, *Pohili*. If this baseball thing doesn't work out, I can see about getting you a job as a line cook at the restaurant."

"I'll be sure to keep that in mind. For now, I might give this professional baseball thing a go. See how it pans out for me."

The table erupted in laughter, a much-needed moment of levity as we enjoyed a normal breakfast, despite the fact there was nothing normal about what was going on outside these four walls.

CHAPTER FIVE

Julia

"Hey, Mom?"

I whipped my head up from where Lachlan and I sat on the couch on his outdoor patio.

Although I wasn't sure "patio" was the correct word. It was so much more than that. Like another room of his extravagant home, complete with fire pit, large-screen television, and built-in exterior grill.

After breakfast, Imogene went up to what had become her room, probably to talk to Roman, who'd texted her practically every hour to check on her after learning of Imogene's connection to the escaped convict. Since we were out of earshot of curious ears, Lachlan and I took the opportunity to fill Nikko in on everything going on.

Until Imogene peeked her head through the sliding glass door, her expression uncertain.

"Is everything okay, sweetie?"

"Yeah. Everything's fine," she assured me, stepping onto the patio. But when she fidgeted with the hem of her shirt, I knew something was up.

Or that she wanted something.

"Umm... A bunch of my friends from school are going to Skyline Park. Roman asked if I could go." Her voice rose in pitch toward the end, dark eyes pleading.

I gazed at her for several moments, my heart squeezing.

But there was no way.

"I'm sorry, Imogene," I said with a sigh, hating to disappoint her. "Any other time, I'd have no problem with you going, provided you checked in every hour and kept your phone tracking enabled. But with Nick's whereabouts unknown, I can't chance it."

"You said you weren't going to allow him to dictate your life," she argued, voice becoming louder. "Refused to go to California and Hawaii because you didn't want him to have that power over you."

"And I don't."

"How is this any different?"

"This is vastly different," I replied calmly, hoping it would temper her own anger and frustration. "Yes, I said I wasn't going to allow Nick to force me into hiding, but I'm still taking precautions. We temporarily moved to Lachlan's." I glanced his way, and he gave me an encouraging smile. "Which was a compromise on my part. On both our parts. So while I don't want to uproot my life because of him, I still must be realistic. And the reality is that Nick is an extremely dangerous individual who poses a true threat to not just my safety, but also yours. So I'm sorry if you don't like my decision, but my priority has and always will be you."

"But everyone's going," she whined, growing increasingly irritated.

"And I'm sure your friends will understand why you can't go."

"So... What?" She placed her hands on her hips, attitude going from irritated to DEFCON 1 in a matter of seconds.

She certainly had my temper.

And my stubbornness.

"I'm supposed to stay a prisoner here while my friends get to have fun?"

"You make it sound like this place is a hellhole. There's a pool. Batting cages. A game room with a pool table and dart board. I've never been arrested, but I'm pretty sure jail cells don't come with these types of amenities."

"I don't care about the *amenities*," she shot back. "I care about my friends. I'll be the *only* one not there. Then tomorrow at school, everyone will be talking about how much fun they had. And I'll feel left out all over again."

"You won't have to worry about that, because you won't be going to school tomorrow," I told her, not thinking it would be a big deal.

I was wrong.

"*What*?!" she shrieked. "You can't be serious."

I glanced at Nikko and Lachlan as they discretely

stood and slipped inside the house, allowing me to handle this on my own. As much as Lachlan had become a part of Imogene's life, I was still her mother. I had to make all the decisions regarding her wellbeing.

Even if those decisions clashed with what she wanted.

Sometimes you had to be the bad guy, even if you wished you didn't.

"I'm very serious, Imogene." Standing, I approached her, running my hands down her arms, but she pushed out of my hold. "It's for your safety. That's all. I don't like it any more than you do."

"But it's ridiculous. If I'm not at school, I can't play in the game on Friday. And I also can't attend the Homecoming dance on Saturday."

"That's still days away. Hopefully this won't last much longer, then we can go back to life as we know it."

"And if it doesn't? If he's still on the run when Friday rolls around, will I be forced to miss out on playing in the game? Miss going to Homecoming?"

"Imogene, I—"

"Just answer me, Mom. Am I going to miss out on the important things in my life because of that sociopath?"

I wanted to argue it wasn't like that. But she *was* missing out on things because of Nick. It was for her safety, though.

"I won't feel comfortable allowing you to be around large gatherings of people. It's too easy for you to get lost in the crowd. For someone to use that to their advantage." I gave her a knowing look, reminding her of all the times Nick did that when she was a child.

All the times I begged, screamed, pleaded for someone to tell me they'd seen my baby girl, to no avail.

"I didn't do anything wrong, yet I'm the one being punished," she choked out. "Do you remember what you said to me when you told me the truth about him all those years ago?"

I swallowed hard, not answering.

"You promised that no matter what, you'd do every-thing to make sure I had a normal life going forward. That you wouldn't let him take that away from me."

"Imogene, baby, I—"

"And now you're breaking that promise."

Before I could open my mouth to remind her it was for her own safety, she stormed back into the house, ignoring Lachlan's attempts to talk to her.

Hopefully he didn't take it personally. Not many people could get through to her on the rare occasions she was like this. From my experience, it never lasted long.

Then again, most of our previous disagreements weren't about her missing something as important as the Homecoming dance, not to mention the soccer game against her school's biggest rival on Friday.

In her teenage world, this was akin to Lachlan's team making the World Series and him being benched because of something someone else on his team did.

"You okay?" Lachlan asked, hesitantly stepping outside.

Nodding, I drew in a deep breath. "I'm sorry you had to see that. I guess we should consider it a win that you haven't had to deal with one of her meltdowns until now."

"You made the right call," he assured me, pulling me into his arms. "Especially considering Nick's history of using Imogene to get to you."

"Then why do I feel like I'm letting her down?"

"She'll get over it."

"Not anytime soon. Things like this, going to Skyline Park... It's a big deal to kids Imogene's age. Especially when everyone else within her circle is going, including the guy she's interested in." Pulling away, I sighed, shaking my head. "She's right."

He arched a brow. "About?"

"I swore I'd do everything in my power to make sure she had a normal childhood. Swore I'd never let Nick take that from her. But I'm doing exactly that. I just... I wish there were something I could do. Some way to let her have this experience with her friends, yet still keep her safe."

"I do, too."

He wrapped me in his comforting embrace once more, holding me for several moments. Then he straightened, a contemplative look on his face.

I tilted my head. "What is it?"

"I..." He licked his lips. "Give me a minute. I think... I'll be right back."

Phone in hand, he rushed from the patio and into the house, disappearing down the hallway.

I stepped inside the living room, meeting Nikko's confused stare. "Any ideas?"

"Your guess is as good as mine." He smiled before his expression sobered. "If you'd like, I'll be happy to speak with the administration at Imogene's school. See what kind of security protocols they have in place. We don't want to think about the possibility, but what happens if days pass and he's still not found?"

"I know," I exhaled, lowering myself onto the couch, squeezing my eyes shut.

I'd considered that scenario more times than I cared to admit. Especially as the hours ticked by and the authorities still hadn't uncovered so much as a hair off Nick's head. Not since the dogs found his prison jumpsuit in the woods. Since then, it's been radio silence.

As if Nick had disappeared into thin air.

But I knew he hadn't.

He was simply waiting.

Planning.

Preparing.

For what, I couldn't be sure.

But I knew whatever it was wouldn't be good.

"She deserves to have some sort of normalcy, Julia. As do you."

I lifted my gaze to his as he sat beside me. "You'd do that? Talk to the director at her academy?"

"Academy? Sounds...fancy."

I snorted. "For the amount of money I pay, it better be. I chose this place because they take security extremely seriously. But with hundreds of kids there, I can't help but worry she'll get lost in the crowd. Then just get lost."

He placed his hand over mine, squeezing. "I'll talk to them. Even if it means personally escorting Imogene around campus, I'll do it."

"Really?"

He shrugged. "That's what I'm here for."

"Thank you, Nikko. Truly."

Noticing movement out of the corner of my eye, I glanced toward the stairs, hoping it was Imogene to apologize for overreacting.

Instead, it was Lachlan.

I slowly stood. "Everything okay?"

"I don't want you to get mad or think I overstepped. And if you want to call it off, we can. I'd be out a bit of money, but so be it."

I frowned, furrowing my brow, glancing at Nikko before returning my gaze to Lachlan. "What are you talking about?"

He approached, grabbing my hands in his. "What you just said made me think."

"W-what did I say?"

"How you wished there were some way you could let Imogene go to Skyline Park with her friends, yet still be assured of her safety."

"Right...," I drew out.

"What if I told you there was?"

I blew out a laugh. "On a Sunday? That place is

packed on the weekends. Especially with the weather being so nice."

"I understand that. But what if I could guarantee there wouldn't be a crowd? That the only people there would be those we invited?"

I gave him a sideways glance, my pulse steadily increasing. "What are you saying?"

He tightened his hold on my hands. "I'm saying I just rented out the place. At least until five o'clock, which is when they kick out anyone who's underage anyway."

I blinked, unsure I heard him correctly. "Are... Are you telling me you rented out Skyline Park for the afternoon so my daughter could still hang out with her friends?"

"It's your decision," he quickly replied. "I can call back and cancel, but since they were getting ready to open, I had to give them an answer right away. So you can think about it. If you still have concerns, I completely understand. I'm not attempting to take your decision-making power away. Just giving you another option. I—"

Before he could utter another syllable, I flung my arms around him. "This may be the sweetest, kindest thing anyone's ever done for her."

He relaxed into my embrace, holding me close. "I love her." He pulled back. "And I think we could all benefit from a break from all of this for a few hours."

"You've got that right."

"So let's take a break. Plus, I've never taken you on an actual date."

I furrowed my brow. "We went out in Hawaii. You

took me to dinner that first night. And to your Little League field. And the farmer's market that one afternoon."

He cupped my cheeks. "Those didn't count. Not in my mind. That was before we decided to do this. When we thought we could experience this amazing connection and still walk away."

He moved his hands from my face, sliding them down my arms and linking his fingers with mine.

"Now that we're really together and you're okay with allowing the world to see us, I'd like to take you out. So please, Julia. Will you go out with me?" He playfully waggled his brows. "It may not be the gourmet meal I treated you to in Hawaii...and if that's what you prefer, I'll make that happen once things settle down a bit...but—"

I pressed my mouth to his. "Yes, Lachlan. I'd love to go out with you." Pulling back, I flashed him a devious grin. "If you're lucky, maybe I'll let you cop a feel on one of the rides."

"Oh, I plan on getting *very* lucky."

CHAPTER SIX

Julia

"Are you ready for this?" I whispered to Lachlan as we stepped off the elevator and made our way to the rooftop area of Skyline Park, the afternoon sun warming my skin.

He tightened his hold on my hand. "I've been waiting for this since you agreed to be my girl. Okay, maybe not *this* scenario..."

He gestured at the carnival-like surroundings, complete with miniature golf course, carnival games, a handful of rides, and plenty of food. It was like an upscale version of the county fairs of my youth. Some of the scents were even the same. Hot dogs. Popcorn. Barbecue. And my personal favorite, funnel cakes.

Lachlan cupped my cheek, bringing my gaze back to

his. "But I want people to see us together. See how happy you make me."

I placed my hands on his chest, snuggling into his embrace. "So do I. I'm sorry I made you wait so long."

"If there's one thing I've learned, it's that you will *always* be worth the wait, love." He gradually lowered his lips, touching his mouth to mine in a sweet kiss. "Always."

I closed my eyes, losing myself in him as I tuned out the rest of the world. There was no Nick. No Dax. No dead girls. Just Lachlan, me, and this love I didn't think existed.

Just as I started to deepen the exchange, excited squeals cut through. I tore away, watching as a group of Imogene's teammates ran toward her.

It would have been an understatement to say she was excited when I informed her that not only could she go to Skyline Park, but that Lachlan had rented it out. I'd lost count of the number of times she hugged both of us, thanking us for making this happen.

But I didn't have much to do with it. It was all Lachlan. All I did was agree.

"Oh, my god, Mo! This is, like, the coolest thing ever!" Mia exclaimed.

"How did your mom's boyfriend pull off something like this?" Abby asked, expression alight with curiosity.

"He must be, like, super loaded," Layla interjected before Imogene could answer, "especially to rent out this place right before they opened."

"He's, well...," Imogene began nervously.

Lachlan sidled up next to her, wrapping an arm around her shoulders. "I don't know if I'd consider myself *super* loaded, but I do fairly well for myself."

Imogene looked up at him, then back at her friends, beaming proudly.

"Mia, Abby, Layla, I'd like you to meet—"

"Lachlan *fucking* Hale!" Mia shrieked.

Lachlan chuckled, looking over his shoulder at me. "I'm beginning to think I should legally change my name to that."

I approached, leaning toward him. "It is a great descriptor for you."

"Your... Your mom's *dating* Lachlan Hale?" Abby asked, mouth agape as she watched Lachlan wrap his other arm around me and kiss my cheek.

Imogene beamed even brighter. "She sure is. And you should see his house. It has a baseball diamond. Batting cages. A pool table. And the pool? It's to *die* for!"

"You've been to Lachlan Hale's house?" they all asked at the same time, as if he weren't standing mere inches away.

As if he were this untouchable idol.

In their minds, he probably was.

"We're staying with him right now. So I guess you can say I'm actually *living* in his house."

Her three friends looked at each other, completely taken aback. Then they all screamed in excitement, as if they were meeting the latest teenage heartthrob.

Then again, he'd amassed quite the following and fan

base...including teenage girls who swooned over how cute he was, even going so far as to hang his poster on their wall.

"What's going on?" a deeper voice asked.

The girls whirled around as a group of guys approached. Including Roman.

When they noticed who stood there, his arm around Imogene and me, they all came to an abrupt stop.

"Holy sh—crap," Roman said, glancing at Imogene before looking back at Lachlan. I wondered if she made him put money into her swear jar, too. It wouldn't surprise me.

"You're... You're Lachlan Hale," another one of the guys said, mouth wide.

"Yes, I am."

I leaned into Lachlan once more. "I get the feeling there's going to be a lot of this today."

"So do I."

"Does it bother you?" I whispered into his ear, although I could see the answer in his brilliant smile, eyes dancing with laughter.

I'd often heard stories about celebrities who were complete assholes to their fans. Who ignored them when in public, often being downright rude if asked for a photo or autograph. While I was sure it was exhausting to be recognized wherever you went, it never seemed to bother Lachlan. Granted, I hadn't been out in public with him much. But the few times I had — when he took me to his Little League field and now today — he didn't appear irritated at all. In fact, he seemed quite enthusiastic about meeting his fans.

"Not in the least. I was once in their shoes. Was excited to meet my favorite baseball players. Sometimes they were great. Other times, not so much. So I made a promise to myself that if I were ever lucky enough to reach the point where people were excited to meet me as *their* favorite player, I'd do my best to be just as excited to meet them. As your meemaw always said, you catch more flies with honey than vinegar." He winked, then stepped away from me, permitting Imogene to make the introductions.

I stood back, heart swelling even more. Not just at his philosophy, but the fact he was able to recite one of my meemaw's sayings. One I'd only told him a few times.

When Roman introduced himself, Lachlan's expression hardened slightly, and he crossed his arms in front of his chest, biceps stretching the fabric of his t-shirt.

"So, you're Roman?" Lachlan said in a deep voice, giving him a stern look.

"Y-yes, sir," Roman answered nervously. "It's an honor to meet you. I'm a huge fan. I'm a pitcher myself. Not nearly as good as you, but—"

"Everyone has to start somewhere."

"Do you mind signing my hat?" he asked, quickly taking it off his head.

"Not at all."

I approached, giving him the marker I'd stuffed into my purse for this very reason.

He was about to sign when he paused, meeting

Roman's gaze. "Before I sign this, I want you to make me a promise."

"What's that?"

"That you'll never treat Imogene with anything less than the utmost respect. I understand you two have been 'talking'. I was once a fifteen-year-old boy myself. I know what goes through a teenage boy's mind. Imogene means the world to me. Do you get what I'm saying, Roman?"

"Oh, my god, Lachlan. Enough. You're embarrassing me...*Dad*," she added as she playfully shoved him.

It was just a joke, but as he stared down at her, there was a gleam in his eyes I'd never seen before.

In the past few months, Lachlan had acted as more of a father to Imogene than her own biological father ever did. He took an interest in her hobbies. I'd even caught him helping her with homework a time or two.

Further proof Lachlan Hale truly was a good person.

"Of course, sir. I'd never do anything to intentionally hurt Imogene. I care about her a great deal."

Lachlan studied him for a beat, as if he possessed some internal bullshit detector. Seemingly satisfied, he nodded and signed the hat, handing it back. Then his expression softened.

"So tell me, Roman... How's your curveball?"

"It could use some work, sir. And my changeup is sh—" He glanced at Imogene again, who gave him a warning look, all but solidifying my assumption she made him contribute to her swear jar. "It's not great. I really struggle with it."

"That is a tough pitch to master." He patted him on the back. "But we'll work on it this winter so you're ready for the spring."

Roman's face lit up. For a teenage boy who had dreams of playing professionally himself, at least according to Imogene, this was probably akin to winning the lottery. "Do you mean it?"

"Absolutely."

"I... I don't know what to say."

"Say you'll be good to Imogene."

"Of course, sir. Even without your offer, I'll always be good to Mo."

"Good answer."

"Come on, Roman." Imogene grabbed his hand, pulling him away. "Let's go on the slides."

He looked at Lachlan, almost as if asking permission. Once Lachlan nodded, Roman turned, he and Imogene joining their friends.

Sauntering up to him, I looped my arm through his. "Pretty sure you just made his day. Hell, his entire year," I remarked as we walked toward a large picnic area, a few of the parents I recognized from Imogene's school sitting there.

He shrugged. "He's a good kid. And Imogene likes him."

"Good kid? If he's such a good kid, why did you just give him the third-degree?"

"I considered myself a good kid. But I also remember what I was like at that age." He gave me a knowing look. "I just wanted to remind him who he'd have to deal with if he hurt Imogene."

I opened my mouth to argue that broken hearts were a part of life as a teenager, but he cut me off.

"And I'm not talking about them breaking up. They're young. I know this is just a teenage romance thing. I'm talking about hurting her deeper than that."

I nodded. He didn't have to say another word. I knew what he was talking about.

I *lived* what he was talking about.

"Thank you," I murmured as I lifted myself onto my toes and brushed my lips against his.

"Just looking out for Imogene."

"That's not what I mean."

"Then what *do* you mean?"

"All of this." I waved my hand around at the teenagers enjoying the park, their laughter and excitement exactly what I needed.

He opened his mouth, but I cut him off before he could give me the response I sensed coming.

"I know. I know. It's not a big deal. For someone with money, this was barely a drop in the bucket. But I'm not thanking you for that. I'm thanking you for the fact that you put in the effort with Imogene. And not just today, but from the beginning. I came into this thing with a shit ton of baggage." I laughed under my breath. "As you're learning more and more every day, especially with recent...developments."

"Not here," he admonished. "Remember. Today's just a normal day."

"I know." I smiled, then glanced toward the slides, watching Imogene and Roman speed down on a pair of blankets. "But you never shied away from all of this. Despite the challenges, you stuck with me when most men would have decided it wasn't worth it. You've treated Imogene as if she were your own daughter." My eyes welled with tears, emotion overtaking me. "I don't think you realize how much that means to me."

He pulled me closer, cupping my face, expression awash with nothing short of absolute sincerity and honest devotion.

"I love you, Julia." He allowed his words to sink in for several seconds before a small smile teased his lips. "And despite her occasional attitude and the minor meltdown earlier, I love your daughter, too. I'll always do everything I can for you. For her. For this strange, unconventional little family we've made."

I tilted my head. "Family?"

He nodded, a peacefulness washing over him. "I know we've only been together a few months. But in that time, you and your daughter have become my family. My *ohana*." He leaned toward me, lips warming mine. "I hope I've become like that to you, too."

"More than I think you realize," I sighed as I succumbed to his kiss. Everything about today, about this moment, felt...perfect.

I knew it wouldn't last. That, at some point, we'd have to face the reality of my ex-husband being on the loose. That he may very well be trying to get to Imogene and me at this exact moment. But for now, I wasn't going to think about that. Wasn't going to let *him* have that kind of power over me.

Instead, I was going to bask in this man's love and savor the gift he gave my daughter.

And me.

"Come on, love..." Lachlan pulled back, grabbing my hand. "How about a round of mini golf? See if either of us can get a hole in one." He flirtatiously waggled his brows.

"Play your cards right, I'm pretty sure you will later on."

CHAPTER SEVEN

Lachlan

"Imogene's going to be talking about today for years to come," Julia said, collapsing onto the bed.

"Is that right?" I met her eyes in the mirror over my dresser as I pulled out a few pairs of briefs and socks, needing to finish packing and get to the airport.

"All her friends will be, too. You made their day. Hell, their year."

I smiled, thrilled I was able to give this to Imogene.

And Julia.

"I think we all needed today, myself included."

Instead of sitting around the house all day, our minds consumed with the uncertainty surrounding Nick's escape as the media covered it to death, we focused on something more important for a few hours. On each other. On smiling. On laughing. On *living*.

Even if only for a little while.

After placing my toiletry bag on top of my clothes, I zipped up my suitcase. Then I grabbed the jeans and shirt I'd set aside and got dressed.

As I finished buttoning my shirt, I glanced at Julia, seeing her frown.

"What's wrong?"

"I thought you always wore a suit when traveling. That it was some team rule."

"Only when we're traveling as a team. Since they're already in California, I can wear whatever I want."

"That's a shame. You know how hot and bothered I get seeing you in a suit."

"That I do." Waggling my brows, I stalked toward her.

She propped herself up on her elbows, green eyes swirling with desire, chest heaving as I slid my hands up her legs and under her skirt.

"Lachlan, what are you—"

"Just seeing if I can get you all hot and bothered even without the suit."

She whimpered as I rubbed my thumb against her panties. "Unless you intend to finish what you're starting, you'd better stop."

When I pulled away and straightened, she pouted. But it was short-lived, her gaze darkening with desire as I slowly unbuttoned my shirt and tossed it onto the floor. I didn't have much time before my driver arrived, but I needed her once more before leaving for the next thirty-six hours.

Returning to the bed, I gently pushed her onto her back, my thumb brushing against her panties once more. "I certainly intend to make sure you finish, love," I murmured, swallowing her moans as I pressed my mouth to hers, our tongues tangling in a searing kiss.

"Then touch me."

"I am touching you." I moved my lips from hers, leaving a trail of kisses along her jawline and collarbone before nibbling on her nipple through her dress.

"No. You're *teasing* me," she admonished. "There's a big difference."

I settled between her thighs. "Am I?"

"You know you are. I need you to touch me."

I slowly circled my thumb against her panties. "I am."

She huffed out an annoyed sigh. "Do you need me to draw you a picture, Hale? Tongue. Pussy. Now."

I laughed, then brought my lips back to hers. "You know I love it when you take charge."

"Well then..." Her hands on my shoulders, she pushed me back down her body, propping up her legs. "Consider me taking charge right now by telling you to get busy eating me out."

I didn't think I could fall any more in love with this woman.

I was wrong.

Hearing her tell me what to do in the bedroom when she refused to give voice to any of her needs and wants mere weeks ago endeared her to me even more.

"Yes, ma'am."

Hooking my hands into her panties, I gradually lowered them down her legs, tossing them onto the floor. When I returned to her, I made a show of licking my lips, drawing out the seconds as I inched toward her, dragging my tongue along the inside of her thigh.

"Lachlan," she whimpered, fingers digging into my hair.

Just as I reached her apex, I paused. Then I retreated, giving her other thigh the same treatment. When I paused again, she squeezed her legs together, locking me in place.

"If you so much as think about backing away again, I'm going to lose my fucking mind."

I glanced up at her with a smirk. "You want my mouth on you?"

"You know I do."

"And you know I'll never deprive you of what you want." I grasped her thighs, spreading them apart. When I slid my tongue along her sex, she exhaled, relishing in that first lick, first touch, first taste.

"You're too fucking good at that," she sighed, moving against me. "This feeling... It should be criminal to feel this damn good."

I paused, eyes briefly meeting hers. "I do have some handcuffs if you'd like."

"I bet you do, you fiend. But not now." She ran her fingers through my hair, nails digging into my scalp, forcing my head back between her thighs. "Right now, I need to touch you. And need you to touch me."

"With pleasure."

I dragged my tongue along her again, focusing on her clit, her breaths increasing with every swirl, every nip, every nibble. When I pushed a finger inside, she arched her back, her motions becoming more frantic until she couldn't fight it any longer and fell apart around me, body quivering and shaking as she succumbed to her orgasm.

Not wanting to waste a single second of what little time I had before my driver pulled up, I shoved my jeans down my legs, thrusting into her before she had a chance to come down from her orgasm.

"God, you feel incredible, love," I groaned, my words coming out breathy and labored. "Love the way you move. Love the way you feel." I leaned down, hooking her leg around my waist as I rocked my hips against her, each thrust and retreat desperate, yet passionate at the same time. "Love the sounds you make when you come. When *I* make you come." I grabbed her nipple through her dress, pinching hard, my lips a breath from hers. "I want you to come again. Want to come with you."

"Harder, Lachlan," she begged.

Never one to deny her anything, I increased my rhythm, the room filled with heavy panting and desperate moans. In seconds, her body tensed, lips parting, breathing increasing. I drove into her harder, faster, unsure how much longer I could hold back. Finally, a new wave of tremors overtook her, every inch of her shuddering around me.

I slammed my mouth against hers, swallowing her cries

as my own orgasm consumed me, both of us riding wave after wave of pure bliss.

When I had nothing left, I collapsed on top of her, holding her for several moments.

"I guess you're able to shoot a hole in one after all," she said breathily.

I pulled back, meeting her gaze.

Then we burst out laughing.

"As you learned today, that's the only hole in one I'm any good at. I'm complete rubbish at miniature golf."

She cupped my cheeks in her hands, bringing my lips to hers. "That's the only one I care about. Feel free to practice your game with me anytime."

Chucking, I rolled onto my side, dragging her body to mine.

It felt wrong to feel something so good, so honest, so pure with everything else going on. But were we supposed to stop experiencing this connection just because Nick's whereabouts were unknown? Were our lives supposed to stop? Were we supposed to deny ourselves what we deserved? If anything, we needed this connection even more right now. Needed this feeling of contentment.

This reminder of the strength of our love.

I took her face in my hands, the post-coital glow replaced by something more serious.

More vulnerable.

"You'd better not do anything crazy while I'm gone," I said, my voice cracking as the fears I'd tried to suppress all day came rushing back. "Promise me you won't do anything that'll put your life in danger. That you'll stay here. That you'll be here when I get back. I can't..." I shook my head. "I can't stomach the thought of losing you." I swallowed hard. "You're my life, Julia."

Sighing, she shook her head, eyes welling with tears. "I swear to you, Lachlan..." She grabbed my hand and placed it over her heart before covering my chest with her hand. "I will always be right here, waiting for you." She leaned toward me, lips skimming mine. "Always."

CHAPTER EIGHT

Julia

The aroma of sugar, vanilla, and chocolate filled the air as I kept myself busy in Lachlan's kitchen Monday afternoon, flour and confectioners' sugar covering much of his island. I'd probably baked more cookies, cupcakes, and pastries than anyone could possibly eat, even with the small group of people I'd invited over to watch the game tonight.

But baking always helped me take my mind off things. And with still no news about Nick's whereabouts, I *needed* to take my mind off things. *Needed* to do something I enjoyed.

Needed to stop seeing Nick's face everywhere I turned.

Plus, I had a few new recipes I wanted to try out. And Lachlan's gourmet kitchen just begged for me to put it to use.

So that was precisely what I'd been doing all day.

When a chiming cut through the *whirring* of my stand mixer, I glanced at my phone, a smile tugging on my lips. Wiping my hands down my apron, I turned off the mixer and hit the answer button, Lachlan's face appearing, the stadium behind him.

"What do you think?" He tilted his phone to give me an unobstructed view of the ballpark. The stands were mostly empty, but the field was abuzz with activity. "Pretty impressive, right?"

I shrugged. "Depends on if you like the Dodgers. Personally, I'm rooting for the other team. Their starting pitcher has an amazing ass that I love to ogle. And occasionally grope."

He laughed. "And this starting pitcher can't wait for you to grope his arse." He waggled his brows before his expression turned serious.

"How are you going? Everything okay?"

"I'm *going* just fine," I said, emphasizing the Australian phrasing. "And nothing's changed since the last time we spoke. Which was just a few hours ago."

He arched a brow. "But in those few hours, Nikko took you to Imogene's school to discuss security measures for her to return to class, correct?"

I propped the phone against a mixing bowl, doing my best to suppress the anxiety filling me over the prospect of sending Imogene back to school.

"He did."

"And?"

I pushed out a long breath. "Nikko said their security is top-notch, which I already knew. It was why I decided to send her there in the first place. They're going to assign a security guard to escort her to each of her classes, as well as keep an eye on her during lunch and any of her free periods. They also have a security plan in place to not only guarantee her safety at her soccer match Friday afternoon, but also at Homecoming Saturday night. She wasn't happy to hear about these additional forms of protection, but I told her it was either that or she stays at your house and completes her lessons there. I'll let you guess which she reluctantly ended up going with."

"Option one?"

"Correct."

"And you? Which option do you feel more comfortable with?"

I exhaled another deep breath. "Honestly, I'd feel more comfortable keeping her locked away until Nick draws his last breath, but I refused to go to California and Hawaii because I didn't want to give him the satisfaction of knowing he forced me out of my home. Didn't want to give him that control. And the same goes for this.

"I almost lost you because I kept letting that asshole dictate all my decisions. Or maybe I allowed my fear of him to cloud those decisions. I don't know which it was exactly. And while we all have to make certain adjustments, like staying at your house because it's safer and ensuring Imogene has a security escort at school, we're not going to put our lives on hold because of him. Not anymore."

I allowed my words to sink in for several seconds before my mouth curved into a smile. "Although, I have to admit, I quite like sleeping in your bed, since it smells like you and makes me miss you just a little less."

"I like the idea of you sleeping in my bed, too. Like the idea of you being in it every night. Even when Nick no longer poses a threat to anyone, which I pray is very soon."

I liked that idea, too. But I didn't tell him that. Not yet. There was too much else going on right now to even think about discussing what Lachlan was implying.

"Regardless of how much longer it takes for the authorities to find him, we need to live as normal a life as possible. Which is why I'm pretending today is just a typical Monday. Except for it being your last regular season game and a win will earn your team a spot in the playoffs."

"But no pressure, right?"

"It's just another game, babe."

He pinched his lips together. "Well... That's different."

I straightened. "What is?"

"You called me 'babe'. I don't think I've ever heard you call me that before." His brows furrowed. "In fact, I don't think I've ever heard you use a pet name for me."

"That can't be right. I'm sure I must have at some point."

"I mean, apart from hearing you scream 'Oh god' when I'm railing you." He flashed me a devious grin, not caring about the people walking by in the background.

"Lachlan!" I exclaimed, eyes widening. "Imogene could have been listening."

"But she wasn't." His playful expression turned panicked. "Was she?"

"No." I smirked. "She and Nikko are in your gym."

"Really?"

I nodded, stirring the batter in the mixing bowl. "Learned he knew jiu-jitsu and asked if he'd show her some moves. So that's what they've been doing. They probably won't be in there much longer since I'm having a little get-together tonight to watch the game. Imogene invited Roman over, too."

"Tell him no funny business in my house," he admonished in a deep voice, expression stern.

"Pretty sure he got that message loud and clear yesterday."

"I'm just looking out for my girl."

I stopped mixing the batter, my heart expanding. "Could you be any more perfect?" I remarked before I could stop myself.

He chuckled, the sound a sexy rumble. "I'm far from perfect, love."

"But you're perfect for me...babe."

"That's all that matters."

I sighed, wishing I could talk to him all night long. But he had a game to get ready for. And I had guests who would start showing up any minute.

"You'd better get going. Give the Dodgers a giant ass whooping on their home turf."

"That's the plan. See you in a few hours." He blew me a kiss.

I pretended to catch it before blowing one back. Then I ended the call.

As I finished whipping the batter for my peanut butter and jelly cookies, I turned the television to the pregame broadcast. The second I did, Lachlan's smiling face appeared on the screen, my heart skipping a beat.

I still couldn't believe I was lucky enough to know him so intimately. The one who got to share a bed, a life, and right now, a home with him. I didn't know what I'd done to deserve his unwavering devotion, even through all the ups and downs. But I wasn't going to obsess over it. Wasn't going to fall into my old habits of thinking everyone had an ulterior motive for wanting to be with me. Instead, I was going to allow myself to be happy.

Finally.

And I'd be damned if I permitted Nick to take that from me.

As soon as the kitchen was back in order, apart from the trays of food I'd prepared for tonight, the doorbell rang. I wiped my hands on the towel and made my way toward the foyer.

"Holy shit. This place is incredible," Naomi said before I even had a chance to open the door all the way, her wide eyes taking in every stunning inch of Lachlan's home.

"Wait until you see the back yard. He's got his own baseball diamond. And batting cages. The patio has an enormous TV, as well as a fire pit. It's where we're going to watch the game. It was either that or the theater room, but I figured it might be nice to be outside. And the kitchen isn't too shabby, either."

I grabbed her hand and pulled her farther into the house, coming to a stop at the kitchen island, allowing her to take in the state-of-the-art appliances, including a double oven and even a bread proofer.

She looked down at the food covering the island. "Seems like you've been taking advantage of this kitchen."

"I'd be crazy not to." I glanced around. "Although, once this is all over, it'll make going back to my house difficult."

"You could just move in together." She waggled her brows.

I shook my head, pushing down my excitement at the thought of this being my life. Of waking up every morning in Lachlan's arms. Of spending hours in this kitchen as I whipped up new, delicious treats.

Of being happy.

The image was so real I could practically taste it. But I had no idea what tomorrow would bring. Hell, I had no idea what life would throw at me in the next few hours. For now, I just needed to take it day by day. Minute by minute.

"Let's deal with one major life event at a time, okay?"

"Speaking of which..." Her expression fell as she ran a hand down my arm. "How are you holding up?"

I forced out an anxious smile.

Today was the first time I'd seen her since she came over to my house immediately after I visited Nick in prison. We talked on the phone and texted as she constantly checked in on me. But when shit hit the fan, she knew the last thing I wanted was a house full of friends and family making sure I was all right. It was why she was such a good friend. She knew when I needed her.

And also when I needed myself.

"All things considered, I'm...okay."

"And Lachlan's okay, too?"

"He's worried. Didn't want to leave. But, as I'm sure you noticed, the security here is extremely tight."

"You've got that right." She rolled her eyes. "I thought the cops down at the gate were going to ask to strip-search me. I was getting ready to bend and spread, if you know what I mean."

I barked out a laugh.

Only Naomi could bring humor to an otherwise shitty situation.

"Nikko also flew out to stay with us, so that's given Lachlan some peace of mind."

"Where is he?"

"In the home gym teaching Imogene some jiu-jitsu. So I'm sure she'll want to start taking classes to add to her already hectic schedule."

"It's good for her to know how to defend herself."

While I hated the idea of my little girl ever being in a situation where she had to, I didn't want her to make the same mistakes I did. Wanted her to be strong, independent, able to speak up for herself when she felt something was wrong.

"Well, I'm glad you're all safe. That you're not letting all this bullshit get to you."

"I need to live my life. Imogene needs to live hers. We've had to make some adjustments, but he doesn't get to control us. Not anymore."

Naomi wrapped her arms around me, pulling me in for a tight hug. "Damn straight he doesn't."

CHAPTER NINE

Julia

"He's pretty amazing," Naomi whispered to me as we sat on the back patio of Lachlan's house watching the game, surrounded by friends and family — Naomi, Imogene, Wes, Londyn, Eli, Nikko, Roman, and even Roman's parents.

But this wasn't simply a gathering of friends and family. It was an escape. A reminder that life would go on, regardless of what it threw at us.

I stared at the screen, watching Lachlan throw another strike for the final out of the fourth inning, preserving his team's one-run lead.

"He really is. I played softball, albeit badly. The skill involved in pitching like he does... You can't teach that. It's nothing short of remarkable."

"Well, he's a pretty remarkable guy."

I sighed. "Yes, he is." My eyes remained glued to the TV, the cameras following Lachlan as he jogged off the field. Just as a commercial came on, the doorbell rang, the sound ominous and foreboding.

Instantly, the light atmosphere shifted, considering everyone I'd invited was already here. Nervous eyes darted around, the air thick with apprehension.

"I'll see who it is." Nikko's gaze drilled into me as he stood. "You stay here."

I nodded, then met Imogene's worried expression. "It'll be okay," I assured her.

"Okay," she replied anxiously, Roman squeezing her hand.

I tried to refocus my attention on the screen, but my thoughts were elsewhere. And glancing at the people around me, I could tell their thoughts were also elsewhere, especially Wes and Londyn, all of us sharing a concerned look.

At the sound of footsteps, I snapped my gaze toward the doorway. My heart plummeted into the pit of my stomach when Nikko appeared, Agent Curran behind him.

"I apologize for the interruption," he began very matter-of-factly, addressing my guests. Then he met my stare. "I need to speak with you. It's urgent."

Naomi clutched my hand, offering me the support and strength I needed right now.

"Is it..." I trailed off, bile rising in my throat.

"Yes," he answered.

Wes quickly stood, his expression unwavering, making it clear he intended on being a part of this conversation.

Agent Curran parted his lips, probably about to tell Wes he needed to speak to me alone. Then he sighed. "Actually, you and your wife should hear this." He looked from Wes to Londyn, then turned to Nikko at his side. "You, as well, Detective Kekoa."

"Do you mind watching over things for a few minutes?" I asked Naomi.

A hint of unease flashed in her eyes, a strange occurrence for a woman who always had tenacity in spades. But even she sensed something big was going on.

"Of course."

I gave her a thankful smile, then stood and made my way toward Imogene.

"Is everything okay, Mama?" she asked shakily.

"Everything will be fine. Don't worry. Just...watch the game. I won't be long." I stole a glimpse at Roman, silently asking him to be there for Imogene since she was on edge.

I was, too. But I had to remain strong, regardless of the dread settling in my stomach.

When he gave me an understanding nod, I continued into the house, leading everyone into Lachlan's study, all of us sitting on the couches and chairs, our attention focused on Agent Curran.

"As I'm sure you've already figured out by my presence here, there's been a development."

A tightness formed in my chest. "What kind of development?"

"Have you found him?" Londyn pressed, her hand firmly enclosed in Wes' grasp, eyes pleading with Agent Curran to give her the answer we all prayed for.

"Yes."

Hope built within in me in response to that one little word. But it soon deflated.

"And no."

I tilted my head. "Meaning?"

"The media hasn't gotten hold of this story just yet, and we're hoping to keep it that way." He gave us all a pointed glare, letting us know that what he was about to share wasn't to leave this room. "My superiors didn't want me to inform you of this, but I felt you deserved to know. But, please, keep it to yourselves. I'm already on thin ice after..." He trailed off, glancing at Londyn before returning his eyes to mine. "Well, after recent events. But if I were in your shoes..." He looked between Londyn and me, "I'd want to know." He kept his gaze on me. "Especially you."

"What happened?" Nikko inquired. "Where did you find him?"

"I'm not sure how much of the news you've caught recently—"

"We've been trying to avoid it," I explained. "Trying to go on as if life is normal. Or as normal as possible, all things considered."

"That's probably for the best." He cleared his throat. "Yesterday, a story broke about a murder-suicide thirty miles north of here. Unfortunately, with Nick's escape dominating the headlines, this story received little to no attention."

"It wasn't a murder-suicide, was it?" I asked, already knowing the answer. "There's more to it, isn't there?"

He slowly nodded. "Correct. There's a lot more to it. There *was* a murder."

"But no suicide."

"No, ma'am."

"Was it Nick?" Londyn asked.

"Yes."

"How can you be sure?" Wes tightened his hold on Londyn's hand. "If it was a murder-suicide, I don't—"

"One of the victims, Christine Griffin, didn't die from the..." He briefly grimaced before finishing, "attack."

His obvious unease gave me pause. This was a man who'd spent his career chasing some of the most notorious and sadistic killers ever to walk the face of the earth. Something about this unsettled him.

And if Agent Curran was unsettled, I couldn't help but be, too.

"As such, Ms. Griffin was able to identify her assailant. Once she did, the local authorities called the GBI, whom I've been helping to track down Jaskulski, considering my history with him."

"What happened?" I asked.

"Saturday evening, a house located ten miles from the scene of the prison transport crash was broken into. At approximately 7:30 p.m., Christine's husband, Jason, went out to the garage to grab a beer from the refrigerator. When he returned, a man who matched Nick's description was behind him, pointing a gun at his head. Nick was free from his handcuffs and shackles, and wore street clothes — a white, button-down shirt, dark jeans, and loafers."

My pulse increased, stomach churning. "He has a gun?"

Agent Curran nodded solemnly. "I'm afraid so. But the gun is the least of my worries. Especially after..." He swallowed hard, expression blanching.

After taking a moment to compose himself, he continued.

"Nick zip-tied Jason to a dining room chair, then forced Christine to go to her bedroom and change into something more appropriate for dinner. He also changed into one of Jason's suits, since they were roughly the same size. Throughout this entire ordeal, he called her..." He closed his eyes and ran a hand through his hair.

I'd known Agent Curran for seven years. I couldn't remember ever seeing him this off. This upset. This...distraught.

"Called her what?" I asked with a quiver, fearing what the answer could be.

He shook his head and lifted his gaze to mine. "Julia."

CHAPTER TEN

Julia

"What happened next?" I asked after a prolonged silence, my insides twisting at the thought of Nick harming this woman because of me.

"They had dinner, during which time he asked about Imogene's studies. Acted as if it were completely normal for him to call this woman Julia and ask about a daughter she didn't have, all while Christine's husband was tied to a chair, bearing witness to all of it. After dinner, Nick took out a cell phone and put a song on repeat, forcing Christine to dance with him—"

"He has a cell phone, too?" Wes pressed, jaw twitching, nostrils flaring.

Agent Curran nodded gravely.

"How?"

"Our guess is there's someone helping him."

"Who? Who could—"

"What song did he play?" I interrupted my brother, needing to know the answer.

Although I feared I already did.

Agent Curran hesitantly turned his eyes to mine, his Adam's apple bobbing up and down. "'Hold me, Thrill me, Kiss me.'"

I expelled a shuttering breath that bordered on a sob. Nikko clutched my hand as I did everything to fight the chills overtaking me.

Just hearing the title of what Nick considered to be "our song" made my skin crawl, bile rising in my throat. Most people would consider it a romantic song about being so in love you felt crazed, detached from reality.

Now knowing what I did about Nick, it had a vastly different meaning.

"He made her dance with him, all the while bringing up memories of dancing to this song on their wedding night... *Your* wedding night," he corrected.

"I know," I replied quickly.

"He made her kiss him. Tell him how much she loved him. How he was the only man for her. And then..."

I drew in a breath, fearing what would come next. I knew Nick killed this poor woman's husband. And tried to kill her, too. I wanted to believe that was it, as horrible as it was. I didn't want to think he'd do anything else.

But knowing Nick, knowing how much he craved power and control, I knew I wouldn't get my wish.

"Then he raped her..."

I squeezed my eyes shut, every muscle in my body stiffening.

"With the blade of a knife."

I released a shuttering cry, my stomach roiling at the thought. I glanced toward Londyn, her own eyes brimming with tears, hands trembling.

"Kept saying something along the lines of 'Now you know how it feels, Julia'. We believe this is his way of seeking revenge for when you stabbed him in the groin, which eventually led to his arrest and imprisonment."

Chills rushed through me, a dizziness overtaking me as a sour taste formed in my mouth.

"When Jason begged him to stop, that he couldn't bear to watch any more cruelty, couldn't stomach listening to her harrowing cries, Nick grabbed his gun, positioned the angle of it in order to make it appear as if it were self-inflicted, and fired. Then he cut Jason free from his restraints, wiped his prints from the gun, and smeared Christine's blood all over her husband's hands and clothing before placing the gun in his right hand. Once he seemed satisfied, Nick approached Christine, the knife in his hand, and plunged it into her stomach. The last thing she remembered before she lost consciousness was Nick saying—"

"'Till death do us part,'" I whispered.

"Yes."

The room fell silent for several moments as we all attempted to absorb everything Agent Curran just shared. No wonder he had paled. The entire ordeal sounded incredibly...sadistic. And the fact she suffered such brutality because Nick deemed her an acceptable replacement for me, at least for the night... It sickened me even more.

Why was he doing this? Why couldn't he just leave me alone?

From the moment I learned the truth about Nick, all I wanted was to be left alone. To raise my daughter to the best of my ability and give her the life I never had. To find my own happiness.

To maybe find love.

Now that I was on the brink of having all those things, Nick was back, threatening to take everything from me again.

"As I suggested a few minutes ago," Agent Curran cut through the silence, "it's my belief Nick has help. His cuffs and shackles were gone. He wore street clothes. Has a cell phone. Neighbors mentioned seeing a work truck parked on the street Saturday morning a few hours after the crash, yet nobody was having work done. Which tells me this may have all been planned."

"Do you think perhaps Daxton Shea might be involved?" I suggested.

"Daxton Shea?" Wes inquired, obviously confused. "What would he have to do with this?"

"Ethan stopped by Saturday morning," I began, doing my best to not reveal too much information since Wes still hadn't shared anything about the recent murders with Londyn.

"Who's Ethan?" Londyn's brows scrunched.

I glanced at Wes, unsure what to say.

"A friend of Lachlan's sister's," Wes stated before anyone else could respond.

I gave him a pointed glare, then looked back at Londyn.

"Ethan found an old incident report Lucy Shea presumably filed with the RA of her dorm while she was attending Brown, which happened to be the same time Nick was getting one of his PhDs there," I explained. "The report documented a rape that had Nick's signature all over it. Based on this and the fact Daxton was born nine months later, it appears Nick may have a son out there. A son who volunteers for the prison outreach ministry that visits inmates. And given the Shea's vast wealth—"

"Let's not go spouting conspiracy theories," Agent Curran admonished, holding up his hand. "I'm going to tell you exactly what I told Ethan when he shared this with me. We need more than a few pieces of circumstantial evidence to implicate anyone in something as serious as this. Especially someone like Daxton Shea."

"Then what are we supposed to do?" I asked, growing more and more frustrated with every passing second. "Sit around and do nothing while Nick could be anywhere? Could be attacking another helpless woman?"

"We've put out an APB on the work truck neighbors saw around the vicinity of the Griffin's house on Saturday. But based on what we know of Nick, it's doubtful he's still driving it, so we're also combing through stolen vehicle reports."

"That's your big plan?" Wes' lips twitched, his own irritation showing. "APBs and stolen vehicle reports? Nick's too smart to steal a car."

"Plus, if Ethan's hunch is right and Daxton *is* involved, he could buy him any number of cars and pay cash," I added.

"I didn't say that was my entire plan. It's merely part of it."

"Then what's the other part?" Londyn asked. "You have to do something to catch him. He can't just—"

"I beleve Nick left the Griffin's house under the impression he killed Jason *and* Christine," Agent Curran interrupted. "Hell, even her sister, a nurse, initially believed her to be dead when she walked into their house Sunday morning to meet Christine for their daily run. It wasn't until she woke up after surgery this afternoon that anyone fully understood what happened."

"What does that have to do with your plan?" My brows furrowed. "And why hasn't this attack been all over the news? Don't you think the public deserves to know what Nick's done? How dangerous he is?"

"I do, but the fact it's been reported as a murder-suicide and not connected to him in any way actually works to our advantage. After all, if he knows we're on to him, he wouldn't fulfill the next part of his ritual."

"The next part of his ritual? You mean giving me a piece of jewelry?"

"No. There's a step before that."

I shook my head. "I don't—"

"With each of his victims, Nick attended their visitation, funeral, burial, or reception. Did he not?"

I blinked, sinking into the couch. "I'd forgotten about that."

"So if we keep with the initial news story that it was a murder-suicide between a couple experiencing marital problems, Nick may attend one of these functions for Christine. So that's what we're going to do. Stage a fake memorial for her. He won't go to a memorial for her husband. He was a necessary casualty."

"Do you really think it'll work?" I asked. "That Nick will risk getting caught in order to attend a memorial service simply because it was once part of his ritual? Correct me if I'm wrong, but raping a woman with a goddamn knife wasn't part of his ritual, yet here we are."

"I don't know anything for certain," Agent Curran replied calmly. "But I do know Nick. Just like you do. I'll be the first to admit he's one of the most intelligent men I've ever dealt with. But let's not forget what drives him. What forces him to act so...sadistically."

"What's that?"

"His obsession. With control. With revenge. With ritual." He paused. "And with you. When torn between one of his obsessions and his rationale, his obsession will always win out. *Always*," he emphasized. "I'm certain it will win out here, too. But this time, we'll be waiting."

CHAPTER ELEVEN

Julia

A gent Curran's visit certainly put a damper on the rest of the evening. He'd apologized profusely for delivering such disturbing news during what should have been a happy evening with friends and family, but I insisted it was okay. That it was better we all knew what was going on instead of being left in the dark.

Nevertheless, I did my best to pretend nothing was wrong. That Nick's escape hadn't resulted in an innocent man's death, his wife being brutally tortured and clinging to life. But even watching Lachlan pitch his team to an incredible win and securing their place in the playoffs couldn't chase away the cloud hovering over me, regardless of how hard I tried to feign enthusiasm, especially in front of Imogene.

I wasn't sure what to tell her about everything Agent

Curran had shared with us tonight. It was one thing to inform her Nick had attacked a woman. It was another to disclose the brutality of it all.

And how he pretended he was torturing me.

Thankfully, Roman kept a constant eye on her. Always asking if she wanted more water or sweet tea. Stealing a glance her way when she wasn't paying attention. Looking out for her.

She needed someone like that in her life now more than ever.

As did I.

"Thanks for inviting us over," Londyn said as the assembled crowd had begun to disperse. "Are you going to be okay?"

"I'll be fine." I gave her bicep a squeeze, forcing a smile. "And you? Will you be okay?"

She looked at Wes, their eyes briefly locking, before she returned her gaze to mine. "I will be."

"Good."

"You'll keep me posted if you hear anything?"

"Of course." I wrapped my arms around her, holding her a little longer than normal. Then she stepped back, allowing Wes to hug me.

"Thanks again for tonight," he said, kissing my cheek. "It was good to do something normal, even with the unexpected interruption."

"It was."

When he dropped his hold and started to retreat, I

touched his arm. "Can I talk to you about something really quick?"

He paused, glancing toward Londyn.

"I'll get Eli into the car," she offered, sensing it was something I needed to discuss with him in private.

"I'll be right out." He leaned down and kissed Londyn's cheek.

Grasping Eli's hand, she made her way toward the foyer, neither of us uttering a word until she disappeared from view.

"I know what you're going to say." Wes turned to me. "That I need to come clean."

"You do."

I briefly looked toward the patio, mindful to keep my voice down so Imogene couldn't overhear. I doubted she would anyway, all her attention devoted to whatever Roman was talking about.

"It's not fair to ask me to keep lying. At first, I understood why you wanted to keep this from Londyn. It all could have amounted to nothing more than coincidence. But I think we all know by now that it's not nothing."

"It's not," Wes sighed.

"Precisely why you need to tell her. She was as much a victim of Nick as I was. Maybe not to the same extent, but that doesn't make what he did to her any less traumatic. I get that the last thing you want to do is cause her any undue stress, considering she's mere weeks away from giving birth, but you have to tell her everything. About the jewelry I've received. About the recent suicides. About what Claire had been looking into. About the possibility there's a copycat repeating Nick's kill cycle. About Nick's demeanor when I went to see him at the prison on Friday."

"I've known I'd eventually have to tell her. I just..." Pinching the bridge of his nose, he pushed out a long breath, the torment he'd been dealing with evident in his expression.

My brother had always been a pretty easy-going guy. Always had an answer to everything.

But there was no answer here.

And the stress of the situation clearly wore on him.

"I guess in my mind she's already been through enough." He lifted his gaze to mine. "I hoped this could be my burden to bear."

I placed my hand on his bicep. "I get that. Hell, I tried to do the same thing with Imogene. And Lachlan. But if there's anything this situation has taught me, it's that you can't always protect the ones you love from the cruelty of the real world. All you can do is offer them your unwavering love, support, and a hand to grasp when life tries to pull them under."

He sighed, shoulders falling in defeat. "She's going to be pissed."

"True. But the sooner you tell her, the easier it'll be for you. It's better to face the music now and make sure she learns the truth from you than risk her finding out on her own. And she *will* find out, Wes. With all this shit going on, there's no way she won't."

"I know." He nodded dejectedly, running his fingers

through his hair, the flecks of gray seeming more numerous than a few weeks ago. "Will you do me a favor, though?"

"Anything."

His mouth curved up into a lazy smile. "Can you keep the couch open for me in case I need it tonight?"

I playfully nudged him. "I'll do you one better. Lachlan has, like, a dozen bedrooms in this place." I waved my hand at my opulent surroundings. "You can take one of them."

"Good to know I'll have a place to stay if need be." He winked.

"You'll always have a place with me."

Wrapping his arms around me, he enclosed me in his tight embrace. Then he pulled back, meeting my eyes.

"Promise you'll be safe. Okay?"

"I don't have any choice," I retorted, trying to lighten the mood, pushing out of his hold. "Have you seen this place? There are cops stationed outside 24/7, not to mention the insane security system Lachlan has. Then there's Nikko..." I gestured toward where he remained on the patio, "who hasn't left my side since he landed."

"And all the security protocols here help ease my worry. But after everything Curran said earlier..." His voice trembled as he shook his head, vein in his neck throbbing. "I just have a bad feeling in my gut that things aren't as they seem. That we're missing something."

"Missing what?"

"I can't explain it, Jules. I just..." He held my biceps, his stare and grip intensifying. "Just swear you'll be safe.

That you won't take any unnecessary risks, no matter what."

I nodded quickly, pushing down the emotions bubbling to the surface. "Of course," I barely managed to squeak out. "I promise."

Relief covered his expression as he pulled me to him once more, hugging me like it was the last time he ever would.

And after everything I learned tonight, I couldn't shake the feeling in the pit of my stomach it very well could be.

CHAPTER TWELVE

Julia

S leep evaded me, regardless of how exhausted I was. I wasn't sure if it was because I missed Lachlan, because of everything Agent Curran had shared, or because of Wes' fears that we were missing some crucial piece in this convoluted puzzle. Perhaps a combination of all three.

After hours of trying and failing to fall asleep, I slipped out of bed and padded down to the kitchen to make some tea, hoping that would help.

But as I walked into the kitchen, I paused when I saw Nikko sitting at the island, the glow from the laptop in front of him illuminating his face.

"Trouble sleeping?" I asked.

He looked my way. "More like my body's still on island

time. It's nearly five in the morning here. Not quite midnight on Oahu."

"So you're a night owl then?" I asked as I walked toward the stove and grabbed the kettle, filling it with water.

"I suppose I'm whatever I need to be at the moment."

I lit the burner, then leaned against the counter, crossing my arms in front of my chest. "You should try to get some sleep, though. If you don't, you'll be exhausted all day. Unless you're planning on heading home once Lachlan gets back." I glanced at the clock on the microwave. "Which should be any minute now, since he hopped on a red-eye instead of flying home with the team in the morning."

"I'm not leaving until I can be assured no harm will come to you or your daughter. No matter how long that takes."

"Thank you. For being here. And spending time in the gym with Imogene today. It means a lot."

"She's a good kid. No wonder Lachlan loves her so much. She's a lot like he was at her age. Strong-willed and a bit of a hothead."

I laughed. "That's most definitely Imogene."

"And that was *Pohili* back then, too. After his father passed away, he had some...anger issues."

"How did he die?"

Nikko hesitated, seemingly unsure what to tell me. I doubted Lachlan kept it from me for a reason. It simply never came up during conversation. There was enough tragedy in our present. No need to dig up more heartache from the past.

"Heart attack. Lachlan was only thirteen. Claire a year younger."

"I'm sorry to hear that. How old was his father? He couldn't have been that old."

"Actually, he was in his sixties."

"He was?" My eyes widened as I did the math. If he was in his sixties when he died, he had to be in his late forties or early fifties when Lachlan was born.

"His mother married an older man. Her parents didn't like it at first. Not only because of the age difference, but also because his mom was a native islander and his father was a white man from Australia. And when I say he was white, I'm talking blond hair, blue eyes, pasty white skin that would turn bright red if exposed to the sun for even a few minutes."

"I know all too well how that is," I laughed under my breath, considering I suffered from the same problem.

When the kettle whistled, I removed it from the burner, poured some water into a cup, then added a bag of green tea. "Would you like some?"

"That would be nice. Thank you."

"Green tea okay?" I grabbed another cup and saucer from the cupboard.

"Perfect."

"Milk? Honey? Sugar?"

"Nothing for me. Just plain."

"You got it."

I finished preparing both cups, then placed them on the island before scooting around to the other side, hoisting myself onto the barstool beside him.

As I blew on my beverage, I stole a glance at his laptop screen. There was a photo of a beach scene, dozens of people sitting on surfboards and kayaks, all arranged in a circle in the brilliant, blue ocean. I'd seen something like this a time or two when I visited Hawaii, just not of this magnitude.

"Is that a paddle-out?"

He nodded solemnly. "It was Piper's memorial service. Hundreds of people came out for it."

"She must have been a remarkable woman."

"She certainly was."

Silence settled over us as we sipped on our tea and Nikko continued scrolling through more photos. I couldn't shake the feeling there was a reason he chose today to take a look at these.

And that it was somehow related to what was currently going on.

"What prompted this walk down memory lane?" I asked hesitantly.

He chewed on his bottom lip, a contemplative expression crossing his brow. "It's probably a waste of time, but I haven't been able to stop thinking about what Agent Curran said earlier."

"Which part?"

He'd said a lot of things, all of which probably led to my own difficulty sleeping.

"About your ex-husband's ritual. How he always attended one of the memorial services for his victims, whether it be the visitation, funeral, burial, or reception."

"And because your sister was possibly attacked by a copycat...or acolyte...you think perhaps he copied this part of Nick's ritual, too?"

"I don't think it's a stretch to consider the possibility," Nikko responded. "While this person may not have followed your ex-husband's rituals to a T, he hit all the important stuff. Killed them on the exact date. Made each death appear to be a suicide. Stole a meaningful piece of jewelry as a souvenir to give to you. There's only one part of Nick's signature Ethan didn't bring up. I'm not sure why. Probably because he didn't know about it, since it wasn't mentioned in the media or during the trial. Which tells us two things."

"And that is?"

"One, there's a possibility this copycat was just as compelled to attend a memorial service as Nick was."

"And two?"

He pinched his lips together, not immediately saying anything. "And two, this person is either close enough to Nick to know he attended each memorial service, even if it was never reported by the media..."

"Or?"

"Or this person is in law enforcement with access to this kind of information."

"You don't think it could be a cop, do you?"

The idea the person behind all these deaths could be

in law enforcement made my stomach churn. But the more I thought about it, the more it made sense. Nick *did* escape a prison transport vehicle after it crashed, losing the cuffs and shackles and changing into street clothes. All evidence pointed to him having help. What if that help came in the form of a cop? Someone who could steer the investigation in a certain direction?

"I honestly don't know what to think. Not anymore. Not when we constantly learn something new that makes me rethink everything. All I do know with any sort of certainty is that I trust very few people right now. And my gut. I always trust my gut."

"And what does your gut say?"

Nikko brought the cup up to his mouth, taking a sip. "It says the answer might be found by looking into the memorials of these latest victims, Piper included. So I'm combing through these photos to see if anyone stands out. Ethan's going to get in touch with the families of some of the other victims to find out if they have anything that could help. Guest lists. Photos. Stuff like that. I'm not sure we'll find anything substantial, since I doubt many people are in the habit of memorializing funerals. Which is why Piper's paddle-out may be the best bet. Our traditions are a bit...different. Memorials are more of a celebration of life than a reminder of death."

"Have you come across anyone who looks like Daxton Shea?"

"Right here." He pointed to a blond man standing on the beach, watching the paddle-out.

He wasn't the only one, many tourists stopping to witness the unique event. But he certainly stood out in his khaki pants and crisp shirt.

"He'd visited Lachlan in the hospital after the attack. Then it appears he stuck around for the memorial a week later."

"Don't you find that odd? At the time of Piper's attack, Lachlan had just been promoted to the majors, right?"

"Correct."

"So why would one of the team's owners fly all the way to Hawaii?"

"Lachlan always said that Dax was just a really good guy. That he'd do the same for any of his players, regardless of whether they made the team millions every year or were barely scraping by in the minors."

I parted my lips to argue my point further, but Nikko held up his hand, cutting me off.

"Do I think it's strange? Yes. And taken together with everything else we know, it *is* suspicious. But like Agent Curran stated earlier, it doesn't measure up to anything remotely close to the burden of proof needed for an arrest warrant. His lawyers would have him released before he's even been read his rights."

I sank into the barstool, feeling defeated. Disheartened. Frustrated.

This was one of the things I hated about this entire situation. Growing hopeful we were on track to getting answers, then being yanked several steps backward.

"Have you shared this with Lachlan?" I dropped my voice. "Including the most recent attack?"

He slowly shook his head. "I figured that was more a conversation to have face-to-face."

I took a sip of my tea, meeting his gaze from over my mug. "I didn't tell him, either."

"It would only worry him unnecessarily. He deserves to enjoy his big win."

I nodded. "You're a good friend."

"I try to be. We may not always see eye to eye, but he's *ohana*. And he always will be."

"Speaking of your long friendship with Lachlan..." I waggled my brows, cutting through the tension. "You've got to have some good stories about him as a kid, don't you? Something incredibly embarrassing."

He chuckled, the deep rumble filling the space. "Do I ever. There was this one time—"

The sound of the door opening interrupted him. We tore our eyes toward the foyer, Lachlan entering. He dropped his suitcase and turned, about to head up the stairs. But when he noticed Nikko and me sitting at the kitchen island, he stopped, expression wide, concern etched on his face as he stalked toward us.

"What happened? What's wrong?"

I slid off my stool, feeling oddly at peace now that Lachlan was back.

"Everything's okay." I ran my hands down his arms.

Things weren't exactly okay. But I didn't want to get into that mere seconds after he walked through the door.

"Why are you awake? Why—"

I wrapped my arms around him, snuggling into his warmth. We hadn't even been apart for forty-eight hours, yet it felt like so much longer. "I've gotten so used to having you in bed with me that I struggle to sleep without you by my side."

He pulled me closer, inhaling deeply. "I missed you, too, love," he murmured, his voice evidencing his exhaustion.

I lifted my eyes, lips brushing his. "Congratulations on your big win."

He smiled shyly, the cocky man I once thought him to be nowhere to be found. "To be honest, I'm surprised I pulled it off with everything going on. But I *really* wanted to win." He laughed under his breath, then glanced toward Nikko. "I knew I had nothing to worry about with Nikko here watching my girls." He gave him a grateful smile. "Thanks, cousin."

"You pitched a hell of a game, *Pohili*. Your mother would have been proud."

Lachlan dropped his hold on me as Nikko approached, patting his back in a bro hug before pulling back and smiling. But then his expression fell, his eyes focused just past Nikko.

We followed his line of sight to see what caused the sudden shift in mood. I should have known.

"Why are you looking at photos of Piper's paddle-out?" Lachlan asked. He wasn't angry. More curious.

And concerned.

I met Nikko's eyes, the two of us nodding slightly. Then he turned toward Lachlan, his expression even, quickly becoming the no-nonsense detective I'd met in Hawaii.

"Agent Curran stopped by earlier today."

"What did he say?"

Nikko and I shared another look before he turned to Lachlan again.

"You might want to sit down for this one, cousin."

CHAPTER THIRTEEN

Lachlan

I stared blankly into space as I listened to what I could only assume to be a truncated version of the information Agent Curran had shared with Nikko and Julia earlier in the evening.

How Nick broke into a couple's home.

How he held them captive for what I imagined to be a harrowing twelve hours.

How he forced that innocent woman to have dinner with him, all the while calling her Julia, pretending she was the ex-wife Nick was still obsessed with.

The woman I loved more than anything.

The woman I was petrified to lose.

How he shot her husband, making it appear like suicide, before stabbing the woman.

It was all so depraved. So brutal. So tragic.

"There's, uh, something else," Nikko stated, pulling my attention back to him, my grip on Julia's hand tightening with every second.

"Something else?" I asked in a shaky voice.

He nodded, his expression even more dire than it was as he informed me of the home invasion that took the life of an innocent man.

When I left for California, my biggest concern was making sure Julia remained within these four walls where I knew she'd be safe from that animal's psychotic obsession. Never did I think something like this would happen.

"Nick also raped Christine."

I squeezed my eyes shut, drawing in a deep breath. I couldn't say I was surprised. With all the deaths attributed to him, he'd raped each woman first. It went without saying that he'd do the same to Christine.

"With a knife."

I flung my eyes open, muscles tensing. "What did you say?"

Julia lifted her gaze to mine. "Nick used the blade of a knife to...to rape her."

I blinked repeatedly, her statement not immediately registering. When it finally did, it felt like an arrow pierced my heart, an indescribable anguish filling me. Standing, I dug my fingers through my hair as I paced around the room, trying to make sense of this.

"A knife?" I repeated after a moment, stopping in my tracks. "He..." I trailed off, unable to finish my question.

Nikko nodded. "Yes. Instead of his genitalia, he used—"

"I got it," I interrupted, feeling queasy.

And not for the poor woman who was forced to endure that, although my heart certainly went out to her.

I was on the brink of expelling the contents of my stomach over the idea this was what Nick wanted to do to Julia.

My Julia.

"When did you learn about this?" I demanded, every muscle in my body quivering as I attempted to remain calm.

"Why does—"

"Agent Curran came over at the start of the fifth inning," Julia interrupted Nikko. "He informed me, Nikko, Wes, and Londyn about the attack."

"The start of the fifth?" I swallowed hard, a painful rock lodging in my throat. "So when we spoke after the game..." I shifted my gaze toward Nikko. "And when I called you right before my flight took off..." I pinched the bridge of my nose. "You both already knew and didn't tell me?"

Julia stood, making her way toward me. "What good would it have done? You deserved to celebrate your win. Not have it tarnished with such...gruesome news."

"Why isn't this all over the internet? Being reported in the media? I haven't heard so much as a bloody peep about something like this, and I've been checking the news. Constantly. Why—"

"Because Agent Curran believes keeping it under wraps, at least for a few more days, could help him track down Nick."

"A few more days? So that animal can do this to even more women?" I searched Julia's eyes, unsure how she could remain so calm about this.

"The FBI, along with the GBI, is doing everything they can to prevent that from happening," Nikko assured me. "In the meantime, the fact Nick believes Christine Griffin died as a result of his assault can work to our advantage."

"How? I—"

"He used to go to funerals. Visitations. Burials," Julia explained. "Liked watching people mourning the women he killed."

"Agent Curran plans to stage a memorial for her," Nikko added. "This Friday."

"And he hopes by not publicizing his involvement in this, Nick will show up?"

Julia nodded. "I don't like it any more than you do. But if Nick's doing this..." She bit her lower lip to stop it from quivering. "If he's torturing and brutalizing innocent women because of me—"

"Don't you dare," I interjected, grabbing her biceps. "Don't you dare put this on you. This is on him, and only him."

She nodded, but I could tell she still felt responsible.

I probably would have in her position, too.

"If Nick's going to these...extremes, I want Agent Curran to do everything in his power to find him. And that's exactly what he plans to do." She rested her hand against my cheek. "He *will* find him. He can't run forever."

I pulled her into my arms, relishing in the feel of her small body against mine. I hated everything about this. Hated the idea of Nick being on the loose and victimizing more women. Hated the idea Julia felt responsible for his actions.

Hated the idea Nick would do the same to Julia if the opportunity presented itself.

The only thing preventing me from having a full-blown panic attack was the fact I knew she was safe here.

"What about Imogene returning to school?" I pulled back to meet her eyes. "You're not going to send her back now, are you? Not with this."

"Yes." She swallowed hard. "I am.

"But—"

"She doesn't know about this. And, right now, I have no intention of telling her about it. This isn't... No four-teen-year-old should have to hear about something like this. Especially when..." She trailed off, attempting to collect her emotions. "I'm not telling her. Not until I have to. I can't suddenly backtrack on my decision to allow her to return to school. She'd know something was up."

"So? Just tell her Nick attacked a woman and leave out the details. Tell her—"

"I don't *want* to backtrack on this decision, Lachlan. Like I said the other day—"

"You refuse to let Nick control you."

She shrugged. "We need to live our lives." She forced out a smile. "Even with these new...developments."

I pulled my lips between my teeth, fearing that living our lives as if nothing were wrong would be our downfall. And I couldn't stomach the idea of anything happening to Julia. To Imogene. To this little family I'd managed to find when I least expected it.

"Come on." Julia linked her fingers with mine. "Let's crawl into bed for a few hours before I need to take Imogene to school."

It seemed selfish to even consider sleeping. But the idea of stealing a few minutes with Julia sounded like exactly what I needed. Then I could figure out what to do.

"Get some rest, *Pohili*. Everything will be fine. I swore I'd keep your girls safe, and I never go back on my word. Promise."

I met Nikko's gaze. "*Mahalo*, cousin."

"Anything for you."

I smiled slightly, then followed Julia up to my bedroom, my mind still consumed with everything going on. With the brutality that poor woman endured. It was all I could think about. I'd never heard of something so depraved. So vile. So appalling.

And the knowledge he did it as he called her Julia only made matters worse.

Only made the despair and anger raging through me increase even more.

As we crossed the threshold and I shut the door, Julia turned to me, green eyes intense and unwavering.

"Don't bring it in here, Lachlan. Leave it outside."

I stared at her, wishing it were that easy. That I could flip a switch and push it from my memory.

"It's so bloody hard." My words came out choked, the fear snaking through me making it difficult to breathe. I dragged her body to mine, enclosing her in my arms, not wanting to let go. "I can't stand the idea of losing you, too."

She pressed a hand to my cheek, forcing my eyes to hers. "You won't."

"How do you know? I saw how he was, Julia. He's... crazed. Obsessed. I fear..." I trailed off, unsure I had the strength to even voice my concerns. A lone tear trickled down my face. "I fear he won't stop until he fulfills his promise to you. Until he does to you what he did to that poor woman. And I can't stomach the possibility. Can't stand the thought of you enduring something so horrendous."

"I'm scared, too. Okay?" She swiped away the tear, then gripped my face in her hands. "But I have to believe it'll all work out. That we didn't come this far only to lose everything." She inched her mouth closer to mine. "That I didn't survive everything I did just to lose the greatest thing that's ever happened to me." Her lips brushed mine before she met my gaze once more.

"I didn't fight hard enough for myself when I was married to Nick. Maybe because I didn't think I had anything to fight for. Maybe because I thought I deserved that life. But now I know nothing could be further from the truth. I *do* deserve to be happy. And you make me so damn happy it almost feels criminal."

I blew out an emotion-filled laugh, all too familiar with what she was talking about. I often felt the same when I reflected on how happy Julia made me. It took a while for me to not feel guilty about it, thinking I didn't deserve to be happy after the role I played in Piper's death.

But now I knew I did deserve this happiness.

And I refused to let anyone take that from me.

Let anyone take *her* from me.

"I promise you, Lachlan..." Her voice turned grave, expression determined. "I will do whatever it takes to protect what we have. To fight for you. For me. For us. No matter what."

I circled my arms around her, my hold on her nearly as tight as a vice. "It fucking hurts, Julia," I confessed. I wanted to find comfort in her assurances. But I couldn't. Not after witnessing Nick's obsession with her first-hand.

"Show me where."

I covered my heart with my hand. "Here."

Eyes darkening, she brought her fingers to my shirt and unbuttoned it, her motions languid and unhurried. The atmosphere shifted from one of frustration and despair to one of lust and hunger. After she pushed my shirt off my shoulders, the material landing on the floor behind me, she ran her fingers along the contours of my abs. Her lips inched toward my chest, tongue tracing circles, her warm, inviting mouth dulling the pain.

I closed my eyes, gripping her hips, slipping my fingers under the material of her shorts.

"Where else?" she murmured huskily.

I returned my gaze to hers. "Here." I touched a finger to my lips.

She clutched my face, pulling my mouth toward hers. At the first taste of her kiss, I moaned, looping an arm around her waist and pulling her closer. I walked backward toward the bed, moving my mouth against hers, our tongues tangling in a desperate dance, both of us doing everything to chase away the pain of our present.

When my legs hit the bed, I unfastened my belt, shoving my pants and briefs down, kicking them to the side. Then I lowered myself onto the mattress, pulling her with me. She straddled me as I remained sitting, running my hand up her back. Grabbing the hem of her t-shirt, I yanked it over her head.

"Where else?" She trailed her fingers down my torso, her hands warm on my skin.

"Everywhere," I whispered.

Touching a hand to my shoulder, she urged me onto my back.

"Then let me heal you." She stood, sliding her shorts down her legs before returning to the bed and crawling on top of me. Curving toward me, her lips whispered against mine. "Let me be your cure."

CHAPTER FOURTEEN

Julia

My eyes fluttered open to the sun streaming into the bedroom, everything bright and vibrant. A complete one-eighty from what felt like only a second ago when I swore I just needed to rest my eyes for a minute before getting up to make sure Imogene was ready for school.

I bolted up, snatching my phone off the nightstand to see it was 7:30. If I had any hope of getting her to school on time, we needed to leave in fifteen minutes.

I glanced to the opposite side of the bed, wanting to let Lachlan know I'd be back in an hour and would take Nikko with me. But he wasn't there. I found it odd, considering how little sleep he'd gotten the past few days. Then again, the news I shared with him last night certainly unsettled him. It unsettled me, too. But I didn't have time to worry about it right now.

Darting out of the bedroom and down the hallway, I peeked my head into what had become Imogene's room, blowing out a relieved breath when I saw she'd gotten up on her own, the room empty.

With quick steps, I hurried down the stairs, hoping she'd managed to at least find some cereal.

Rounding the corner, I came to an abrupt stop, seeing Lachlan and Imogene sitting at the kitchen island together, a coffee in front of him, a plate of bacon and eggs in front of her.

Well, that wasn't entirely true.

The eggs were gone, apart from a few streaks of yoke, and she currently chewed on the last piece of bacon.

"Morning, Mama," she said brightly, as if it were normal for her to be sitting in Lachlan's kitchen, eating a breakfast he made for her before she left for school. While it wasn't completely out of the ordinary, it still felt...different. Maybe because he did all of this on his own without me lifting a finger. Hell, I slept through most of it.

"You're up," Lachlan commented as he met my gaze from over his coffee cup.

"What's going on?"

"Breakfast." He stood and strode toward me. "Want me to make you something?"

"Why didn't you wake me up? I could have fixed Imogene breakfast. She's not your responsibility."

He pressed a chaste kiss to my cheek. "I figured you could use some rest. And even if Imogene isn't my responsibility, I can still help. So I got up to make her breakfast and take her to school. Give you a break for once in your life."

"You were going to take her to school?"

"Of course." He stepped back. "Want some eggs?"

"Maybe just coffee for now. I need to get dressed and make her lunch."

Lachlan grabbed Imogene's lunch bag, placing it on the island beside her. "All done. Yogurt. Granola bar. A banana. And a turkey sandwich."

I blinked repeatedly, jaw dropping. "You... You packed her lunch, too?"

He shrugged. "It wasn't that hard. I've seen you do it a bunch of times."

"And now I get to brag to all my friends that Lachlan Hale made my lunch," Imogene muttered around a mouthful of bacon. "Can he still drive me to school, Mama? He was going to take me in the Mustang. And I really, *really* want to go in the Mustang." She practically bounced in her chair with excitement.

"I'm sure Lachlan's tired. He pitched yesterday. Then took a red-eye to get home. He needs to rest."

Her expression immediately fell.

"I don't mind," Lachlan insisted. "You can come, too, of course."

I looked from Lachlan to Imogene, her excitement returning. I didn't want to put the responsibility of taking care of Imogene on his shoulders simply because we were living here temporarily.

At the same time, I didn't want to deprive Imogene of something she really wanted. She was going through enough at the moment.

And I feared it was only going to get worse before it got better.

"Are you sure?" I asked Lachlan once more. "You don't have to if you'd rather—"

He pressed a kiss to my lips, silencing me. "I'm more than sure. Let me do this for Imogene. And you."

I met his gaze, unable to stop the smile from pulling on my mouth, my heart feeling fuller than it should, considering everything going on.

But none of that mattered. Not now. Maybe we were setting ourselves up for failure by not worrying about Nick with every passing second.

But I'd done that for years.

I refused to give him the satisfaction anymore.

"Okay. We'll all go in the Mustang."

"Yes!" Imogene cheered excitedly.

"But you'd better go brush your teeth and finish getting ready. We need to leave in five minutes."

"You got it." She bolted off her barstool and rushed up the stairs.

I couldn't remember the last time I saw her move so quickly to get to school. Not since kindergarten when she cried after learning she couldn't go to school on the weekends because it was closed.

"Here." Lachlan handed me my coffee in a travel mug.

"You really don't have to do all this."

He wrapped an arm around my waist. "I know I don't have to. I *want* to. Want to be a part of both of your lives. Want to help you out when I can. Plus, that stubborn, headstrong kid of yours has grown on me." He winked.

"I'm just so used to having to do everything on my own. I don't know how to react when someone offers to help."

"You say thank you."

"In that case..." I lifted myself onto my toes and skimmed my lips against his. "Thank you."

"Anything for you, love." He pulled me closer, deepening the kiss. But I cut it short before it turned from a PG kiss into more R-rated territory.

"I need to get ready. Just give me a few minutes."

"Of course."

Leaving my coffee on the island, I dashed up to the bedroom.

More than aware all eyes would be on us this morning...not just because of Lachlan's flashy car, but also because of the news surrounding Nick's escape...I tugged on a pair of jeans and traded my t-shirt with "It's a throat punch kind of day" on it for a black V-neck.

After arranging my auburn waves into some semblance of a bun on the top of my head and applying some eyeliner, I headed back downstairs, Lachlan and Imogene waiting.

"Ready?" Lachlan asked.

"Ready."

I grabbed my coffee as Lachlan took Imogene's book bag and slung it over his shoulder. Then he led us out to the garage, helping me into the back seat before helping Imogene into the front so she could get the "full Mustang experience", as he put it.

As we talked and laughed during the fifteen-minute drive, it felt so...normal. Like we were a real family driving to school. It may be unconventional, but just because we didn't fit the mold of what someone thought an ideal family should look like didn't mean our love for each other was any less valid. If anything, it was even stronger because of all the struggles we'd been through to get to where we were.

When we pulled into the parking lot, quite a few students and faculty looked our way. While it wasn't odd to see the lot filled with luxury cars — Mercedes, Lexus, Audi, BMW — a 1968 Mustang Shelby Cobra wasn't your typical car, especially when the engine rumbled loudly as Lachlan maneuvered through the parking lot.

And the man driving wasn't some stuffy CEO or politician, either.

For the first time, I didn't care about standing out, about people looking at us.

I wanted people to see us together.

All of us.

Lachlan pulled to a stop in front of the school and jumped out, darting over to Imogene's side to help her to her feet. Several students streaming into the school stopped to gawk. A few even took some photos, which I was certain would end up on their social media sites within minutes. Perhaps sooner.

But that didn't make Lachlan act any differently than he would have had it only been us. To him, it was just background noise. Not something he paid much attention to.

"Are you going to stay back there, or do you want to ride up front with me?" he asked, pushing the front seat forward and extending his hand.

"The front. Definitely."

I placed my hand in his and climbed out, turning toward Imogene.

"Have a good day. Remember the rules. No going anywhere you're not supposed to, and certainly nowhere without your assigned escort."

I stole a glimpse at the front doors where the director of the academy stood beside an intimidating man dressed in a suit whom I recognized as one of the school's many security guards. After offering them a grateful smile, I returned my attention to Imogene.

"And I want you to text me between every class period. No matter what."

"I'll be fine," she assured me with a roll of her eyes.

Then, to my surprise, she wrapped her arms around me, even though the entire school was watching. I suppose when baseball's hottest pitcher drives you to school in his sexy muscle car, it was okay to make a few teenage faux pas, like hugging your mom.

"Love you, Mama." She dropped her hold. "I promise

to text between every class. And the tracking on my phone, watch, and tag on my backpack is enabled."

"Good."

It might have been overkill, but in my mind, there was no such thing. Not when it came to Imogene. While I didn't want Nick to interfere with her ability to go to school like a normal teenager, I did have to be realistic, especially after the news Agent Curran shared last night. Being able to track her offered me some peace of mind.

She gave me one last smile before turning toward Lachlan and hugging him. "Thanks for the ride, Hale."

"You got it, kid. Love ya." He kissed the top of her head.

"Love ya, too."

As if my ovaries hadn't already exploded this morning when I walked into the kitchen to see Lachlan had made breakfast for my daughter, then packed her lunch, seeing them hug and say they loved each other... It filled me with more appreciation and respect for these two amazing people than I thought possible. More love than I should have felt, given everything going on.

But maybe that was exactly why I should have felt this way. Despite current events, we had each other. We had this love. As long as we found strength in the bond we shared, I was confident we'd get through anything.

Once Imogene disappeared through the front doors of the school, the director and security guard close on her heels, Lachlan helped me into the front seat before making his way around to the driver's side. He was about to shift into first and lower the parking brake when I grabbed his face and brought his mouth to mine.

He stiffened, seemingly unsure what to think of me kissing him like this in front of Imogene's school where anyone could see us.

Where anyone could take our photo and post it on social media.

While I had no problem kissing him at Skyline Park on Sunday, that was different. We were surrounded by friends. That wasn't the case now.

But I didn't care who saw us. Not anymore. I was done living in fear of what people would think. Done pretending to be someone I wasn't just to be accepted.

Lachlan made me realize I was good enough as I was. And maybe I was the type of person who wanted to kiss her ridiculously sexy boyfriend in the school parking lot.

"If you don't stop kissing me, I'm going to need to find some abandoned street so we can christen this car," he murmured against my mouth.

I cocked my head. "You've never christened it?"

"Can't say as I have."

"Well then..." I leaned back into the seat, pulling the seat belt across my chest. "I know the perfect spot."

CHAPTER FIFTEEN

Julia

O ver the next few days, life returned to some sort of normalcy.

Or at least as normal as possible.

Whenever the phone rang, Lachlan, Nikko, and I would jump, hoping it was Agent Curran delivering the news that Nick had finally been caught and we could all breathe again. Or that it was Ethan calling to tell us he'd received photos from some of the other funerals and Dax was at every single one.

That never happened, though.

Instead, Ethan confirmed what Nikko feared would happen. That the families didn't take many pictures, considering it wasn't exactly an event they wanted to remember. Agent Curran hadn't received any viable leads on Nick's location, either. I tried to not wonder if that was because he'd found a new woman to brutalize. When I voiced my concerns, Agent Curran claimed there hadn't been any additional attacks of a similar nature.

I tried to find comfort in that. But I wondered if it was because this time, Nick actually *did* kill the woman and no one had discovered her body just yet.

I didn't voice that concern to Curran, though. Or Lachlan.

I didn't want to burst our bubble. Because, despite everything going on, things were going great.

I woke up in Lachlan's arms every morning. After we made love, he'd get up to cook Imogene breakfast before we drove her to school in the Mustang. Always in the Mustang.

Once we returned to his house, he'd disappear into the home gym. Sometimes I'd join him for a quick run on the treadmill or just to watch him lift weights, which was certainly a sight to behold. After a shower together, we'd have lunch before he headed to the field for a few hours of conditioning. Even though their first playoff game wasn't until Saturday and Lachlan wasn't scheduled to pitch until Tuesday, they still did some light drills every day so they were ready.

While Lachlan was at the field, I'd spend my day experimenting with new recipes, using Nikko as my very willing guinea pig. I'd regale him with stories about my meemaw and her love of food, and he'd share snippets from when Lachlan was a small boy, as well as teach me a bit about Hawaiian culture.

I couldn't remember the last time I'd spent so much time in the kitchen experimenting. No board meetings. No advertising pitches. No looking at sales figures.

For the first time in years, I actually felt happy again.

And for the first time, I considered accepting one of the many offers I'd received from various restaurants vying to own my brand.

I'd built The Mad Batter as a tribute to my meemaw. Somewhere along the way, however, I veered off the original path I'd set out on.

I didn't want to own a bakery on every street corner. Didn't want my cupcakes packaged and sold in grocery stores. But that was what happened. The brand had been diluted so much it was no longer the unique, independent bakery I once imagined where I'd shower people with love through food.

But if I'd learned anything after my crazy love affair with Lachlan it was that it was never too late for a fresh start.

I found that fresh start in love.

Maybe I could find it in my career, too.

Friday afternoon, as Nikko and I were about to head out, the door opened, Lachlan walking in.

I furrowed my brows, confused. He was supposed to be at the field for one last day of conditioning before their first division championship game.

"What are you doing back? It's only 2:30."

"But Imogene has a soccer game at three today, yeah?"

"Yeah...," I drew out, looking between Nikko and Lachlan.

"That's why I'm home early. They took it easy on us today anyway, since they want us all rested and ready for tomorrow. Now that we're essentially 'out' as a couple, I didn't want to miss the opportunity to watch Imogene play."

"You left practice early so you could go to a high school soccer game?"

"Of course," he replied, as if it were completely normal. "You don't mind, do you? I guess I should have made sure you'd be okay with this. I just—"

"Of course I don't mind. I just thought..." I shook my head, words seeming to escape me. "I'm not sure *what* I thought. But I do know you wanting to sit through her game never crossed my mind. I didn't think it would interest you."

He looped his arm around my waist. "I love you. And I also love your daughter. This is important to her. Therefore, it's important to me. I can't promise I'll always be able to make it to her games, but I'll do my best to support both of you any way I can."

I parted my lips, searching for something just as meaningful to say in response. But nothing seemed adequate. Instead, I brushed my mouth against his, not caring that Nikko stood just a few feet away. At this point, he was used to seeing us kiss.

"Can you be any more perfect?" I sighed against him.

And just like every other time I made a similar comment, he laughed. "I have my faults, but I'm glad you think I'm perfect."

"You're perfect for me. That's all that matters."

"I hope that's all that will ever matter."

CHAPTER SIXTEEN

Lachlan

"Well, isn't this a surprise." Naomi sauntered up as I helped Julia out of the Range Rover.

I considered taking the Mustang, simply because I knew how much Imogene loved that car. But since Nikko was with us, I figured we'd all be much more comfortable in my SUV.

"Hey, Naomi." Julia wrapped her in a hug. "Thanks for coming out for the game."

She waved her off. "Anything for my niece. Plus, my boss has been out of the office all week, so I can pretty much do whatever the hell I want."

Julia rolled her eyes. "You can pretty much do whatever you want even when your boss *is* in the office."

"True." She winked, then glanced my way.

"Good to see you again, Lachlan. Congrats on the win on Monday."

"Thanks," I said, feigning enthusiasm.

It was hard to be excited about having a place in the playoffs with everything else going on. But I tried to do what Julia had been doing — living her life, despite the constant threat of Nick hanging over us like a tumultuous storm cloud.

"Have you met Nikko?" I asked. "He's—"

"Of course." She gave him a smile. "Good to see you again."

"You, too."

She held his gaze for a beat, then tore her attention back to me, frowning. "Wait a minute. You're here."

"Yes...," I drew out.

"And so are you," she directed at Julia.

"I am."

"In public."

"It would appear so." Julia glanced my way before looking back at her friend.

"With Lachlan."

"Yes."

"Does this mean you're finally telling the world you're together?" Naomi asked excitedly.

There wasn't so much as a hint of hesitation as Julia nodded, a wide smile forming on her mouth. She hooked an arm around my waist.

"Yes, Naomi. It does." She craned her head back, eyes briefly locking with mine, before she looked back at

Naomi. "Although, I'm fairly certain the world already knows, considering Lachlan's driven Imogene to school in his Mustang every morning and the other students haven't been shy about posting photos and videos on their social media."

"So you're telling me you're not just openly dating, but you're also social media official?" Her voice kicked up at the end as she struggled to reel in her excitement.

Julia laughed, joy, happiness, and contentment crossing her expression. What I wouldn't do to keep that look on her face for the rest of her days.

"Yes, Naomi. We're together. In all ways a couple can be together. No more secrets. No more pretending. No more hiding."

"Well, halle-*fucking*-lujah!" she exclaimed, pulling Julia into a hug so tight I was certain it was going to cut off her oxygen. "It's about damn time."

"Naomi," Julia admonished. "You're in the parking lot of a school."

Naomi pulled back, rolling her eyes. "I'm in the parking lot of a *high* school. Trust me. These little fuckers say much worse than me."

"I seriously can't take you anywhere," Julia muttered under her breath as she waved at a couple with two elementary-aged kids walking by.

"You can pretend you're embarrassed all you want, but I know the truth." She flashed Julia a smile. "You'd be lost without me."

"That I would."

"Now that *that's* settled, let's go watch my niece kick some serious ass on the field."

My fingers locked with Julia's, we made our way toward the athletic fields located behind the massive, brick building of Brookhaven Academy.

As we walked, I noticed quite a few people looking our way and whispering to each other. Especially the women. It didn't take a mind reader to know what they were saying, their upturned noses and crossed arms making it clear they wondered what someone like me would see in Julia.

I kept expecting her to shy away, maybe increase her distance from me. But she didn't. If anything, she held her head higher, waving at a group of moms who were obviously talking about her.

Just as we were about to climb the bleachers to find a seat, I tightened my grip on her hand and yanked her body to mine, treating her to a sweet kiss. It wasn't deep or full of longing. Just a simple kiss to let her know how much I appreciated her. Plus, a part of me wanted to make all those catty mothers jealous.

When I stepped back and saw the shocked, borderline envious expressions on their faces, I knew I'd succeeded.

Once we made our way up the bleachers and found some seats, Julia pointed toward where Imogene was warming up on the field.

I watched as she bounced the ball from knee to knee, her quick footwork rather impressive. This was a vastly different game than baseball. While there were times it called for fast reflexes, especially when going for a double play or attempting to throw out a runner heading home, it wasn't remotely close to the constant action of football — or soccer, as Americans called it. And the fact Imogene made the varsity team as a sophomore meant she was pretty damn talented at the sport.

"People are definitely figuring out who you are," Julia whispered into my ear when the coaches called the kids over to the sidelines for a pre-game pep talk.

I tore my attention away from the field for the first time, too proud and excited for Imogene to look anywhere else. But now that I did, I observed quite a few people looking our way, as well as several younger kids and teens holding hats and a marker as they timidly approached, obviously hoping for an autograph or photo.

"Shite," I murmured. "I didn't even think." I shook my head, meeting Julia's gaze. "I'm sorry. I shouldn't have come. I just wanted to watch Imogene play..."

"Hey." She placed her hand on my leg. "It's okay. I'm thrilled you're here." She nodded toward the field. I followed her line of sight, smiling when I saw Imogene waving excitedly at me. "She's thrilled you're here, too. It means a lot to her."

I waved back, then returned my eyes to Julia's. "Well, *she* means a lot to *me*."

"Then stay. Maybe just tell your adoring fans you'll sign autographs and take photos *after* the game."

I chuckled. "And here I thought styling my hair and wearing a button-down shirt would be enough of a disguise."

"Maybe if my daughter weren't a teenage girl, it would have been."

I looked at her quizzically. "What does that have to do with anything?"

"Because teenage girls *love* to talk. When she first learned I was dating you, it killed her that she couldn't say anything to her friends. Now that she can, I guarantee she drops your name every chance she gets."

"I'm sorry. I—"

"You have nothing to apologize for, Lachlan. She's a huge fan. And she's proud of you."

"I'm proud of her, too. She's just... She's an awesome kid." I nudged Julia. "But that's to be expected."

"Why's that?"

"Because she has you for a mum. And if you ask me, I think you're pretty awesome." I pressed a soft kiss to her cheek, then stood, slowly making my way toward the growing group of students hoping for an autograph.

After telling them I would happily sign autographs at the end of the game, I made my way back to Julia just as the ref blew the first whistle.

Over the past few months, I'd watched Imogene practice different drills in her back yard. Even did some drills with her, although I was complete rubbish when it came to football.

But watching her in an actual match was incredible. I couldn't help but feel a sense of pride as I watched her block any ball that came remotely close to her. It was similar to how I felt whenever I learned one of the kids in my Little League had achieved something that hadn't been possible before they joined, whether it be higher grades, turning a double play on the field, or getting into college.

But here, the pride was even more profound.

Because, in the past few months, Imogene had become important to me.

She may not have been my biological kid, but I felt a deep connection to her.

I'd do anything to protect her and this little family I'd managed to find when I didn't think I'd ever have a family again.

When I didn't think I ever *wanted* a family.

Now I did.

And I'd be damned if I let anyone attempt to take them from me.

CHAPTER SEVENTEEN

Julia

"Way to go, Imogene!" Lachlan exclaimed as we made our way onto the field after their win, thanks to my daughter being an impenetrable wall on the field.

As always.

"You were incredible out there." He wrapped his arms around her, kissing the top of her sweaty head, as if she were his own daughter.

And that was precisely what it felt like as I watched Imogene's game.

Or, more accurately, as I watched *Lachlan* watch Imogene's game.

The way he cheered for her, supported her, encouraged her was exactly what a father would do.

It was exactly how I always hoped a father would act

around her. Never would I have imagined finding such an incredible role model for her in a twenty-seven-year-old professional baseball player.

"Thanks," she replied somewhat shyly, sensing quite a few pairs of eyes on her. But that didn't seem to affect Lachlan. He tuned it out, all his attention focused on Imogene as he celebrated in her win, as if she'd just won the World Series. Not an inconsequential high school soccer game.

"You did great, sweetie," I added. After getting praise from Lachlan Hale, my approval didn't matter in the least. "How do you feel? You didn't overdo it, did you?" I raked my gaze over her, always the concerned mother of a heart patient.

"I'm fine. You don't need to worry about me." She toyed with her necklace of a mended heart, knowing where my anxiety came from.

"It's my job to worry about you."

"I know." She rolled her eyes, feigning aggravation. Then her expression brightened.

"Roman!" she shouted as she waved.

I followed her line of sight to see Roman standing off to the side, as well as dozens of others waiting to ask Lachlan for his autograph, baseballs, hats, and even a few gloves in their hands.

Roman jogged toward Imogene, a sincere smile on his face. "Great game, Mo. You're one heck of a defender."

Her cheeks reddened under his compliment. "Thanks."

"Ms. Prescott," he said politely. "Mr. Hale. Good to see you again."

Lachlan shook his outstretched hand. "You can just call me Lachlan."

A wide smile tugged on Roman's lips, eyes lighting up. "Thank you, Mr., uh... Lachlan."

"Or you can just call him Hale." Imogene crossed her arms in front of her chest, pretending as if Lachlan weren't the celebrity he was. "That's what I do."

"I think I'll stick to Lachlan," Roman replied nervously, obviously remembering the warning Lachlan gave him days ago. "Are you staying for the football game?" he asked Imogene.

She gave me a pleading look. "Can I?"

"I don't know, sweetie," I said with a sigh, hating to be the bad guy yet again. "You haven't had dinner yet."

"I can get her something at the concession stand. They have hot dogs, burgers, stuff like that."

"That's very kind of you," I told Roman, then addressed Imogene again. "Don't you want to shower after your game?"

"I can do that in the locker room."

I pulled my bottom lip between my teeth, wishing one of my previous reasons would work to discourage her. The last thing I wanted was to tell her she couldn't stay for the Homecoming game when practically the entire school would be there. Any other day, I would have happily agreed. Would have encouraged her to go.

But with Nick on the run, everything was different.

"I could stay," Nikko said softly behind me.

I whirled around, having forgotten he and Naomi stood nearby.

"You shouldn't have—"

"Or we could stay," Lachlan suggested.

I turned toward him, eyes wide. "*We* could?" I questioned. "As in you and me attend a high school football game?"

"A distraction might be good for us." He gave me a knowing look.

It *was* Friday. The night Agent Curran planned to stage Christine Griffin's memorial in the hopes of catching Nick.

"Please, Mama." Imogene clasped her hands in front of her, expression imploring. "It's the Homecoming game."

"Are you sure about this?" I asked Lachlan. "You have a big game tomorrow."

"I'm not pitching until Tuesday. It'll be fun. I haven't been to a high school football game since, well...high school." He chuckled. "I think we all deserve a normal Friday night."

I looked into his eyes, unable to believe the brooding man who barely uttered two words to me after I was stung by that jellyfish all those months ago was the same man suggesting we attend a high school football game so my teenage daughter could hang out with her boyfriend.

Sighing, I returned my gaze to Imogene's dark eyes. "Fine. You can stay."

Unable to contain her excitement, she wrapped her

arms around me, hugging me tightly, not caring who saw. Then again, what could her friends possibly say, considering her close connection to the one and only Lachlan Hale?

I pulled her toward me, savoring in my little girl's embrace. With everything going on, her hugs were even more meaningful.

Even more necessary.

As I breathed her in, I scrunched up my nose. "But you *definitely* need a shower."

Imogene laughed, pulling away. "Going now." She glanced at Roman. "I'll be out in twenty minutes."

"I'll save you a seat."

She smiled, then turned, her ponytail bouncing as she jogged off the field and toward the athletic building.

"Straight to the locker room," I called after her, my anxiety waning slightly when her assigned escort followed close behind. "And straight back. No detours."

Glancing my way, she saluted. "Yes, ma'am."

CHAPTER EIGHTEEN

Julia

"I suck at telling her no," I said to Lachlan once Imogene disappeared into the athletic building.

"No, you don't. You're a good mum." He arched a brow. "If all this stuff with Nick weren't going on, would you have let her stay?"

"No question."

"Then you made the right decision." He leaned down, lips touching mine.

It was freeing to be able to kiss him anytime without worrying about who could see us. While we couldn't exactly make out, at least not here, I still liked the idea of kissing him anytime and anywhere I wanted.

Lachlan pulled back and glanced past me, pushing out a long breath.

"Well, if Imogene's only going to be twenty minutes, I

should probably start signing a few things."

I placed my hands on his chest, hoisting myself onto my toes. "Do your thing." I pressed another kiss to his lips, then turned toward Naomi.

"Come on. Let's people watch and talk shit."

She clapped excitedly. "Two of my absolute favorite things to do." She hooked her arm in mine as we walked toward the empty bleachers.

Any other day, no one would be lingering, all the students having left or gone toward the football field in preparation for tonight's game. But today wasn't a normal day. Instead, dozens of students waited to meet Lachlan and get his autograph.

And just like in Hawaii, he happily signed anything the kids asked of him, Nikko keeping everything running smoothly.

"It's really sweet of him to do this."

"What? Sign all those autographs? That's normal for him. I haven't been out in public with him much, but I imagine this is pretty typical."

"No." Naomi shook her head. "I'm talking about the fact he came to Imogene's game tonight when he has his own to get ready for. The way he cheered for her... The pride in his eyes..." She licked her lips, struggling to come up with the words to explain it.

She didn't have to, though.

I lifted my gaze to hers, emotion tightening my throat. "I know..."

She squeezed my hand. "I'm so happy for both of you.

He's truly an incredible man, Jules. And exactly the type of person you deserve. That *Imogene* deserves, too. I'm glad you finally allowed yourself to be happy. Finally allowed someone to love you. And allowed yourself to love someone in return."

"And I'm glad you finally smacked some sense into me." I nudged her, lightening the tension.

"That's what I'm here for."

The minutes passed in comfortable silence as we watched Lachlan easily interact with everyone waiting to meet him. He truly was a remarkable man. And completely unlike the image most people probably had of the young pitcher who had a propensity for being a bit of a hothead, at least on the mound. Instead, it was obvious how much he appreciated each and every one of his fans. How grateful he was to have the opportunity he did.

I was so mesmerized by watching Lachlan that I didn't realize how much time had gone by until Roman approached, brows scrunched in concern.

"I'm sorry, Ms. Prescott." He ran a hand through his hair. "But has Imogene come out of the athletic building yet? I tried texting and calling, but she hasn't answered. Or even read my texts."

I glanced at my watch, seeing it had been over a half-hour. Her game ended a little after six. It was now approaching seven, and the football game would be starting soon.

Granted, she was taking a shower. And since she had plans to spend time with Roman, she could have been putting in a bit more effort than normal in styling her hair and applying her makeup.

That didn't stop the worry from creeping in, even after I checked the location of her phone, watch, and backpack tag, all of them in the same place — the general vicinity of the locker room.

"I'm sure everything's fine," Naomi offered, sensing my growing unease. "Her security escort has barely left her side. Hell, I thought he was going to step onto the field and shadow Imogene during the game."

"You're probably right. But I'll go check on her anyway."

I pulled my phone from my purse and pressed Imogene's contact, holding it up to my ear as I stood and made my way across the field. When her voicemail picked up, I called again, not so much as glancing Lachlan's way as I passed. All my attention was focused on the athletic building, searching for anything that appeared out of place.

But nothing did.

Everything, from the sound of the marching band warming up in the distance to the excited voices of people arriving for the game, was completely normal.

Still, I couldn't shake the feeling in my gut that something wasn't right. It was the same, sinking sensation I experienced whenever I'd return from the bathroom at the mall. Or from grabbing a snack at the beach. Or from talking to a childhood friend at a county fair, only to learn Imogene wasn't where I'd left her. That she'd vanished into thin air.

I tried to convince myself I was overreacting. That she had a security escort with her. But her escort couldn't go into the shower with her. What if something happened to her there?

I quickened my steps, my anxiety increasing with every passing moment. Suddenly, a hand grasped my arm, stopping me in my tracks.

"What's wrong? What happened?"

I blinked, meeting Lachlan's concerned gaze.

"Nothing." I shook my head, not wanting to worry him if this were simply a result of spending years living in a constant state of fear that Nick would find a way to take my daughter from me. "I just... Imogene hasn't come out yet, and it's been much longer than twenty minutes. She's probably just taking her time getting ready." I forced a smile. "But I want to make sure."

"Take Nikko with you," he insisted, glancing around at the growing crowd descending on the football field. "I'll be right behind you."

I nodded, still in a daze as I set off toward the athletic building once more, Nikko at my side. We only made it a few feet when his phone rang. He paused, checking the screen.

"Agent Curran."

"The memorial," I murmured.

Nikko brought his cell up to his ear. "Detective Kekoa."

"We got fucking played!" I heard Agent Curran shout.

Adrenaline shot through me at the outrage in his voice.

In the seven years I'd known this man, I'd never heard him show this much emotion.

"What happened?" Nikko looked my way, putting the call on speaker, then glanced in Lachlan's direction. In an instant, Lachlan jogged toward us.

"He figured out our plan! He knew all along! Probably even knew Christine was still alive!"

With every word he spoke, my anxiety increased even more, dread filling me that even Lachlan's reassuring touch on my lower back couldn't diminish.

"He knew it was a setup. Even knew exactly where I'd stationed a lookout."

"How?" Nikko asked. "What happened to make you say that?"

"He sent a fucking courier. Gave me a book."

"A...book?"

"*The Count of Monte Cristo*. When I went to visit Nick in prison last month, I gave him a copy, since he'd been asking for one. It's not the one I gave him, but there's no doubt in my mind it's from him. The message inside, though... I can't make sense of it."

"What does it say?"

"'Smile'. All I can think is maybe he's watching us? Recording us? What else could that mean?"

I pushed out a quivering breath, feeling like all the oxygen had been ripped from my body. "Oh god..."

I spun around, taking off at a sprint, legs pumping, heart racing as I screamed Imogene's name.

I didn't care if I made a scene. Didn't care if I were

overreacting and ended up embarrassing her. If I did, so be it. It was a small price to pay to ensure she was still here. That she was still with me.

But I knew she wasn't.

I threw open the doors to the athletic building, my flip-flops slapping against the linoleum as I raced down the hallway. The short distance felt like miles as I hurried toward the locker room. As I feared, her escort wasn't guarding the door, like I'd been assured he would be.

I burst inside, praying with everything I had that she'd be there. That this was simply a case of my separation anxiety rearing its ugly head.

But emptiness greeted me, no sign of life to be found.

At least initially.

As I stepped farther into the locker room, I could make out a faint sound. It was muffled and unclear, but it sounded like...music.

"Hello?" I called out, every fiber of my being telling me to turn back.

But that was at odds with the mother in me who would do anything for her child. Who would never be able to live with herself if something happened to Imogene because she'd hesitated. Retreated.

So I continued into the room, nothing seeming out of place.

All the lockers were closed, some decorated with posters of encouragement for tonight's game. As I walked past rows of bathroom stalls, the music became louder, clearer, the melody all too familiar.

Because it was the same song I once sang to Imogene when I crawled into bed with her after Nick played his twisted version of hide-and-seek.

A boulder lodged in my throat as I ran toward the sound, sliding to a stop at a pile of clothes on the floor near a bench, Imogene's number on the back of her stained jersey.

"No...," I whimpered, carefully lifting her clothes off the floor to reveal a phone.

On the screen was a photo of my little girl, unconscious and gagged, wrists and ankles bound, lying in what appeared to be the trunk of a car.

A wail I didn't recognize as my own ripped from me as I fell to the floor, my cries echoing in the empty room.

"Julia!" Lachlan shouted as the door to the locker room crashed open, followed by heavy footsteps. "Are you—"

He came to an abrupt stop when he took in the scene. Imogene's uniform. A cell phone playing "Smile". A photo of her in some asshole's trunk.

"Oh god, no..."

"He has her!" I sobbed as he knelt beside me, wrapping me in his arms. "He has my baby." Each word felt like a knife plunging into my heart. "What if he's—"

"It'll be okay," he attempted to assure me, preventing me from voicing my concerns. "I won't let that happen." He pulled back and cupped my cheeks in his hands, tears cascading down both our faces. "I swear to you, Julia. I will *not* let that bastard hurt her. I will find him. And when I do, I *will* kill him."

CHAPTER NINETEEN

Lachlan

Within minutes, the entire campus was locked down while police swarmed the area. We'd told them Imogene wasn't here, that she'd been abducted, but they refused to listen. Until a search of every last inch of the campus turned up empty.

While the football game was canceled, no one was allowed to leave until they were questioned by the police. When I heard some of the cops complain about having to interview hundreds of people, I lost it, screaming that there was a teenage girl missing and the mild inconvenience of having to interview everyone here in the hopes someone had seen something was a small price to pay if it ended up saving her life.

Just as I finished tearing into one of the uniformed cops

to stop bitching and do his damn job, a voice I really didn't want to hear cut through.

"Well, well, well. Good to see you've worked on that anger issue since the last time I had the pleasure of being in your presence, Mr. Hale."

I whirled around, glowering at Detective Walker as he nonchalantly strode toward where I stood with Julia, Nikko, and Naomi. "What the fuck are you doing here?" I hissed.

He was the absolute last person I wanted to see right now, or ever, especially considering the last time I saw him, he more or less implied I intentionally killed Piper and stabbed Claire on the night of that home invasion. To say my confidence in him actually being able to help find Imogene was low was an understatement. At least I had Nikko and Agent Curran on my side, both of whom I knew would do everything they could to bring her home safely.

"Pleasure to see you, as well, Mr. Hale. Although, I must admit, it's a bit surprising. Is there a reason you're at a high school football game?"

I wrapped my arm around Julia's shoulders, pulling her closer. Despite her breakdown in the locker room earlier, she'd shown amazing strength, answering questions with a clarity I didn't think myself capable of at the moment.

"Imogene, the missing girl..." My voice briefly caught. I paused, not wanting to show this bastard a hint of emotion. "I'm dating her mum, Julia."

He glanced Julia's way. "Is that right?"

"Yes," she answered, head held high. "That's right."

He studied her for a beat before lifting his analytical gaze to me. "Why is it that people around you tend to end up dead?"

Julia inhaled a sharp breath, body tensing. "What are you saying?" she asked shakily. "Is Imogene—"

"I apologize, ma'am," Detective Walker interjected quickly. "I shouldn't have said that. I assure you. I have every reason to believe your daughter is perfectly safe."

I snorted. "Safe. Abducted by a serial rapist and killer, but sure. That sounds perfectly safe to me!"

He gave me a warning glare before looking back at Julia, his smile congenial. "I'm Detective Walker with Major Crimes here in Atlanta. We're going to do everything we possibly can to bring Imogene home safely. I'm sure the uniformed officers have already asked you what she was wearing, but if you don't mind coming with me to answer a few more questions..." He glanced my way, then added, "Alone."

Julia met my eyes, uncertain. "But—"

"I must insist," Detective Walker interrupted. "Right now, everyone here is a potential suspect."

"Lachlan was with me the entire time Imogene was supposed to be in the locker room. He—"

"If you want to find your daughter, I just need a few minutes."

She nodded, blowing out a breath. "Of course."

"I'll be right here," I promised her, sensing she needed my assurance that I wouldn't disappear on her, too. Then I brushed a soft kiss to her temple before dropping my hold, watching as she followed Walker several yards away.

I kept my eyes trained on them as I sidled up beside Nikko.

"I don't bloody trust that guy," I muttered, glowering at him.

"Cool it, bruh. Let bygones be bygones. He didn't want to look into Claire's death because all the physical evidence, including the ME's report, indicated she committed suicide. So what? He's not the only one who didn't want to reopen the investigation into these supposed suicides. They've all based their decision off the evidence present at the time. Just like my lieutenant did."

I tore my eyes toward his, brows scrunched. "What are you talking about? Your lieutenant *did* reopen the investigation. Didn't she? You said you were going to speak with her."

"And I did. But after I presented what I knew, she decided to leave it alone, at least for the time being. Said she needed more than some tenuous theory. Much like Curran's superiors at the Bureau told him."

"No." I vehemently shook my head, stomach churning. Something wasn't right. Something seemed...off. "Walker came over my house not even two weeks ago. Claimed a Detective Marshall with HPD had been trying to reach out to me."

Nikko looked at me quizzically. "We do have a Detective Marshall, but—"

"Walker claimed she'd been looking into the night

Piper died. Made it sound like she was in charge of the investigation and wanted to clear up my statement. When she couldn't get in touch with me, he told me she asked him to come talk to me, since Marshall once worked with Walker in Atlanta before she moved to Hawaii."

He frowned. "What else did he say?"

"That Marshall reached out to Aaliyah."

"Aaliyah Downs?"

I nodded. "And that Aaliyah mentioned a little... disagreement Piper and I had gotten into that afternoon."

"Disagreement? What disagreement? I don't remember you saying anything about—"

"I didn't think it was important. Not after she was attacked in our own goddamn home."

"What was it about?" Nikko widened his stance, crossing his arms in front of his chest.

"It was stupid," I sighed, scrubbing a hand over my face. "When I arrived home that day to tell Piper about being promoted to the majors, I was all excited. Thought she would be, too, considering I'd achieved everything I'd ever dreamed of."

"Let me guess. She was...less than enthusiastic about your success." He arched a brow.

"That about sums it up. Especially when I suggested we live in Atlanta during the season, then in Hawaii the rest of the year."

"And Detective Walker liked the idea of you arguing."

"He did. You know I'd never do anything to hurt Piper. He implied I did, though. Even implied I was the one who stabbed Claire, since the trajectory of the stab wound indicated it was inflicted by someone who was left-handed."

"Which Caleb was," he reminded me. "It was one of the reasons he was arrested. Couple that with the fact his semen was found on Piper's body, his height and build matched the description you gave, and his truck was observed running a red light near your house in the minutes following the time of the assault, and it looked like a pretty open-and-shut case."

He pinched his lips together, a contemplative expression crossing his brow. "But why would Marshall go hunting this when the lieutenant told me not to just yet. I didn't even think anyone else in the department knew I'd spoken to her about it."

"There's something off about this." I nodded toward Walker. "Something off about him. I always thought it strange he didn't press charges against me for punching him when he was adamant about seeing me 'hang', as he'd said. But nothing. Not even a civil suit. Why? There's got to be a reason, other than the fact my agent insisted I pay all medical expenses."

Nikko stared into the distance, the solemn air a stark contrast from the energized atmosphere less than an hour ago.

"I'm normally not one for conspiracy theories, but you're right. Something stinks about all of this. I'll see what I can find out on my end. Reach out to some other detectives, as well as Curran and Ethan. See what they can dig up on Walker and Marshall."

I slapped him on the back. "Thanks, cousin."

"You bet." He pulled me in for a quick hug. "In the meantime, you need to focus on Julia." He met my eyes. "Nothing else. You got it?"

"That's the plan."

"We'll find Imogene. And then we'll make whoever took her wish he were never born."

My fists clenched. "That's *also* the plan."

CHAPTER TWENTY

Julia

Lachlan grasped my hand as he led me from his garage and toward the house. When we approached the door, I hesitated, unsure if I could walk inside, cross that threshold and see everything just as it was the last time I was here.

When I still had my daughter.

It would serve as a reminder that she was gone.

That Nick had won yet again.

As her mother, I had one job. To keep her safe.

I'd failed.

Sensing my unease, Lachlan squeezed my hand. "Are you okay?"

I blew out something between a laugh and a cry.

"Sorry. Of course you're not okay. Nothing about any of this is okay. I just..."

He palmed my lower back, wrapping me in his embrace. I didn't know if it were because he sensed I needed to feel him or because he needed to feel me. Needed this reminder that we still had each other.

As he drew in a deep breath, he pinched my chin, tilting up my head to meet his eyes. "I just need to know you're as okay as you can be."

I gave him my best attempt at a smile. "I'm okay as I can be."

He nodded slightly, swiping a few tears from my cheeks with his thumbs. "We don't have to stay here. If it's too much..." His Adam's apple bobbed up and down in a hard swallow, Imogene's disappearance nearly as difficult for him to cope with as it was for me. "We can go somewhere else. Stay in a hotel."

While the idea of staying someplace where I wouldn't be surrounded by physical reminders of my daughter was appealing, I doubted it would make a difference. Imogene was a part of me. Every time I looked at my reflection, I'd see her.

"I appreciate the offer..." I pressed my hand to his cheek, savoring in the scruff of his unshaven jawline. "But like I said last week. I'm not going to let Nick chase me out of my home."

"Then let's go home." He lowered his lips to mine, treating me to a sweet kiss. Then he pulled back, his hold on my hand tighter than normal as we walked into the house.

I paused just inside the foyer, my gaze sweeping over

the open living space. Everything was precisely as it was when we left for Imogene's soccer game. Trays of my latest sweet concoctions sat on the kitchen island. The television we'd forgotten to turn off earlier flickered, the news not only covering Nick's escape, but also Imogene's disappearance, a montage of photos I'd given the police appearing on the screen. But that wasn't what stopped me in my tracks, the weight of everything finally crushing me.

It was the shoes I nearly tripped over in the foyer.

Imogene's shoes.

As if able to sense my impending breakdown, Lachlan strode over and quickly turned off the television before returning to me and pulling me into his arms.

"We'll find her," he assured me for what felt like the hundredth time in the past few hours. And each time, his determination seemed to increase.

As did his anger.

"I swear to you, Julia. I am going to do everything I can to bring her home to you. To us. To the people who love her." He cupped my cheeks in his hands. "Make no mistake. I love that smart-ass daughter of yours. You don't get to hurt the people I love and not suffer the consequences. He *will* pay for this. For everything he's done and gotten away with. This time, he's fucked with the wrong person."

I wrapped my arms around him, resting my head against his chest, drawing strength from his conviction.

While part of me feared Nick would end up victorious,

no matter what we did to catch him and get my daughter back, I couldn't dwell on that. Couldn't give up.

Not when Imogene needed me the most.

"Thank you, Lachlan. If you weren't here…" I choked out a sob. "I'd be a fucking wreck if it weren't for you." I lifted my eyes to his.

"I love you," he said with a quiver. "So fucking much."

"And I love you."

His lips touched mine, the tenderness in his kiss briefly subduing the heartache. "Let's get some rest."

"I'm not sure I can sleep tonight."

"I didn't say sleep. But you need to rest." He ran his hands down my arms. "Agent Curran and Nikko are chasing down every single lead they can right now. I guarantee the second they find anything, they'll call."

"Okay." I gave him a small smile. "Let's rest."

Fingers interlocking with mine, he led me through the house that felt devoid of any life. Even when Imogene hid away in what had become her room, earbuds in, music blaring, I still felt her presence.

Now that was gone.

Would I ever have that again?

Once Lachlan and I were locked away in his bedroom, we undressed in the dark, the faint light from the moon streaming through the windows. I grabbed one of Lachlan's t-shirts from his dresser and pulled it over my head before crawling into bed.

When Lachlan slipped in behind me, I turned to face him, staring at him in the darkness. He pushed a tendril of hair out of my face. Now that the frenzy of spending hours answering questions about Imogene and Nick was done, I was finally able to process it for the first time.

Finally able to allow myself to *feel* it for the first time.

My throat tightened, my emotions slowly creeping in.

"Show me where it hurts," Lachlan whispered, just like I did days ago after he learned what Nick had done to Christine Griffin.

How it appeared Nick hoped to do the same thing to me if the opportunity presented itself.

My eyes not leaving his, I covered my stomach where I'd carried Imogene for nine months.

He pushed me onto my back, snaking down my body and lifting my shirt. His lips were warm on my flesh as he peppered kisses along my waistline, starting at the pink scar on one side before slowly and sensually making his way to the opposite side.

He raised his gaze to mine. "Where else?"

Tears slid down my cheeks as I brought my hand to my breast, covering my heart.

He lifted my shirt higher, the warmth of his tongue tracing circles around my nipple briefly chasing away the all-consuming emptiness.

He met my eyes once more. "Where else?"

"Everywhere, Lachlan," I choked out, allowing my emotions to spill forward.

He hovered over me. "Then let me take it away."

I grabbed his face, hooking a leg around his waist. "Make it stop hurting. Please."

He made quick work of pushing his briefs down his legs, my underwear joining them on the floor. When he returned to me, he held me in his arms.

"Give me all of it, love," Lachlan said, kissing away my tears. "Your bad days. Your heartache. Your pain. Your anger. Your despair. Your nightmares." He held my face, determination within his eyes as he eased inside of me, a noiseless gasp escaping my throat. "Let me carry the burden."

I wrapped my arms and legs around him, tears streaming down both our faces, but we didn't stop. We couldn't. We needed this connection. Needed this reminder of our love.

As he moved inside of me, doing what he could to take it all away, he dropped his forehead to mine, both of us breathing in the other as we connected *alo* to *alo*.

Soul to soul.

Heart to heart.

Pain to pain.

When we got home, sex was the last thing on my mind, especially with my daughter missing. But this wasn't sex.

This was two people demonstrating the love they had for each other.

Two people giving each other the strength to continue on when they wanted to give up.

Two people promising to stand by each other's side.

No matter what.

CHAPTER TWENTY-ONE

Julia

Most of Saturday passed in a blur as law enforcement ramped up their efforts to find Imogene. Detective Walker organized a search in the wooded area surrounding the school, and every single student and faculty member showed up to assist in the efforts. Lachlan and I were there, too, along with Wes, while Londyn stayed home with Eli, attempting to shield him from the news that his cousin was missing.

I suppose that was one good thing to come out of this. Londyn finally understood why Wes had kept the truth about Nick's possible connection to a slew of recent deaths from her. It wasn't for any reason but to protect her.

Regardless, I knew they wouldn't find anything during the search.

After all, when I found Imogene's phone in the locker

room, the screen showed a photo of her tied up and lying in what looked like a trunk.

While my confidence in Detective Walker actually doing what was necessary to find my daughter was somewhat lacking, I found comfort in the fact that Agent Curran was making progress in locating my ex-husband's whereabouts, thanks to the courier who was hired to deliver the book at Christine Griffin's memorial.

He claimed to be a rideshare driver who answered a request for a pickup at Brookhaven Park Friday afternoon. When he got there, a blond man wearing a suit approached. He paid him $5,000 to bring a book to a specific location and deliver it to a certain individual.

Agent Curran had put in a request for the surveillance footage from the cameras located around the park and was confident he'd receive the files sometime today. Once he did, he hoped to be able to run facial recognition software on whomever it was, bringing us one step closer to finding Nick. And Imogene.

In the meantime, he encouraged us to do the two things mentioned in the last line of Alexander Dumas' *The Count of Monte Cristo*, as ironic as that was. He told us to simply wait and hope.

So that was what I did. Waited and hoped.

And baked.

I didn't know what else to do, feeling completely helpless. So I did what I could to take my mind off things, making all of Imogene's favorite sweet treats so I could shower her with them when she came home.

And she *would* come home.

I refused to consider the alternative.

Just as I was about to zest a lemon for my lemon blueberry scones, the doorbell rang, my pulse increasing. Lachlan looked up from where he stood beside me, helping. It probably took his mind off things, too.

Despite my insistence, he refused to go to Tampa with the rest of the team for tonight's game. While I hated the idea of him missing his team's first playoff game, I liked having him here.

"It's Curran," Lachlan said to Nikko after checking the camera app on his phone. "Along with some woman."

"Probably Agent Hawkins." Nikko stood from the table. "She's the GBI agent he's been assisting to track down Nick."

After wiping his hands on a towel, Lachlan made his way toward the front door, Nikko and I following closely behind. To say we'd been anxiously waiting for any sort of update would be putting it mildly.

"Mr. Hale," Agent Curran said once Lachlan opened the door. "Ms. Prescott. May we come in?"

"Of course." Lachlan stepped back, allowing Curran and the GBI agent to enter his home.

"This is Agent Hawkins with the Georgia Bureau of Investigation. We've been working together on locating Nick." He looked my way. "And now Imogene."

The slender brunette held out her hand. "Ms. Prescott."

"Thank you for your help," I said as we shook.

"Of course, ma'am." She looked at Lachlan, the two briefly shaking. "Pleasure to meet you, Mr. Hale. Although I wish it were under different circumstances."

"Don't we all."

"And you remember Detective Kekoa," Agent Curran stated.

"Yes. Good to see you again, Detective."

"Did you find something on the surveillance footage?" I asked, cutting through the formalities.

"We did." Agent Curran glanced at Agent Hawkins before returning his attention to me. "I wanted you all to hear it from me first."

"Hear what?" Lachlan crossed his arms in front of his chest.

"The footage showed a man matching the description the courier gave — approximately six feet, maybe six-two, blond hair, wearing a suit. He was observed approaching the courier's vehicle. After a conversation lasting less than a minute, this individual gave the courier a thick envelope, presumably the cash, as well as a book. Then the courier drove off in one direction while the individual walked away in another."

"Did you run facial recognition on this guy?" Nikko asked.

"We couldn't," Agent Hawkins stated. "He kept his face obscured, as if knowing precisely where the cameras were located."

"Which we expected," Agent Curran interjected.

"So you don't know who it was?" I asked, despair tightening my throat. I didn't know how much more of this I could take.

"I wouldn't say that. While he never looked at the camera, a few seconds after the courier left, another vehicle was seen leaving the parking lot. A Mercedes. We ran the plates."

Nikko arched a brow. "And?"

"The car is registered to Daxton Shea," Agent Curran stated.

A brief silence filled the room as we processed the information.

"That fucking bastard," Lachlan seethed, breaking through the quiet. The muscles in his jaw twitched, nostrils flared, hands clenched. I placed a hand on his arm, attempting to calm him, but his anger was palpable.

"Due to who his family is," Agent Hawkins continued, "we thought it best to be as certain as possible before pursuing a search and arrest warrant. So we sat the courier down with a photo array."

Lachlan's brows scrunched. "Photo array?"

"It's exactly what it sounds like," Nikko explained. "You present a handful of photos to the witness, all of whom match the general description of the person in question, and see who they pick."

"Precisely," Agent Curran said. "We showed the courier a half-dozen different arrays containing photos of individuals fitting the description he provided. And each time, I'll give you one guess who he chose."

"Daxton Shea," Lachlan ground out.

"I've shared all this with the DA," Agent Hawkins explained. "She was more than satisfied that this evidence was sufficient to present before a judge for a search warrant under the theory he may be harboring a dangerous fugitive. Because of the extenuating circumstances, she found a judge who'd hear the petition today. As we speak, to be precise. I have teams standing by, so we're ready to go once we have a signed warrant, which should be within the hour."

I exhaled a tiny breath, a sense of relief filling me. It didn't matter they weren't here to tell me they'd found Imogene. While I longed to receive that news, at least this was *something*. After what felt like a constant stream of bad news, one setback after another, this was a step in the right direction.

Finally.

"I want to be there," I declared. "Lachlan, too." I glanced his way.

"I..." Agent Curran shared a look with Agent Hawkins.

"Based on everything we've learned, it's clear Daxton Shea's been helping my ex-husband," I stated matter-of-factly. "He sent a courier to deliver a copy of the book you gave him in prison, which contained an inscription that only he'd know the meaning of."

"True," Agent Curran agreed. "Or at least there's sufficient evidence to believe there's a connection."

"Exactly." I held my head high, squaring my shoulders. "Based on what I know about my ex and the evidence found in the locker room, namely Imogene's cell phone playing the song I used to sing to her as a child, the same song title that was inscribed in the book you received, I have every reason to believe Nick is involved. So if Daxton's helping him, there's a possibility she may be at his house. Correct?"

Curran and Hawkins both nodded.

"So I want to be there. If Imogene's there..." My resolve cracked, lower lip trembling. "If something's happened to her..." I closed my eyes, swallowing hard, pushing down a new wave of emotion.

Lachlan wrapped an arm around me, pulling me into his embrace, comforting me. I inhaled deeply, drawing strength from him.

"I don't want the next time I see my daughter to be on some cold, metal table."

"It won't be," Agent Curran attempted to assure me.

"I hope you're right. I really do. But the second I learned she was missing, all I could think about was what Nick had done to Christine Griffin. If he's done the same thing..." I squeezed my eyes shut again as Lachlan held me tighter. Then I returned my determined gaze to Agent Curran. "Just grant me this one request. Please."

"It's not protocol," he stated.

"*Fuck* protocol," I argued. "Last I checked, you didn't exactly follow protocol when you paid Nick a visit in prison. Or when you set up my meeting with him."

"That may be true, but I'm not in charge of this investigation. I'm simply assisting. I can't make that call." He nodded at the woman to his side. "Only Agent Hawkins can."

I turned my pleading gaze toward her. "I'm begging you. Let me be there. If by some miracle my daughter is there and we can put an end to all of this, don't you think she deserves to have her mother nearby? She's been through so much already. More in her fourteen years than anyone should have to endure in a lifetime. She's going to want her mother. Not some cop she doesn't know if she can trust." I glanced toward her left hand, noticing a wedding band. "Do you have kids?"

She smiled slightly. "Three girls. The oldest is, well... She's Imogene's age."

"If it were your daughter, wouldn't you want to be the first face she saw? Wouldn't you want to hug her, assure her nothing bad would ever happen again? And Lachlan's just as torn up about this as I am. Please. If she's there, we don't want to wait one more second than necessary to hug her."

She stared at me, parting her lips, obviously conflicted between following the rules and doing what she knew was right. Finally, she sighed.

"Fine. You can be there. But under no circumstances are you to get out of the car unless I say so." She looked from me to Lachlan. "That goes for you, too. Do you understand?"

"Of course." I offered her a grateful smile. "Thank you."

"I'd want to be there, too," she admitted softly.

CHAPTER TWENTY-TWO

Lachlan

This entire experience was an exercise in extreme restraint, especially when Agent Hawkins knocked on the door to serve the search warrant, expecting Dax to be in Tampa for the game. Where I should have been.

So to see him answer the door when he'd never missed a playoff game before unsettled me. Made me want to jump out of the back of Agent Hawkins' SUV and storm up to him as he sat on his front porch, an officer watching over him, while the police searched his house for anything that could connect him to Domenic Jaskulski, all while Dax claimed to know absolutely nothing.

To make matters worse, Detective Walker showed up and, after a brief argument with Agent Hawkins, was allowed to be part of the search.

"I guess no news is good news, right?" Julia remarked

nervously as she rubbed her hands down her jeans, unable to mask her apprehension. "Then again, in my case, no news is probably bad news."

"Hey." I cupped her cheeks, leaning my forehead against hers, hoping this gesture, this connection, gave her the strength she needed.

Hoping it gave me the strength I needed.

"It's going to be okay. Curran isn't going to give up until Imogene is home. You can't, either." I narrowed my gaze on her. "You just have to..." I trailed off when I noticed movement out of the corner of my eye, glancing over Julia's shoulder as a crime scene tech exited the house carrying a large evidence bag.

And in that bag was a familiar backpack.

Imogene's backpack.

"No...," I exhaled before realizing it.

"What?" Julia turned in her seat, eyes following my line of sight, releasing a cry.

I wrapped my arms around her, kissing the top of her head, hoping to offer some comfort in a world that was spinning more and more out of control with every passing moment.

I tried to keep my anger in check. Tried to focus on what Julia needed.

But I couldn't stay silent. Not anymore. I'd kept it to myself ever since Ethan came over and informed us of his theory about Dax.

But it wasn't just a theory anymore.

I didn't do enough to stand up for Claire when she was alive.

I'd be damned if I made that same mistake where Julia was concerned.

And Imogene.

Releasing Julia from my hold, I opened the door and jumped from the SUV, ignoring her reminders that Agent Hawkins insisted we stay here. With every step I took, my nostrils flared a little more, fists clenching and unclenching.

"Lachlan?" Dax began as I approached. "What are you—"

Before he could utter another syllable, I reeled back, fist connecting with his face, a crack echoing in the night air.

"Where the fuck is she?" I demanded, my face inches from his, finding a sick sort of satisfaction in the blood spilling from his nose.

"I don't know what you're talking about!" Dax insisted, expression contorted in pain as he scrambled to get away from me.

A group of uniformed officers rushed toward me, attempting to restrain me. It took four of them to finally handle my strength.

"Bullshite, Dax," I seethed as another officer tended to the blood dripping onto his crisp, white shirt. "Bull-*fucking*-shite. I know everything. Know who you really are. Know your biological father is Domenic Jaskulski. Know you volunteer for the same outreach ministry that visited the prison where that sick fuck's been an inmate the past several years. Know you dated Autumn Quinn in the months before she allegedly took her own life. Except she didn't, did she? She was killed!" I shouted as I fought against the officers restraining me, kicking up dirt as my ears pounded, pulse elevated.

"You killed her! Just like you tried to kill Piper. And me. And Claire." I sucked in a shaky breath, everything coming full circle. "Then you really *did* kill Claire, didn't you? She figured it all out. She saw you for who you really were, so you killed her. You killed my sister, you sick son of a bitch!"

My fury seeming to give me even more strength, I managed to break free from the officers and reeled back.

Just as I was about to connect with his face again, he shouted, "I didn't kill her! I fucking loved her!"

I paused, mid-strike, his words ringing out around me.

"What did you say?"

He drew in a deep breath, his eyes unwavering, not a hint of hesitation within. "I said I loved her. Claire and I were... We were dating."

"Dating?" My voice rose in pitch, unsure what to believe. If they were together, why didn't she say anything?

"For the past year until..." He trailed off, swallowing hard, taking a moment to collect himself. "She didn't want to say anything. Not yet." He blew out a subtle laugh, a nostalgic smile tugging on his lips. "I guess she was kind of worried about how you'd react. Reminded me you had a bit of a temper and she didn't want me to be on the receiving end." He used his shirt to wipe the blood that continued to spill from his nose. "Seems she had a point."

I blinked, shocked. But the fact he was supposedly in love with my sister had nothing to do with all the other evidence.

"Okay then. Fine. You loved Claire. That doesn't explain how the backpack belonging to my girlfriend's missing daughter ended up in your goddamn house."

"It was actually found in his car."

I spun around as Detective Walker approached, that same, smug expression plastered on his face.

"The trunk, to be precise."

A sob echoed. I looked to see Julia standing mere feet from me. I rushed over and pulled her into my arms. What I wouldn't give to snap my fingers and go back in time. Insist we take Imogene home immediately following her soccer game.

If I had, we'd still be together.

But like Nikko had attempted to assure me, if Nick were behind this, and we were all but certain he was, he would have found a way to get Imogene, no matter what.

"I have no idea how it got there," Dax argued. "I've never seen that backpack before."

"Where were you from the hours of five to seven yesterday evening?" Detective Walker asked, flipping open his small notepad.

"At the gym."

"What gym is that?"

"Lifetime Fitness. In North Brookhaven."

"So you were at a gym in North Brookhaven. Which is where Imogene Prescott attends school. And near the park where surveillance cameras captured footage of a man matching your description hiring a courier to deliver a book to Agent Curran at the memorial he staged for a woman Domenic Jaskulski brutally raped and left for dead. A book Agent Curran had given Jaskulski in prison. And the Mercedes this backpack was found in was also seen on that surveillance footage."

"And like I already told Agent Hawkins... I have several cars. Since the weather's been nice, I've been driving the Wrangler lately." His lips curved into a sad smile. "Claire loved that car."

"So you're saying you *weren't* driving your Mercedes yesterday evening in the North Brookhaven area?"

"That's correct."

"Then how do you explain the fact a man matching your description and driving your car was seen at Brookhaven Park?"

"I can't. Someone could have taken the Mercedes, then returned it before I even knew it was gone."

"And just so happened to leave the missing girl's backpack in the trunk?"

"I didn't kidnap her. And I certainly didn't drive my Mercedes to Brookhaven Park yesterday."

"Can you tell me what you did at the gym?"

"Why does it matter? I went to the gym. Worked out. Came back here. Fell asleep. I swear to you. I have no idea where that girl is." He turned his pleading eyes toward

Julia. "I am so sorry your daughter is missing. I can't even imagine how difficult this must be for you. But I had nothing to do with it. Someone must have stolen my car to make it look like I was involved."

Julia opened her mouth to say something, but before she could, Detective Walker interjected.

"So your theory is that someone stole your car, used it to deliver a package to a courier and kidnap Imogene Prescott, then returned the car, leaving the backpack in it to make it appear like you were involved."

"I don't know," he exclaimed, becoming increasingly frustrated. But he still made no move to insist on calling his lawyer before answering any more questions. "All I do know is I didn't take the poor girl. I would never do something like that. Would never do anything to harm another person. It's not in my nature."

"Can you tell me why you went to a gym twenty minutes away when you have a home gym? And it's quite a nice gym, too, if I might add. Nicer than the one we have at the station." He looked at some of the officers standing there. "It has a treadmill, elliptical, one of those fancy stationary bikes, several weights and weight machines. Everything you could ask for in not just a home gym, but a professional health club. Which is why I find it odd you'd go to a public gym when you have all the convenience of a gym in your own home. So want to tell me where you *really* were between the hours of five and seven on Friday night?"

Dax parted his lips, sweat beading on his brow. "I—"

At the sound of a commotion from inside the house, we turned our attention toward the open front door as a man in a forensics jacket peeked his head outside.

"I think we've got something, Detective. You're going to want to see this." He glanced my way before looking back at Walker.

"Don't let him out of your sight," Walker instructed one of the uniformed cops, pointing at Dax. Then he gestured to me. "Him, either. If he feels the need to throw any more punches, cuff him." He gave me a warning look before spinning and hurrying into the house.

"What do you think they found?" Julia asked, eyes awash with tears. "You don't think it's—"

"Shh..." I pulled her close, running my hand up and down her back. "Imogene's fine. I can feel it," I attempted to reassure her, despite my own fears that they found a body inside.

If they did, I didn't care what Detective Walker would do to me. I would kill Dax. And it would take a lot more than a couple uniformed officers to pull me off the bastard.

"Lachlan, I swear to you," Dax's voice cut through my increasingly morose thoughts. I lifted my penetrating stare to his. "I didn't take her. I'm not involved in any of this. You have to believe me."

It took every ounce of resolve I possessed to not storm over there and wrap my hands around his throat. But I wouldn't. Strangling him was too quick a death. If he were behind this, he deserved a far worse fate than that.

And I would make sure he got what he deserved.

"I don't have to believe anything right now," I spat. "All I know is a little girl who is my world is missing and her backpack was found in your bloody car!"

"Like I said, I—"

Before Dax could offer the same excuse he had all evening, Detective Walker strode out of the house carrying a Bankers Box. Agent Curran and Agent Hawkins followed closely behind, grim expressions on their faces.

I pulled Julia closer, unsure what it meant.

Or what was in the box.

Scenes from the movie *Seven* flashed in my mind. All I could do was hope the outcome here wasn't the same as in the movie.

"Okay, Mr. Shea. Since you had such an illuminating explanation as to why Imogene Prescott's backpack was found in your car, let's put your extraordinary investigative skills to the test again, shall we? How do you explain the fact the forensics team found this in a hollowed-out floorboard in your library? To be clear, they heard a creak and pulled up a board, thinking perhaps that was where you were holding the girl. Imagine my surprise when they showed me this."

Detective Walker set the box down, then pulled out a file. Julia and I inched closer. I squinted, able to make out the name *Autumn Quinn* on the tab.

"I've got a detailed surveillance report. Photos. Background check. Bank records. Lease agreements." He whistled as he shook his head. "I'm impressed. It's all extremely thorough. More thorough than some of the background investigations I ask my team to provide. Incredibly meticulous." He flipped through the file. "The attention to detail is astounding. It includes everything anyone could possibly want to know about a person."

"I don't know where that came from," Dax declared nervously, but Detective Walker simply ignored him.

"I could perhaps understand why you'd do a background check on Autumn Quinn. After all, you dated her a while back. Correct?"

Dax nodded subtly.

"Considering who your family is, it's probably best to know what kind of girl you're getting involved with. Make sure there aren't any skeletons that could leave a mark on your otherwise upstanding family. But what I can't understand is why you'd also have background checks on twenty other women. All of whom are now dead, including Claire Hale."

Dax opened his mouth to argue. But Detective Walker cut him off yet again.

"I know. I know. Maybe you just had a fascination with these women who allegedly committed suicide."

I arched a brow in Agent Curran's direction, surprised to hear Detective Walker call their suicides "alleged" when for months, he'd insisted there was nothing alleged about them. Curran didn't give anything away, though. Instead, he seemed...troubled.

"But do you want to know what I find extremely questionable?"

This time, Dax didn't even attempt to respond. He simply stared at the ground, resigned.

"Why photos of their dead, naked bodies were included in these background checks. Photos that weren't taken by crime scene technicians. Including one photo in particular I find quite interesting."

I held my breath as Detective Walker pulled out a folder marked "Claire Hale" and took out a photo. When my eyes fell on my sister's naked body submerged in a tub, blood staining the floor, I bit back a sob. But the sight of her wasn't what caught me off-guard. It was the hand placed on her head, the touch almost...affectionate.

And on the pinky finger of that hand sat a ring with a giant S... Much like the one Dax always wore.

Detective Walker grabbed Dax's hand and held the photograph up to it, the rings identical.

"You'll be getting your wish after all, Mr. Hale," Detective Walker directed at me. "It looks like we'll be reopening the investigation into your sister's death. And making an immediate arrest."

Yanking Dax to his feet, he pulled his arms behind his back and secured a pair of handcuffs to his wrists.

"Daxton Shea, you're under arrest for the murder of Claire Hale, Autumn Quinn, and what looks like quite a few other women," he stated as he led Dax away from the house and toward a waiting police car. "You have the right to remain silent. If I were you, I would highly consider exercising that right."

Agent Curran approached, his analytical gaze studying

Detective Walker's every move as he shoved Dax into the back seat of the cruiser.

"So this is good, right?" I asked. "Apart from the fact we still don't know where Imogene is. At least we confirmed Ethan's theory."

He pinched his lips together, shaking his head.

"You're not convinced, are you?" Julia remarked.

"It seems too easy. Too convenient. And Dax's reaction seemed too..."

"Authentic," Julia offered.

Agent Curran met her gaze. "Exactly." He ran a hand over his face. "I guess one good thing came out of it, though."

"What's that?"

"We've got a serial killer on our hands. Officially."

"Meaning the FBI can now get involved."

"It appears so."

CHAPTER TWENTY-THREE

Lachlan

The second Julia and I stepped into the living room of my house, Nikko snapped his head up from his laptop, various files spread over the kitchen island.

He'd apparently spent the past few hours doing his own investigation. Into what, I wasn't sure.

He jumped to his feet. "What happened, bruh? I got a call from my lieutenant saying they're officially reopening Piper's case because of evidence found in Daxton Shea's possession. What the fuck is going on?"

I met Julia's eyes before looking back at Nikko. "A lot."

He crossed his arms in front of his chest, his biceps bulging. "Care to share?"

"You might want to sit down for this." I ran a hand over my face, still trying to process everything we'd learned. "And maybe grab a drink."

After we made ourselves comfortable around the table, I proceeded to tell Nikko everything that had happened at Dax's house.

How the search team found Imogene's backpack in his Mercedes.

How they found a Bankers Box containing background checks on all the murder victims.

How one photo in particular directly linked Dax to those murders, thanks to the photo showing a pinky ring identical to the one Dax wore.

Then I told Nikko about the phone call Curran received while driving us back to my house. How Agent Hawkins warned Curran that Walker was on a rampage after his captain ordered him to walk away from the investigation and leave it to those with extensive experience in serial murders. Namely Agent Curran.

"Have you told Ethan?" Nikko asked after I finished. "I'm sure he'd be thrilled."

"Curran tried to call him from the car, let him know what was going on, but he couldn't get a hold of him."

Concern wrinkled his brow. "You don't think anything—"

I shook my head. "I highly doubt it. Honestly, when Ethan's down the 'rabbit hole', as he calls it, it takes an act of God to pull him back to reality. He's probably trying to make sense of Claire's research. Or searching for pictures from the various memorial services. See if one person shows up at all of them."

"But he can stop now, right? They've got the guy." Nikko narrowed his gaze. "Don't they?"

I glanced at Julia, who simply shrugged.

"Curran's not sure," I admitted. "Said Dax's denial seemed too authentic."

He nodded, his expression thoughtful. "And what do you think?"

I blew out a breath, just as conflicted as I was when Curran initially voiced his doubts at Dax's house.

"I want to go to sleep tonight knowing we're closer to finding Nick and bringing Imogene home." I rested my hand on Julia's leg and gave her a small smile. "All the physical evidence points to him being involved."

"But...," Nikko drew out, sensing there was more.

"But all the physical evidence *also* pointed to Caleb assaulting Piper. All the physical evidence *also* pointed to Claire committing suicide. And Autumn. And more than a dozen other women. When I saw that crime scene tech come out, Imogene's backpack in an evidence bag, then that Bankers Box full of background checks and photos, there wasn't a question in my mind it was Dax. I mean, that's a lot of physical evidence directly tying him to killing these women, as well as abducting Imogene."

"But the more you thought about it..."

"The more my gut says there's another explanation."

"Just like it did with Claire," he stated.

"Just like it did with Claire."

He studied me a moment before nodding. "Then we

keep going. Keep turning over every single rock until we can prove without a shadow of a doubt that Daxton is involved." His gaze shifted to Julia. "Keep going until we bring Imogene home."

She gave Nikko a grateful smile, but it wavered.

I could tell she was disheartened that nothing more had come out of tonight's search. We were no closer to learning where Imogene was than we were before. We knew we shouldn't get our hopes up of finding her at Dax's house. Even so, it still stung.

And now that she had been missing for twenty-four hours, the situation seemed to become increasingly helpless with every passing minute.

When a chiming cut through the silence, I tore my eyes toward Julia, hope filling my gaze as she pulled her cell out of her purse and looked at the screen.

"It's Wes. Probably calling to find out what happened at Dax's."

She stood and walked toward the kitchen, bringing the phone up to her ear.

"Hey, Wes. I..." She frowned. "Wait. Calm down. You're breaking up." She squinted, covering her free ear with her hand in the hopes of hearing better. Then she hitched a breath. "Oh no," she exhaled.

"What is it?" I jumped out of my chair and strode toward her, praying it wasn't more bad news. I didn't think any of us could take anything else going wrong.

She held up a finger. "It's okay, Wes. It'll all be okay. You hang tight, and I'll be right there."

I heard Wes' muffled voice say something in response, yet couldn't make out what it was.

"No. I told you I'd be there. Told Londyn I'd be there. Considering the circumstances, it's even more important I'm there since I've been through this before. Stay calm. I'll be there soon." She ended the call.

"What's going on?" I asked, trying to mask my anxiety.

"Londyn's in labor," she explained.

"I thought she wasn't due until around Thanksgiving."

"She's not. She's only thirty-four weeks, so this is a bit unexpected. And scary. I need to get to the hospital so I can be there for them."

"What?" I barked out, my fear sounding like anger. "Right now? With everything going on?"

"Wes will be with me the entire time. Plus, you should see security in a maternity ward." She snorted a laugh. "Pretty sure it's tighter than Fort Knox. After I delivered Imogene, I couldn't go near her in the NICU unless they scanned my wristband and made sure it matched hers. Sometimes it was the same nurse who watched me push that baby out of my vagina." She glanced at Nikko. "Sorry for the visual."

Nikko blushed, averting his gaze. "No worries."

"Trust me. They don't fuck around with security on the maternity ward."

She ran her hands down my arms, attempting to ease my fears, as baseless as they probably were. That still didn't make me worry any less.

"Plus, I could really use the distraction. I don't know if

I can stand staying cooped up in this house waiting for news on Imogene. If I go to the hospital, at least I can think about something else for a while. Londyn's about to experience what it's like to deliver a baby who will need immediate medical treatment. Just like Imogene did."

"I understand that. But—"

"Nothing prepares you for enduring hours of labor, only to have that baby whisked away before you can even hold her. Londyn's delivering a baby at thirty-four weeks. That means her lungs aren't fully developed yet, so she'll need assistance to breathe." Her lower lip quivered. "Trust me when I say that seeing your newborn baby hooked up to machines is absolutely earth-shattering. I'd like to be there for Londyn as she goes through that. Just like I wish I had someone there for me when I had to go through it. When every day seemed to bring an entirely new set of challenges I was unprepared to handle, especially after the stress of giving birth. When I say it is exhausting, that's putting it mildly. So while I appreciate your concern, Lachlan, and know exactly where it's coming from, I have to do this."

I studied her, her determination unwavering. I knew that look in her eyes. No amount of protest on my part would get her to change her mind. There was no compromising. I could either get on board or get out of her way.

"You promise you won't leave the hospital? Will text every hour?"

She rolled her eyes, but eventually nodded. "Of course."

"Okay." I wrapped her in my arms. "Be there for Londyn. But I'm driving you."

"I expected nothing less."

CHAPTER TWENTY-FOUR

Julia

"You don't have to stay, Jules," Wes whispered as we sat in the NICU Sunday while Londyn rested in her recovery room, the hours of labor having wiped her out. "I'm sure you're exhausted."

"I did nap for a bit before Londyn was ready to push. I'm fine." I fought against a yawn.

"I just don't want you to feel like you have to stay here. I'm sure you have more pressing matters on your mind." He stroked Ellery's head as she lay in the incubator, wires and tubes monitoring her vitals and helping her breathe.

Ellery Jane Bradford was born at 6:12 this morning, weighing in at a whopping five pounds, two ounces, and measuring a mere sixteen inches.

While seeing any tiny baby hooked up to wires and lying in an incubator was difficult, the doctors were optimistic, especially since she was born at a higher weight than other preemies at thirty-four weeks. Her lungs weren't fully developed, so she needed help breathing for the time being. And she was a bit jaundiced. But aside from that, she was doing great.

Another miracle baby.

Just like my own.

"Your troubles will always be my troubles, Wes." I rested my hand on his arm and gave it a reassuring squeeze. "Just like mine will always be yours."

He met my gaze. "You know they will."

"Which is why I'm exactly where I want to be. If Curran finds anything, he'll call. For now, I just want to be with you guys." I smiled at Ellery. "And my beautiful little niece." I looked back at Wes. "If I go back home, I'll lose my ever-loving shit," I admitted with a laugh. "I like being here. Like feeling useful."

Wes tilted his head. "That's interesting."

"What is? You know I love you and Londyn. I—"

"No." He grinned deviously. "How you referred to Lachlan's house as your home."

I blinked. I hadn't even realized I'd done that. It felt right, though. When I conjured up the image of home in my head, it was no longer my house. It was wherever Lachlan was.

"I guess it kind of feels like home now. Or at least it will once—"

Wes grabbed my hand. "I know," he interrupted. "She's okay. She's a fighter. Just like her mama."

I gave him a small smile, although I secretly prayed with everything I had that my daughter was stronger than her mama.

Pulling my hand from Wes', I stood. "I'm going to get a coffee. Do you want anything?"

He studied me for a beat, his analytical gaze sweeping over me. But if he saw anything that worried him, he didn't mention it.

"If I drink any more coffee, it'll overtake my bloodstream," he chuckled, his drooping eyes evidencing his exhaustion.

And it would only get worse before it got better.

But I didn't want to tell him that.

He had enough on his mind right now.

"Okay. I'll be right back."

"You sure you'll be okay?" he asked in a low voice, giving me a knowing look.

"This place is crawling with security. They don't let you go anywhere without checking this." I pointed to my visitor's sticker. "Especially around here. I'll be back soon."

I leaned down and kissed his cheek. Then I kissed my fingers and touched them to Ellery's tiny foot.

"Be a fighter, baby girl. There's a big world out there just waiting for you to make your mark." I admired her for a moment, then headed toward the door.

"Hey, Jules?"

I glanced over my shoulder. "Yeah?"

"I love you."

"I love you, too."

I held his gaze, then continued out of the NICU, doing my best to keep my emotions in check.

I loved my brother and Londyn, and I meant what told him. I truly wanted to be here.

But being in the NICU again brought back memories of those days after Imogene was born.

Which only made me miss her even more.

On more than one occasion throughout the night and early morning, I was on the verge of breaking down at all the reminders. But I couldn't. I had to stay strong for Wes. For Londyn. Their daughter was fighting for her life right now.

Just as I feared mine was.

Needing to breathe something other than the stench of sickness and cleaning supplies, I made my way past the cafeteria and out the front doors, sucking in a deep breath. After being cooped up in a hospital for the past twelve hours, it was a welcome feeling, the fresh air reinvigorating me more than the copious amounts of coffee I'd consumed throughout the night.

So instead of heading back inside right away, I lingered by the entrance, watching people come and go — doctors, nurses, patients. I also took the opportunity to text Lachlan, since cell service was spotty inside, who told me he was taking Nikko out for a traditional Southern breakfast.

I couldn't wait to find out what he thought of it, especially compared to his mother's cooking.

When about fifteen minutes had passed of simply enjoying the fresh air and sunshine, my phone pinged with a text from Wes, making sure I was okay. Not wanting to tell him I'd just stepped out for a minute, which I knew would only add to his concerns, I responded I was fine and would be back up soon.

Returning my phone to my pocket, I was about to head inside when I noticed a Starbucks just down the block. While I typically preferred to support locally owned coffee shops, Starbucks was a welcome sight after being forced to consume weak hospital coffee all night. I needed something stronger.

I jogged up the street and slipped inside, the familiar scent of robust coffee wrapping around me as I waited in line behind about a dozen people, mostly hospital employees and individuals wearing visitor stickers on their shirts.

"Julia?"

I whirled around, a moment of panic passing that a reporter had followed me to ask questions, something I'd avoided since Imogene went missing. Relief filled me at the familiar smile that greeted me.

"Ethan..." I stepped into his embrace that lasted a little longer than normal. "How are you?"

He squeezed me tighter. "I should probably be asking *you* that. How are you holding up?"

I met his gaze. "I'm hanging in there."

"Good." He gave me an encouraging look, then stepped back.

"What are you doing out here?" I asked. "I thought you lived closer to Midtown."

"I do." Averting his gaze, he shoved his hands into his pockets. "With everything going on, I went out for a few drinks last night to decompress. One thing led to another and, well... I didn't feel comfortable taking her back to my place with all the research lying around. Didn't want her to see something she shouldn't and go to the media. So we went back to her place, which is right around the corner."

"Good for you. You deserve a nice girl."

"Eh." He lifted his eyes to mine and shrugged. "She's sweet and all, but I'm not sure there's a future there."

"You're still young." I gave his arm a gentle squeeze. "You've got your entire life to find 'the one'. Believe me. You'll find her when you least expect it."

"That's what I hear. How about you? What brings you out this way?" He zeroed in on the visitor sticker attached to my t-shirt. "Is everything okay?"

"Londyn went into labor last night."

His brows scrunched. "I didn't know she was due so soon."

"She wasn't. So I came to be with her and Wes."

"Even with everything else going on?"

"I thought I could use a distraction."

"I hear that."

"What can I get started for you?"

I looked over, seeing I was next in line, the barista waiting. I approached the counter. "Grande Americano with an extra shot and steamed milk, please."

"Make it two," Ethan said from behind me, handing the woman a twenty. Then he glanced my way. "My treat."

"Thanks."

"Of course."

After Ethan paid, we stepped to the side to wait for our drinks, trying to find a spot to stand where we weren't in everyone's way. Something that was becoming increasingly difficult as the shop filled up.

"If you want to hang out over by the door, I'll grab our order."

"Are you sure?"

"It's two cups." He winked. "I think I can manage."

"Thank you."

I walked toward the lounge area, leaning against the wall and briefly closing my eyes. I didn't think it possible to fall asleep standing up, but I was so exhausted. It felt like I could sleep for days and it still wouldn't be enough.

"Here you go." The sound of Ethan's voice forced my eyes open as he approached, drinks in hand. "Grande Americano with an extra shot and steamed milk."

"Thanks." Flashing him a smile, I took the cup, fighting a yawn as I raised it to my lips and savored in the taste of the strong coffee. "I should probably head back. I promised Lachlan I wouldn't leave the hospital. Plus, Wes is expecting me."

"Before you go, I could use your help. Pick your brain, so to speak. I'd planned on stopping by Lachlan's this morning to talk to you." He leaned toward me, lowering his voice. "I think I may have found something."

"What?"

"It may be nothing. But I uncovered some photos from

Autumn Quinn's memorial service. I hoped you might be able to help me identify a few people."

"Why me?"

"Because they were other volunteers from Homes for the Homeless. Your brother's charity. After doing a bit more digging, I learned there was a homebuilding project going on in each of the cities around the time of each of the murders. Since I know you're quite involved with his charity and help him run it, I thought you might recognize some of these individuals."

"You think it could be someone tied to Wes' charity?" I asked. "What about Dax Shea?"

"We need to explore every possible angle. I spoke to Agent Curran this morning. He spent hours last night interrogating Daxton Shea. He doesn't believe he did this, even though there's overwhelming evidence pointing his way."

I swallowed hard, the thought of it being someone connected to my brother's charity unsettling me. Especially since Imogene spent a great deal of time working with the charity.

"Of course. I'm happy to take a look."

"I have the file in my car parked out back. It'll only take a minute. Then I'll escort you back to the hospital myself."

"Thank you."

Placing his hand on my back, Ethan led me out of the coffee shop and toward the parking garage, sipping on my coffee as we walked.

After he helped me into the passenger seat of his Cadillac SUV, I glanced around the interior, which was as clean as I expected. It even still had that new car smell.

Ethan probably would have been horrified if he saw the inside of my car. While it wasn't filled with junk and trash, it was nowhere near as immaculate as this. If I didn't know any better, I would have thought it a rental.

"This is so comfortable," I said when he slid in behind the wheel.

I took another large sip of my coffee, then set it in the cupholder in the center console. I turned toward him, sighing, my eyes feeling unusually heavy as I leaned my head against the headrest.

"I'm beat."

"Why don't you take a few minutes to rest? You won't be any good to anyone if you don't sleep. Especially Imogene when you finally see her again. And I promise you, Julia... You *will* see her again."

"You're right," I mumbled, my words practically indecipherable. "I'll rest. But only for a min..."

CHAPTER TWENTY-FIVE

Agent Curran

"What do we have?" Agent John Curran approached Agent Hawkins as he slipped past the established perimeter around a quaint, two-story house located in a suburb of Atlanta.

"It's a mess. A treasure trove of trace evidence."

"Give me the bullet points," he stated, the two walking past the house and into the gated back yard.

It was a typical back yard, about a half-acre and impeccably maintained. Flowerbeds lined the exterior of the house, a few lawn chairs circling a fire pit. In the far corner sat a large shed Agent Curran estimated to be roughly three hundred square feet, a handful of crime scene techs walking in and out, carrying boxes marked as evidence.

"At approximately eight this morning, we got a call

from Lieutenant Kelly with Atlanta PD, informing us of a potential lead relating to both Imogene Prescott and Domenic Jaskulski. And it came from none other than Rosario Walker."

"Walker?" He tilted his head. "As in..."

She nodded. "The wife of Detective Shawn Walker. She's been in Los Angeles for the past month on a production," she explained as they trudged through the grass, the dew dampening the hems of his slacks.

"Production?"

"Ms. Walker is a set designer on some TV show. They shot the first few seasons out here, then moved it back to LA, so she heads out there when they shoot. Anyway, when she got home at six this morning, Walker wasn't in bed, even though his work vehicle was parked out front. So she came out here, since he likes to do a bit of woodworking. Walker wasn't here. But she did find something."

"What's that?"

Agent Hawkins strode toward a long table set up along the fence where one of the techs was cataloguing all the evidence into a laptop. She grabbed a small bag and held it up.

"This."

John's eyes skated over the silver chain, focusing on the charm — a heart mended with stitches.

Just like the one Imogene Prescott wore in many of the photos her mother had provided to help with the search.

"Look familiar?"

John took the bag, closely examining it. "Not just familiar." His fingers traced the date etched on the back of the charm. The date of Imogene Prescott's first heart surgery when she was no more than a few months old. "Identical."

"Mrs. Walker recognized it, too. After she couldn't reach her husband, she called the station to inform them of her discovery."

"So Imogene was here." John exhaled a relieved breath, thankful they were getting closer to finding the poor girl.

Agent Hawkins nodded. "Appears so. They're still processing everything, but so far, they've uncovered various journals containing handwriting that matches Jaskulski's. They've also found clothing that matches the description of the suit Christine Griffin claimed he changed into after he broke into their home. They're stained with what appears to be blood."

"And Walker's involvement?"

"We're still trying to figure that out. But I don't think it's a stretch to theorize he's involved in some capacity."

She flipped open her notebook. "I spoke with some of the neighbors. Several claimed to have seen Detective Walker coming and going from the shed over the past week, as well as overheard some heated arguments. His neighbor to the right..." She nodded at the house next door, "a Mr. Jacob Mueller, claimed to have heard three distinct voices, one of which he recognized as Walker's. The other two were unfamiliar."

"Any idea where he is?"

She shook her head, returning her small notebook to her back pocket. "Not yet. His work vehicle is out front. We've frozen all his bank and credit card accounts. We've also put out an APB for his personal vehicle, coupled with an Amber Alert for Imogene Prescott. In the meantime, we're combing through every inch of this property to see if we can figure out where he would have taken her."

"This is a good start. More than we've had to work with so far."

John swept his gaze over Detective Walker's property, everything charming and decidedly middle-class. The perfect place to raise a family. There were even a few bricks with painted handprints along the patio, presumably his daughters' handprints from when they were young.

"Why would he do this?" John mused. "Why would he get involved in something like this? He was less than a year away from retiring with a full pension. To throw all that away now? And for what?"

"In my experience, people make stupid decisions when money's involved. Or blackmail."

"Or both," John stated.

"Or both."

John heaved a sigh, about to hand back the small bag containing Imogene Prescott's necklace when he paused, squinting at the delicate chain.

"What is it?" she asked.

"Was the necklace found this way?"

"Yes. The benefit of a cop's wife uncovering it, I

suppose. She knew the importance of not disturbing it, so she left it where it was in the grass. After it was properly photographed, I placed it into this evidence bag."

"Just like this?"

"Just like this," she confirmed. "Why?"

"The clasp." He manipulated the chain, showing Agent Hawkins what he was referring to.

"What about it?"

"It's attached."

"And..." She furrowed her brow, not understanding what he was getting at.

"If it fell off as she was being moved from this location to another, as one would assume was the reason it was found in the grass, either the chain would be broken or the clasp would be undone." The more he spoke, the more excited he became. "That's not the case here. This is together."

"What do you think it means?"

He licked his lips, wracking his brain. He didn't know much about Imogene, but he'd picked up on a few things from talking with her mother. One thing was certain. They were quite a lot alike. Tenacious. Determined. Resourceful. Even under pressure.

"I think this was intentional," he stated. "The girl's version of leaving a trail of breadcrumbs."

Spinning on his heel, he strode toward the shed, a half-dozen techs bagging anything they deemed relevant.

"Everyone stop what you're doing right now," he ordered, voice echoing against the rafters.

A silence fell over the shed, not so much as a camera shutter to be heard.

"What is it?" Agent Hawkins pressed.

"This necklace." John lifted the bag. "What if it's not the only one?"

"We looked. We haven't uncovered any more necklaces. Or other jewelry. It—"

"No." He quickly shook his head. "Not a necklace. Anything strange or unusual. Imogene Prescott is a very bright girl. She may have been young when she learned who her father truly was, but she still remembers certain things. Like how he used to play hide-and-seek, where he'd hide Imogene and make Julia find her."

"What does that have to do with this?" Agent Hawkins frowned. "I'm not sure I—"

"Because as Imogene got older, she realized what her father was doing. Realized he was intentionally hiding her from her mother. I could be wrong, but I think this necklace is part of a trail Imogene left behind to lead us to something important."

"Maybe to where they took her?" Agent Hawkins suggested.

"Let's hope so." John scanned the shed, analyzing every nail, every footprint, every piece of wood.

"What are we looking for?"

"She wouldn't have made it obvious," he suggested, hoping his theory was correct. "It would be out of place, but not entirely conspicuous." He surveyed the cramped space, dust floating in the air as rays of sunlight filtered through the cracks between the siding. Then he squinted, stepping cautiously toward the workbench, a small piece of colored tape stuck to the edge.

He sucked in a breath, yanking his cell from his pocket and finding the photo that had been on Imogene's phone when Julia learned she'd been taken — Imogene bound and gagged in what looked like a trunk. And around her wrists was blue tape.

This tape.

"Here," John said excitedly, pointing to the small piece adhered to the workbench. "This is our trail. Find another piece of tape."

Everyone started searching for tiny pieces of tape. And they found them. From the workbench. To the tool cabinet. To the gun safe. To the folded-up lawn chairs. To the bags of potting soil. To the sawhorses. To the garden tools hanging on the wall. To a dehumidifier.

Which was where the trail went cold, no more tape nearby.

"Did she run out of time?" Agent Hawkins inquired.

John worried his bottom lip, something nagging at him.

"Maybe this was where she wanted to lead us..."

He whirled around, addressing one of the crime scene techs. "Open this up. Now."

"Yes, sir."

He rushed over and started to remove the water tank. But instead of being filled with water, it was filled with photos.

And not just any photos.

Photos nearly identical to the ones found in the files uncovered in Daxton Shea's house less than twenty-four hours ago.

"Holy shit," Agent Hawkins exhaled, eyes going wide. "But how is this supposed to help us find the girl?"

John placed his hands on his hips as he peered into the distance, sweat beading on his brow from the muggy air.

"What if it weren't to find her, but someone else?" he speculated.

"Someone else?"

"The neighbor said he'd heard arguing. That means Imogene must have *also* heard arguing. And the 'trail of breadcrumbs' we can only assume she left led us to a dehumidifier filled with photos similar to those found at Daxton Shea's last night."

"Maybe she wanted us to know he's not involved?" Agent Hawkins offered.

"Perhaps." John grabbed the container, striding toward the workbench and clearing a space. He got to work separating the photos into piles, one for each girl featured in them.

And they weren't all photos of their dead bodies. Much like was found in Daxton's house, some were obviously for surveillance purposes, the woman in question going about her daily life with no knowledge she was being watched. Observed.

Stalked.

Once he finished sorting the photos, John stepped back, studying the three rows of seven piles.

"That's twenty-one girls," Agent Hawkins announced.

"Twenty-one girls," John repeated. Then he arched a brow. "There were only *twenty* files found in Daxton Shea's possession. Only twenty confirmed deaths, at least according to my research."

"So you're saying there's one you don't know about?"

John looked up, blowing out a breath through his nose. Why would Imogene put her own life at risk in the hopes of leading whomever might find her necklace to these photos?

Was it to free Daxton Shea?

While John was skeptical of his involvement, this wasn't exactly the exculpatory evidence needed to point the finger at someone else. These photos being in Walker's possession could mean Daxton Shea either paid or black-mailed him to conduct this surveillance.

But John couldn't shake the feeling it was something more than that.

"It's today's kill...," he mused absentmindedly.

"What?"

"It's October thirteenth. The anniversary of the date Jaskulski killed a hotel clerk. Meaning this guy needs to kill a hotel clerk today to continue the ritual. What if the extra girl is the woman this guy plans on killing today?" He checked his watch, seeing it was already nearing noon. "If he hasn't already."

"How do we figure out which one of these women it is?"

John refocused his attention on the stacks of photos.

Over the past several months of investigating this series of murders, he'd become quite familiar with each of the victims. Could draw their faces from memory. Which was why he found it odd that one didn't stand out as he sorted the photos.

He went through the list of victims in his head, looking at each pile of photos. Emily Scott... Lillian King... Autumn Quinn... Everly Flores... Alice Marks... Simone Prentiss... Piper Kekoa... Claire Hale... Justine Connors...

They were all here.

But as he focused on each of the women, he realized one was not like the others. And why this woman's photos didn't stand out as someone he didn't recognize.

Because he *did* recognize her.

Because he *knew* her.

"Shit," he cursed, snatching the pile of photos.

"What is it?"

"This woman..." He held up the photo of a young blonde working the concierge desk at what appeared to be an upscale hotel.

"You think that's his next target?"

He nodded gravely. "I do."

"I can try to run facial recognition," Agent Hawkins offered. "See if something comes back, but there's no guarantee."

John slowly shook his head. "That won't be necessary."

"Why? I—"

"Because in addition to the hotel she's photographed in here, this woman has another job."

Agent Hawkins' brow furrowed. "How do you—"

"Her name's Katherine McCurdy, although most people call her Rina. She works in the corporate offices of The Mad Batter as the personal assistant to the CEO. Who just so happens to be Julia Prescott."

CHAPTER TWENTY-SIX

Julia

"What time is it?" I murmured, rousing myself from sleep, exhaustion consuming me.

I couldn't be sure how long I'd dozed off. Hopefully not too long. But I needed sleep. I'd never been so worn out in my life.

"'Come what come may. Time and the hour runs through the roughest day.'"

At the sound of that smooth, refined accent quoting what I recognized as a line from Shakespeare's *Macbeth*, I snapped my eyes open. A chill rushed down my spine when I was met with Nick's cold stare.

But that wasn't all.

Imogene was bound and gagged in a chair in front of him.

"*Imogene!*" I shrieked and attempted to stand, but I

couldn't, duct tape securing me to a chair that was similar to the ones I purchased for my dining room. I struggled against my bindings, to no avail. I vaguely remembered Londyn's former neighbor, Diego, a self-defense teacher, showing me what to do if ever in this scenario.

But for the life of me, I couldn't remember what it was, my panic overshadowing all rational thought.

Imogene called out for me, her cries muted by the gag in her mouth, tears streaming down her face.

"It's going to be okay, baby," I assured her through my own tears.

For the past forty-eight hours, I wanted nothing more than to see my daughter again.

I didn't expect it to be like this, though.

I lifted my gaze to Nick, glowering at him as he made his way around the dining room table.

My dining room table.

The bastard was keeping us hostage in my own fucking house.

The house I bought so I could have a place free from memories of him.

Now he was tainting what had become my sanctuary. My respite. My second chance.

Which was precisely why he brought us here when anyone else would consider it too risky.

Further proof Nick didn't care about being caught. Not anymore. Not now that he had me.

"What have you done?" I seethed.

He dropped down to his knees in front of me, gripping

my face in his hands. At the feel of his flesh on mine for the first time in over seven years, I cringed, bile rising in my throat. But that didn't deter him. If anything, he only gripped me tighter.

More possessively.

"What I had to in order to protect our family."

"Ethan..." My voice quivered. "Is he... Did you kill him?"

"Now why would I do that?"

"Because you murdered that poor man whose house you broke into last week. Shot him in the head and made it look like he killed himself. Did you see me with Ethan and kill him, too? It's the—"

"Ethan," Nick called out, standing. "Can you please come here for a moment?"

I furrowed my brow, my pulse steadily increasing as heat washed over me. Something about this scenario didn't sit right with me. Both Imogene and I were tied up. Why wasn't Ethan?

"Julia's worried I killed you."

A laugh echoed from upstairs, followed by footsteps. I floated my gaze to the stairs, watching as Ethan descended wearing a crisp suit that just screamed money.

Something I'd never seen him wear before.

What the hell was going on?

But when my eyes went to the pinky ring on his left hand, the same ring Dax wore, I had my answer.

"You?" I squeaked out.

He clapped slowly as he walked toward us, a conniving

smile on his face. He barely resembled the Ethan I knew. The geeky, somewhat awkward man I'd grown to admire and respect.

Was it all an act?

"It's a bit of a shock, isn't it?"

Even his voice was different. Smoother. More refined. More...sinister.

Much like Nick's.

"All those girls...," I began. "Piper... Claire..."

"I had no choice about Claire." He laughed under his breath. "She was much smarter than I gave her credit for. After she announced on her podcast that she thought there might be someone out there copying Nick's crimes, I figured I'd offer to help in the hopes of throwing her off the scent, so to speak." He gritted out something that looked like a pained smile. "But she was just too smart for her own good. So she had to die. Just like you." His expression brightened. "But I'm going to let Nick do the honors, considering he's been waiting for this day for quite some time now. Since I first started visiting him and sharing my... extra-curricular activities."

"Ethan has quite the imagination," Nick offered, beaming with pride. "But his technique was a little rough."

"So you helped him?" I squeaked out.

"I prefer to consider myself a mentor, something he was in need of, especially after the unfortunate incident involving Ms. Kekoa. But over the years, he's really come into his own. I'm quite impressed with how far he's come since those early days."

Ethan looked at Nick, a creepy sort of appreciation passing between them. "Thank you. That..." He trailed off, as if overcome with emotion. "That means a lot."

"I mean it. It's been a true honor."

As the two men stared at each other, my stomach churned. This didn't make sense. Why would Ethan go through the trouble of flying all the way out to Hawaii to tell Lachlan what he knew about Claire's death and what she'd been looking into? If he hadn't, who knew if we would have ever figured out the connection between the deaths and the gifts I'd received.

"Speaking of which," Ethan began, looking back at me. "I must take my leave of this little...family reunion. Sadly, I do have some business to attend to. It *is* the thirteenth after all." A smile twisted on his face.

"I understand completely," Nick said.

"What are you going to do?" I asked, even though I knew the answer.

"What I must," Ethan responded, expression almost crazed. Like he didn't have a choice. Like it was an obsession. A compulsion.

Exactly as he had suggested it was for whomever was behind these deaths.

It sickened me to think he was talking about himself and none of us knew. We simply accepted his help because he had the answers we needed at the time. All along, he was probably doing it so we'd never be the wiser. So we'd look anywhere other than at the truth staring at us with cold, calculating eyes.

"The ritual must be completed." He buttoned his suit jacket, heading toward the door leading to the garage. Then he paused, glancing over his shoulder. "That assistant of yours? Katherine, isn't it?"

"Rina," I corrected, unsure what he was getting at. "But yes. Her given name is Katherine."

The corners of his lips curved up, eyes dancing with amusement. "She works at a hotel on the weekends, doesn't she?"

"No," I exhaled, throat closing up, stomach churning, knowing exactly why he asked.

"And that necklace she wears is quite lovely."

With that, he disappeared into the garage as I fought against my restraints, Imogene's cries becoming more desperate.

I wanted to assure her it would be okay. That I'd find a way to get us out of here.

But I feared I wouldn't.

That Nick would finally fulfill the promise he made all those years ago.

And there was nothing I could do to stop him.

CHAPTER TWENTY-SEVEN

Julia

"Why are you doing this?" I asked, a knot forming in my throat from frustration and anger, along with a hint of fear. Especially when I noticed the knife in Nick's hand. "Why couldn't you just let us live our lives in peace?"

"Oh, my darling..." Nick placed the knife on the table and kneeled in front of me, cupping my face. "Do you think I like being forced to do this? I hate seeing you like this. You have no idea how much it truly pains me. But after our little interlude at the prison, I realized I couldn't put it off any longer. I had no choice. You pushed me to the edge, my love. When Imogene was born, I swore I'd do whatever it took to protect our little family. So that's what I'm doing." He narrowed his eyes on me, his stare turning malevolent, menacing. "Protecting our family. Taking back what's mine."

"We're not yours, Nick!" I countered, my voice becoming increasingly aggravated and desperate. "We don't belong to you. We're divorced. I had your parental rights terminated."

He abruptly stood, nostrils flaring, jaw twitching. I knew that would irritate him. After all, Nick was obsessed with being in control. The idea he had no power over us, at least in the legal sense, infuriated him to no end.

"And like I told you last week...," he began through a clenched mouth, grabbing the knife, "I don't care what the State of Georgia has to say. In my heart, you will *always* belong to me." He trailed the blade along my neck, forcing my head up.

When Imogene whimpered, I flicked my eyes her way, trying to assure her it would be okay. But all I could think about was what Nick had done to Christine Griffin.

God, I hoped Imogene hadn't learned about that.

"After all, you are my eternal beloved." Nick slowly lowered his lips, my heart thrashing in my chest as I fought against my restraints. "My Hera. My wife."

He covered my mouth with his, blade piercing my skin, but I refused to open for him, keeping my lips pressed tightly together.

Pulling back, he stared at me, eyes cold, the knife still digging into my neck.

Finally, he stood and increased the distance between us. I pushed out the breath I'd been holding.

"Perhaps we're going about this wrong," he said thoughtfully, pacing in front of me as if lecturing one of his college classes. "After all, it *has* been quite a few years since we've been a family. I can't expect things to just go back to the way they were. We need time to get to know each other again. See who we've become over the past seven years." He stopped pacing, spinning to face me. "Perhaps a nice Sunday dinner as a family could ease the...tension."

"Sunday dinner?" I asked, feeling like I was in some sort of alternate universe.

Then again, as I prepared for my visit with Nick a few weeks ago, Dr. Fields had reminded me that my version of reality and Nick's version were vastly different. That to be on an even playing field, it would be advantageous to subscribe to Nick's version of reality. At least temporarily.

I didn't take her advice then, and it had ended in disaster.

I couldn't let that happen today.

Not when my daughter's life hung in the balance.

"Yes," Nick stated. "I believe it's the perfect opportunity to give us a chance to reconnect."

I paused for a moment, needing to play this right. If I was too eager, he'd become suspicious. And I couldn't have that.

I snorted. "I'm not sure how you expect us to have Sunday dinner when we're tied up. Not to mention you have our daughter gagged."

Nick tapped the knife against his lips, brows furrowed

in contemplation. "I suppose that might make things difficult."

"But I'm happy to cook you dinner," I offered, giving Imogene a nervous smile. "Cook all of us dinner. Like I used to."

Nick studied me for a protracted moment, debating. All I could do was pray he'd agree. That he wouldn't sense the plot currently forming in my mind. My only chance at getting Imogene out of here depended on my ability to convince Nick to undo our restraints. If he refused, I didn't know what I'd do.

Didn't know how we'd get out of this with our lives.

Swiftly, he kneeled in front of me again, brandishing the knife. I sucked in a breath, pulse skyrocketing. Then he brought it up to my wrists, slashing through the tape securing me to the chair.

"You're right, my love. We can't have Sunday dinner with you both tied up."

After cutting the tape around my ankles, he made his way to Imogene, slicing through her restraints. Just as he was about to pull the gag from her mouth, he paused, pressing the blade against her throat.

"*Nick, no!*" I shrieked as more tears slid down Imogene's cheeks, her entire body trembling.

He turned his threatening gaze to mine. "But if you so much as even think about trying to make a run for it, I will cut her throat and make you watch her draw her last breath. Got it?"

I swallowed hard, heart pounding in my chest, on the verge of expelling what little food I had in my stomach.

"Of course," I said quickly, voice dripping with desperation. "I won't make a run for it. Promise."

He swept his analytical gaze over my face, the seconds stretching. Finally, he pulled the knife away and yanked the gag from Imogene's mouth.

"Thank you, Nick," I breathed out, wobbling slightly as I made my way toward Imogene. "I'll just take her upstairs so we can get changed."

"Changed?"

"Look at me." I gestured to the clothes I'd been wearing for over twenty-four hours. "I remember how you prefer us to be dressed for dinner, especially on Sundays. A t-shirt and shorts isn't exactly appropriate, is it? You look so dashing in that suit. Let us look nice for you."

He raked his eyes over me, as if trying to work out my angle.

"I never much cared for such…unflattering attire," he finally said. "I'll allow it. But I'm coming with you."

"Of course." I gritted out a smile, clasping Imogene's hand.

As I pulled her up the stairs, I sighed in relief at the feeling of my baby girl's skin against mine. A reminder she was still here. Was still alive. And I'd do whatever I needed in order to ensure she stayed that way.

"I'll just be a minute," I told Nick as I pulled Imogene into her bedroom.

He placed a hand on the door, preventing me from

closing it all the way. "I'm not leaving you unattended."

"Mama, I'm bleeding," Imogene said under her breath, giving me a knowing look.

"It's okay, sweetie," I assured her, bringing my eyes back to Nick. "I need to see to our daughter. In private. Unless you have experience in helping a teenage girl with her very first period."

His eyes widened, uncertainty flashing within. "I don't... I—"

"I need to help her. Show her how to use feminine products. I'm sure she'll want to take a shower to clean herself." I narrowed my gaze on her, silently urging her to agree.

"Yes. I definitely need a shower. Or a bath. My back hurts a little."

"I know. Cramps aren't fun." I looked back at Nick, his unease visibly increasing the more I spoke about what women went through each month. "So shall I show our daughter how to secure a pad to her undergarments, or would you like to do the honors?"

He quickly shook his head. "You can go." Then his expression hardened. "But if you're not out in ten minutes, I'm coming in."

"I'll be out in five."

With a smile, I closed the door, grabbed Imogene's arm, and hauled her toward the windows.

Once we were as far away from the door as we could get, I pulled her into my arms and squeezed tightly.

"I'm so sorry, Mama," she sobbed against me. "I didn't

mean for any of this to happen. I—"

"It's okay, baby," I whispered, kissing the top of her head. "It'll all be okay."

I held her a moment longer before pulling back, knowing we didn't have much time. "Are you hurt?"

She shook her head, blinking back tears. "I thought *you* were hurt. That's why I went with that police officer Friday night. He said you were hurt and I needed to come with him."

I furrowed my brow. "Police officer?"

"I think he said his name was Detective Walker."

"That fuck," I hissed, anger bubbling inside me. But I couldn't waste time worrying about that right now. "It's okay. It'll all be okay. I'm going to get us out of this."

"How?"

I parted my lips, shaking my head as I looked out the window. As was typically the case on Sunday afternoon, the street was quiet. Then a flickering light caught my eye. I looked at my front yard, Imogene's bike lying there, the sun reflecting off the handlebars.

I darted my gaze to her. "Your bike is out front."

She rolled her eyes. "Pretty sure now's not the time to yell at me for that. I know I'm not supposed to leave it out. I—"

"I'm not yelling. I'm saying. Your bike is out front. Easily accessible."

"I'm not sure I—"

"Listen to me very carefully." I ran my hands down her arms. "When I walk back into the hallway, you keep your ear up to that wall." I pointed to the shared wall between our rooms. "When you hear me say something like 'I have the perfect dress in mind', you turn on your bath—"

"I'm not *really* bleeding. I just said that in the hopes he'd give us some privacy."

"I know," I responded quickly. "But I want you to make it seem as if you are taking a bath. So once you hear the signal, turn on the bath, then leave."

"Leave?"

"Yes."

"But Nick will—"

"I'm going to distract him."

"How?"

When I gave her a knowing look, horror immediately crossed her expression.

"No." She vehemently shook her head, tears sliding down her cheeks once more. "You can't. I know what he did to that woman. Christine. And there are more, too."

"More?"

"More women he...hurt. Every night. The police never found them because that detective—"

I clutched her hands. "Don't worry about that. I'll be fine. This is the only way to get you out of here safely. And hopefully me, too. But I need you to do exactly what I say."

I glanced at the clock on the wall, seeing I'd already been in here for two minutes. My time was running out.

"Once I give you the signal, I need you to turn on the water, then quietly go downstairs and into my office. Behind the photo of Meemaw and Gampy on the wall is a hidden safe. The code is your birthday. In it are four guns. All are loaded, so you need to be *extremely* careful. Keep them pointed at the floor. I want you to leave one in that drawer." I gestured to the top left drawer of her dresser, the one closest to the door leading to the en-suite bathroom. "Leave another in the junk drawer in the kitchen. Another in the entryway table. And the last one in the console table on the second-floor landing. Do you understand?"

She quickly nodded, her body trembling. "Dresser. Junk drawer. Entryway. Console," she repeated.

"Good. Once you do all that, get the hell out of this house, grab your bike, and ride as fast as you can to Lachlan's."

"Why not Uncle Wes' house? It's closer."

"Because he's at the hospital. Londyn went into labor early. Plus, Nick knows where Uncle Wes lives. But he doesn't know where Lachlan lives. Or at least it won't be the first place Nick looks when he realizes you're gone. And he eventually *will* realize you're gone. I won't be able to distract him forever. So you need to work as quickly and quietly as possible, then ride your bike as if your life depends on it. Okay?"

More tears streamed down her cheeks. "Okay."

"Okay." I pulled her against me, swallowing down my own tears threatening to fall. "I love you, Imogene," I choked out. "No matter what happens, I am so proud of the amazing woman you've become. Never forget that."

"I won't," she sobbed as I inhaled her scent, praying it wasn't the last time I'd ever hold my baby girl.

CHAPTER TWENTY-EIGHT

Agent Curran

"Shit!" Agent John Curran cursed as he tossed his cell into the center console after calling the hotel where Katherine McCurdy worked on the weekends.

"What did they say?" Agent Hawkins asked, glancing his way, pressing her hand to the dashboard as John took a turn at a high rate of speed, barely slowing down.

"She called out sick this morning. Said she felt dizzy. Had difficulty standing."

"Do you think he already got to her?"

"I hope not." John pressed the gas harder, skillfully maneuvering through traffic.

After a drive that felt like it took hours instead of mere minutes, John finally pulled into the parking lot of the townhome complex where Katherine lived, his tires screeching as he slammed on the brakes.

He jumped out of the SUV, Agent Hawkins close behind as he jogged toward the correct unit, gun drawn, eyes scanning the area for anything that looked out of the ordinary.

But nothing did.

To anyone else, it was a typical Sunday afternoon. The sun was shining. Birds chirping. A slight breeze rustling the trees.

But John feared Katherine's Sunday afternoon was anything but typical.

Approaching the door to her townhome, he paused, glancing at Agent Hawkins.

"Do we knock?" she whispered. "If he's in there and alerted to our presence..."

"He might kill her," John finished, voice soft. "If he hasn't already."

"Exactly."

John tried the knob. Locked. He put his ear up to the door, listening for sounds to indicate any movement from within. Anything to indicate a struggle.

But there was nothing. No feet padding on the floor. No rustling of clothes.

No life.

Were they too late?

"There are sliding glass doors in the rear of these units," Agent Hawkins offered.

"Let's go."

They took off at a sprint, running around the building

and into the back alley, counting to make sure they entered the correct one. Jumping the short, stone wall onto Katherine's back patio, John cautiously approached the rear sliding door, expecting to have to break the glass to enter.

But it was slightly ajar.

After giving Agent Hawkins a look, he slowly slid it open, doing his best to remain as quiet as possible. As he stepped into Katherine's living area, his gaze methodically scanned the space for any movement or evidence that something was amiss, but everything appeared normal.

A stack of mail sat on the kitchen counter. A few wine glasses were in the sink. A blanket was sprawled along the couch. Other than that, everything was neat. Orderly. Peaceful.

Until a muffled cry pierced the air, the sound sending a chill through John. He didn't hesitate, rushing toward the source, gun raised as he flung open the bedroom door.

A pair of petrified, blue-gray eyes met his, gag over her mouth, wrists tied to the headboard, a tall man between her legs holding a knife to her throat.

"Put it down," John demanded, gun trained on the man, something familiar about him.

"I must do this. She has to die."

His voice was crazed, obsessed. Just as John knew this man was. Hell, you had to be in order to devote the past five years of your life to carrying out a series of methodical murders. It required a level of compulsion he couldn't even begin to understand.

From the moment he realized there was something more to the necklaces Julia Prescott had received, John believed this guy's compulsion would end up being his downfall.

Just like it was Nick's.

"No, she doesn't. You don't have to do this." John inched closer. The second he did, the man dug the knife deeper into Katherine's throat, blood seeping out.

"Don't take another step. And lower your weapons. I'm close to her carotid. Believe me. You don't want me to keep going, because it'll get *really* messy."

John met Agent Hawkins' gaze, giving her a nod. They slowly crouched, placing their weapons on the floor.

"Kick 'em over."

The agents did as requested, and the man relaxed the pressure of the knife.

"It's okay, my beautiful Katherine." He kissed her tears away. "I didn't want to do it that way, either. Death comes much too quickly then." There was a creepy sort of awe in his voice as he moved the blade from Katherine's throat, along her cheek, and up her arm, pausing along the underside of her left forearm. "I much prefer the radial artery. It's slower. Allows me to watch the life slowly leave your body over the course of what could be hours."

Katherine released a cry, squeezing her eyes shut as her frame trembled, tears streaming down her cheeks.

"It's not as easy as it seems. It's why so many suicide attempts are unsuccessful. You have to know exactly where to cut. And it can't be superficial, although I certainly make a few shallow cuts before the big one. Makes medical examiners believe it truly was suicide." He slowly turned his head, his sinister eyes meeting John's for the first time.

It felt like all the oxygen had been ripped from the room, the truth like a punch to his gut.

"Ethan," he exhaled, fighting against the dizziness consuming him.

"Crazy, right?" Ethan's lips twisted into a smile. "Who would have thought the same guy you pretty much handed the investigation to would be the one behind it?" He laughed, eyes brightening with excitement. "Quite the epic twist, isn't it? You never saw it coming, did you? I'll let you in on a little secret, though."

"What's that?"

Ethan leaned closer, lowering his voice. "Neither did Julia."

Heat washed over John's face, dread settling in his stomach. "What did you do?"

"She was so concerned for my safety," he continued, not bothering to answer John's question. "Thought Nick had killed me before taking her. But Nick would never hurt me." There was a frenzied, hysterical quality to his voice, making John believe someone in Ethan's past *had* hurt him.

It wasn't a surprise. After all, childhood abuse was often a common factor in serial killers' backgrounds. But

John couldn't focus on that. Not right now. His only thought was to get Katherine out of here safely.

And finding out what Ethan had done to Julia.

"Where is she?" John demanded. "Where's Julia?"

"Where she belongs." Ethan turned his eyes back to Katherine, running the knife along her arm, her sobs growing louder as he traced her wrist.

"And where's that?"

"Why, with her family, of course." He briefly looked John's way. "I've reunited them." His gaze drifted to Katherine once more. "Just like I'm about to reunite Katherine with hers."

Katherine wailed as she fought against her restraints.

"It will all be over soon, my darling Katherine." He dragged his tongue along her cheeks, licking her tears. "After all, you told me how much you missed your family. How guilty you felt that your parents and brother had died in a car crash after coming to visit you at Emory your freshman year. How you'd give anything to see them one more time. Have one more chance to tell them how much you love them. I'm going to give you your wish."

His grip on the knife tightened as he gouged the blade into her skin. This time, it wasn't merely a superficial cut. It was deep. Penetrating.

Deadly.

Reacting swiftly, Agent Curran reached into the holster hidden beneath his suit jacket and grabbed his other weapon, quickly firing.

Several seconds passed, the gunshot echoing in the room.

Finally, Ethan collapsed onto the bed beside Katherine, blood pouring from the wound in his back as John watched the life drain from *his* eyes.

Not Katherine's.

CHAPTER TWENTY-NINE

Julia

I paused to pull myself together, not wanting Nick to become suspicious. The only thing going for me was the fact he really didn't know anything about Imogene.

Didn't know she'd been a survivor since birth.

Didn't know how hard she'd fight for those she loved.

Didn't know she was a complete badass.

And because of that, I had no doubt she'd get herself out of here.

Forcing a subtle smile onto my face, I stepped into the hallway, nearly slamming into Nick, who stood inches from Imogene's door.

"Did you...take care of it?"

I rolled my eyes. "It's her period. Not a feral animal. But yes. I explained what she needed to do and how to minimize any discomfort. She's getting ready to soak in the tub." I continued past him, making my way down the hall and into my room, Nick following.

I slipped inside, turning around to close the door, pausing at Nick's intimidating presence.

I arched a brow. "I assume you want to keep an eye on me?"

"You assume correctly."

Heaving out a sigh, I stepped back to allow him into my room. "Come on in then. You can have a seat on the bed."

After he brushed past me, I shut the door, blowing out a relieved breath that it was all going according to plan.

So far.

"Is this okay?" I asked quickly, glancing over my shoulder at him. "The door being closed? It's just a habit, I suppose. I can leave it open, if you'd prefer," I added, hoping I wasn't overplaying my hand.

"You may leave it closed," he instructed, a sly smirk curving his lips. "Some alone time might do us good. After all, isn't that what that crackpot therapist we went to suggested? That we spend some time together, just the two of us?"

I faced him, doing everything I could to keep my hands from trembling. "That is what she suggested. Now..." I made my way toward the closet that shared a wall with Imogene's room. "I think I have the perfect dress in mind for dinner," I said loudly, as if wanting to be sure Nick could hear me.

In reality, there was only one person I cared about hearing me.

When the sound of running water filtered from the other side of the wall, I knew Imogene had.

Quickly selecting a dress I knew Nick would appreciate, I returned to the bedroom.

"What do you think of this one?" I held it in front of my body.

He pinched his lips together, studying it carefully. "It's hard to say. It looks good on the hanger. But I'd like to see it on you before I decide."

I chewed on my bottom lip, hesitating. I had to play this smart. If I appeared too eager, he'd know something was amiss. But if I was too resistant, he might call an end to this entire charade and pull me back downstairs. I couldn't have that. I needed him to stay in this room. At least until Imogene had enough time to get as far away as possible.

"If that's what you'd like." I smiled, turning toward the en-suite bathroom.

But I didn't make it more than a few feet before he jumped up and grasped my arm, stopping me in my tracks.

"Here," he demanded.

"W-what?"

His dark eyes locked on mine. "You'll undress and dress in here. In front of me. So I can make sure you're not trying to hide a weapon anywhere. Forgive me, my love, but our a certain past encounter has left me a tad...distrustful. I'd rather not have a repeat of that little incident."

Reminding myself I was doing this for Imogene, I

stepped out of my sneakers and pulled off my socks. I refused to look directly at Nick as I lifted the t-shirt over my head and slid off my shorts.

"Oh, Julia..."

His hungry gaze swept over my frame as he stepped closer. He brushed my hair behind my shoulders, the feeling of his hands on my body making my stomach churn.

"You are so beautiful. And this skin..." He lowered his mouth toward my neck, every inch he erased causing my muscles to tighten even more. "I've spent the past seven years fantasizing about tasting it once more."

I fought against the scream begging to be set free when he dragged his tongue along my neck, teeth biting my flesh.

"About doing so much more than just tasting it."

"Please, Nick," I begged, playing the subservient wife he always wished me to be.

The subservient wife he'd manipulated me into becoming throughout our marriage.

"Let me put on this dress. See if it meets your approval."

He lingered for a beat, then retreated. "You may continue."

Doing my best to not show even a hint of relief, I grabbed the dress off the bed. As I was about to slip it off the hanger, Nick stopped me with a firm grip on my wrist once more.

"Has it really been so long that you've forgotten what I prefer?"

I blinked, brows furrowed.

Nick narrowed his gaze on my bra, skimming the blade of his knife along the material before sliding it down my stomach and along the waistband of my panties.

"No undergarments. I like access to my wife whenever and wherever I choose."

"But Imogene will—"

The pinch of the blade digging into my hip cut me off, a whimper escaping.

"Otherwise, I'll just have to cut them off."

He moved the knife farther south, my entire body shaking as he used it to lift the material of my panties, ghosting it against my center. I bit my lower lip to stop my chin from quivering, panic racing through me.

"I wouldn't want to cut something I shouldn't. At least not yet."

I held my breath, doing everything in my power to stop the tears from welling in my eyes as a new wave of tremors overtook me.

"O-of course," I agreed shakily, returning my gaze to his. "No undergarments. I'll take them off."

He didn't move for several moments, a sick look of satisfaction crossing his expression when he pressed the blade against me. It wasn't hard enough to draw blood, but enough to be borderline painful. I didn't even want to think what Christine Griffin must have endured.

What *all* the women must have endured.

"Good decision," he finally remarked.

When he pulled the knife away, I pushed out a breath, turning around and increasing the distance between us.

"Face me. I want you to look at me as you undress."

I briefly squeezed my eyes shut, then did as he asked, my heart hammering in my chest as I reached behind my body to unclasp my bra.

"Come closer."

Legs wobbling, I timidly closed the distance a few inches, hoping it was enough to satisfy him.

It wasn't.

With a chilling grin, he slowly shook his head, using a finger to summon me. "Keep coming, Julia. I'll tell you when you can stop."

I took several more steps until there was barely enough space between us for me to undress without bumping into him.

"This is sufficient. Now, you may undress for your husband."

Goosebumps prickled my skin, the way he looked at me with animalistic need making me feel like I was going to throw up. But I had to do this.

For Imogene.

I risked a glance out the window to see if her bike was still there, praying she was on the brink of getting out of here.

I *needed* her to get the hell out of here.

When I spied her slender body peddling down the street as quickly as she possibly could, I exhaled, a grateful smile tugging on my lips.

"What are you—"

Whirling around, my back facing Nick, I pulled my hair over my shoulder. "Can you unclasp me?" I asked, voice slightly higher than normal, evidencing my nerves.

My heart thrashed in my chest, adrenaline pumping through my veins. I prayed he didn't catch on. That he'd be so distracted by the fact I was willing to let him touch me that he wouldn't look outside and notice Imogene racing away.

My anxious breaths echoed in the room, the only other sound that of the clock on the wall.

After several tense moments, his hands covered my back, slowly sliding up my spine. He unfastened the clasp, then pushed the straps down my arms, tossing it onto the floor.

"Let me see you, Julia."

Summoning my resolve, I faced him once more, his appreciation evident as his gaze raked over my body.

"Now the panties." He tapped the knife against my hip. "Unless you'd like me to do the honors."

"I'll do it."

"Then do it."

I kept my stare trained on his, trying to ignore the devious glimmer in his eyes. All I could do was pray with everything I had that Imogene would get as far away as quickly as possible.

I feared she was the only chance I now had of making it out of here alive.

CHAPTER THIRTY

Lachlan

I slung my duffel bag over my shoulder, hating the idea of going to the ballpark for the game when Imogene was still missing. At the very least, I would have felt better if Julia were home. It didn't matter how many times she assured me she was perfectly safe. I couldn't shake the feeling in my gut that something was off. It had been there all morning and into the afternoon, despite receiving text messages saying she was okay.

As much as I wanted her here, I didn't know what it was like to carry a child, then watch the baby fight for life. If this was what gave her purpose, what took her mind off Imogene, I wasn't going to deny her that.

"You'll go get Julia when she needs a ride home?" I asked Nikko, confirming what he'd repeatedly promised me.

He glanced up from his laptop where he was having another look at the photos from Piper's paddle-out.

"You know I will," he assured me. "You just focus on the game. I'll take care of things around here."

"Thanks, cousin."

"You bet, *Pohili*."

I was about to head to the door when a chiming cut through.

I peeked at Nikko's cell on the kitchen island, seeing Agent Curran's name on the screen.

I dropped my duffel bag and waited, not caring if staying made me late for pre-game warmups.

Nikko answered the call, placing it on speaker.

"Hey, John. I—"

"It was Ethan!" Agent Curran shouted, his voice frantic.

"What are you talking about?" Nikko asked calmly.

"The copycat! I'm still trying to piece it all together, and it's a much longer story than I have time for right now, but we uncovered a lead about who this guy's next target could be. So we went to her apartment and found Ethan *fucking* Shore there, about to slice her wrists!"

With every word he spoke, my rage increased, frustration forming in my throat over the idea it was Ethan. The guy was a goddamn vegetarian who startled during thunderstorms, for crying out loud. I was supposed to believe geeky Ethan Shore could have been behind it all?

Plus, we never would have gotten this far in determining what happened to Claire if it weren't for him. Hell, we would have probably still been trying to figure out who Lucretia was from the cryptic voicemail she left me. I didn't want to believe it.

Couldn't believe it.

"Please tell me you've spoken with Julia." Agent Curran's question forced me out of my thoughts.

"Why?" I asked nervously, heat washing over my face.

"Have you?"

"She's texted me off and on all day. The last one I received was about a half-hour ago."

"But have *spoken* to her? Heard her voice?"

"Why?"

The more questions he asked, the more uneasy I became, a knot forming in my stomach.

"Because Ethan said something that leads me to believe that, well... That Nick has her."

"What did he say?" I asked, muscles trembling, throat aching.

Agent Curran blew out a long breath, sounding resigned. "That he reunited her with her family."

I pulled my phone out of my pocket and pushed her contact information, pacing as I listened to it ring.

And ring.

And ring.

I hung up and navigated toward our messages, reading through them, hoping it would prove Curran wrong.

But as I scanned the latest text she sent, I could no longer deny it.

Nick had Julia.

Julia: *I'll be careful, my darling. Don't worry about me. I'm exactly where I belong.*

I should have realized. Should have known it sounded nothing like Julia. She didn't use pet names. That should have been enough for me to see the truth screaming at me.

"Where the fuck did that bastard take her?!" I bellowed, my voice echoing against the high ceilings of my home. My chest squeezed. Throat ached. Muscles cramped.

"We're working on that as we speak."

"Ask Ethan," I begged. "Beat it out of him if you have to. I don't give a fuck. Just find out where my bloody girlfriend is!"

"He's dead."

"*What*?! He told you Nick took Julia and you...you... you fucking *killed* him?"

"I didn't have a choice. It was either shoot him or watch him murder an innocent girl."

"Oh god!" I wailed, doubling over, an excruciating pain shooting through me. "So you're saying you have no idea where she is?"

"We'll find her."

"How?!" I roared, digging my hands through my hair. "How exactly do you plan on doing that? You heard what he said at that prison. 'Till death do us part'. It was a fucking threat." I swallowed the bile rising in my throat. "And what he did to that woman? Christine? What if he's..." I trailed off, unable to say it.

"Julia's a smart woman. She survived being married to him. She'll survive this, too. She knows him better than anyone. I have every faith in her ability to outsmart him again. In the meantime, I'm heading to the hospital, since it's the last place anyone can confirm seeing her. Hospitals have a ton of security cameras. I'm hoping one of them picked up something that can lead us to her."

"We're on our way," Nikko stated, not even asking what I wanted to do. He knew there was no way I planned to sit idle while the love of my fucking life was missing.

"No," Curran replied firmly. "You will both stay where you are. I understand you care about her, but I can't afford any interference. *Julia* can't afford any interference. The best thing you can do for her is to let me conduct my investigation as quickly and efficiently as possible. If you do show up, I won't hesitate to have you arrested. Not when an innocent woman's life is at stake. I assure you, Mr. Hale, the second I learn anything, you'll be the first to know. For now, let me do my job and bring your girlfriend and her daughter home."

I squeezed my eyes shut, feeling completely helpless. But I wouldn't know where to even begin looking for them.

"You'd better bring them home," I ground out. "Alive."

"I plan on it."

When the line went dead, I doubled over, releasing an anguished cry, needing to do something to make it stop hurting.

And right now, the only person who ever made it stop hurting was currently fighting for her life.

Or worse.

"He'll find them," Nikko attempted to assure me.

"How?" I advanced, nostrils flaring, body vibrating. "How the fuck do you know that?"

"I don't. But I refuse to give up hope. You can't, either. Julia needs all the hope she can get right now."

I clenched and unclenched my fists, trying to stop my mind from thinking about what she could be going through right now, each thought darker and more depraved than the last. What made it worse was that I couldn't do anything. That I had to sit on the sidelines while Agent Curran attempted to put the pieces together.

It was like Piper's attack all over again. Like being knocked out and rendered useless while she was assaulted.

Which only served as a reminder that Ethan was involved. That I'd allowed him into my home, my family, my life, only to learn he was the reason Piper was dead.

That Claire was dead.

And that Julia may very well be dead, too.

It was a good thing Agent Curran killed him. If he hadn't, I would have taken care of him myself. And it wouldn't have been as quick as a bullet to the chest. Or head. Or wherever he was shot. I would have made him suffer. Made him beg for his life.

At the muffled sound of the front gate opening and slamming shut, I snapped out of my thoughts.

"You expecting anyone?" Nikko asked, a single brow arched. "Your driver maybe?"

I shook my head. "I drive myself to home games. Plus, whoever it is has a code to unlock the gate."

Grabbing my phone, I pulled up the app for my security system, navigating to the exterior cameras.

When I saw the slender figure sprinting up the driveway toward the front door, I dropped my cell and darted out of the house as fast as my legs could carry me.

"What is it?" Nikko called after me, following close on my heels.

My arms pumped, heart raced, lungs burned. But I didn't stop.

Not until my body collided with Imogene's. I wrapped my arms around her, hugging her tightly. Sobs wracked through her as she clung to me, tears drenching my shirt. But I didn't care. All I did care about was that she was safe. That she was here.

That she was home.

"Shh... It's okay, sweetie," I quivered, smoothing her blonde waves. "You're safe. I got you. Nothing bad's ever going to happen to you again. I swear to you, Imogene."

"He has Mama," she cried out, pulling away and meeting my eyes. "She sacrificed herself so I could get out. And now..." Her chin trembled. "Now I'm worried he's doing what he—"

"Where were you?" I interrupted, not allowing her to voice the same concerns I had since I'd learned Nick had her.

Hell, since I'd learned about Nick's assault on Christine Griffin.

"At the house."

"What house?"

"Our house."

I pushed out a relieved breath, a weight momentarily lifting. "It's going to be okay." I pulled Imogene into my arms again. "Your mama did the right thing in getting you out of there and sending you here."

I kissed the top of her head, then stepped back. "I want you to go with Nikko. He's going to take you to the hospital to make sure you're okay."

"But—"

"You've been missing for forty-eight hours, Imogene. I need to make sure this didn't put undue stress on your heart. So he's taking you. No argument."

"And where will you be?" Nikko asked.

"Where do you think?"

"I'll call Curran. He should handle it."

"He's near Emory. That's twenty minutes away on a good day with no traffic. I'm only five."

"Lachlan, be smart. You're not—"

"Smart?" I interjected, my voice rising in pitch, coming out almost crazed. "Smart went out the window the second that bastard hurt my *ohana*. And now the woman I love is enduring God knows what. So while I appreciate your concern, I'm going. This. Ends. Now."

"But—"

"*No.* There's no but here. And I'm not going to waste time arguing. I need to get to her before..." I swallowed hard. "Before he does any more damage than he already has." I spun on my heels, sprinting toward my garage.

"*Pohili*, wait!"

"I told you," I shouted over my shoulder. "I—"

"If you insist on doing this..." He jogged toward me, pulling his gun from his belt and handing it to me. "Take this."

A chill rushed through me, my mouth growing dry at the memory of the last time I tried to save the life of someone I cared about.

But things were different this time.

I didn't have a concussion.

My knee wasn't injured.

I was thinking clearly.

And right now, the only thought in my mind was putting an end to Domenic Jaskulski.

Once and for all.

CHAPTER THIRTY-ONE

Julia

"Now, let's see you in this dress," Nick said once I stepped out of my panties, the last barrier between us gone. "I do hope it pleases me." As he dragged the blade up my leg, the cold metal skating against my apex, I whimpered. "The dress Christine Griffin chose for dinner was so distasteful. A short, skimpy thing. So I treated her like the whore she dressed like."

He swept his menacing stare over my naked frame, the knife scraping across my hipbone before traveling up to my breasts, circling a nipple. I sucked in a breath, my legs shaking.

"But you wouldn't buy a dress that makes you look like a whore. Not when you're married." He curved toward me. "Would you, Julia?"

"Of course not," I answered nervously. "The only man

I want to look good for is my husband. The only man I want to please is my husband."

"Quite right." Nick slid his tongue along his lips as his gaze raked over me once more. It made me feel like nothing more than a piece of meat he was getting ready to devour.

Or an animal he was about to slaughter.

"May I dress for you now?" I swallowed down the bile in my throat at playing the submissive wife he probably hoped he'd married. It pained me to do so, but if this bought Imogene more time to get to safety, I'd happily do it.

"You may."

I gave him a small smile, then stepped back, my fingers trembling as I lowered the zipper. I was about to pull the material over my head when Nick's voice stopped me.

"Where are my manners?"

I tore my gaze toward his, fearful of what sick, twisted path he was about to force me to travel.

"You shouldn't be doing that."

"I... I shouldn't?"

"You're my queen." Setting the knife on the bed, he stepped toward me. "Royalty doesn't dress themselves. They have someone who does that for them. As well as undresses them. They also have someone who bathes them, at least in more historic times. If you're my queen, I should take on those roles. Should bathe you. Dress you. Worship you. Now..." He extended his hand, a single brow arched in expectation. "May I?"

My stomach churned at the idea, sweat beading on my

forehead, despite the chills rushing along my spine. But I pushed down my trepidation, doing my best to remain in Nick's convoluted version of reality. At the very least, he had put the knife down, if only for a few seconds.

I handed him my dress, my chest rising and falling in a quicker pattern when he stepped closer, the fabric of his suit jacket skimming my nipples.

"Lift your arms, my love."

I did as he asked, my pulse increasing with every second he didn't make a move to pull the dress over my head. Instead, he licked his lips, eyeing me with hunger. Want.

Depravity.

Finally, he lowered the material over my head and guided my arms through the openings. Once he smoothed the flowing, green dress over my hips, he turned me around, raising the zipper. Then he pressed a hand to my stomach, pulling me to him. I couldn't escape the image of us together in the full-length mirror on the opposite wall, even though I would have given anything to squeeze my eyes shut and go somewhere else, even if only in my mind.

He brushed his thumb along the underside of my breasts, sensually circling his hips against me. When I felt his arousal, I whimpered, my teeth chattering, limbs trembling.

"No need to be nervous, my love."

"I'm sorry. It's just... It's been a while," I lied.

He didn't call me out on it, though, happy to stay in this alternate reality where we were still married.

Where I was still devoted to him.

Where I was still the meek wife who was petrified of stepping out of line.

"I guess I'm just nervous you won't be...satisfied with me after all this time."

He spun me around, pinching my chin, directing my gaze to his.

"Impossible, my beloved." His mouth slowly descended, every inch he erased causing fear to spike through me. "I'll always crave you above everyone else. I could never find you to be anything less than perfect. You're the love of my life. My soul mate." He paused, lips poised over mine. "My Hera."

He moved his mouth against mine, coaxing my lips apart. As much as I wanted to resist, to bite his tongue so hard it drew blood and make my escape, it was too soon. Lachlan's house was about fifteen or twenty minutes away on bike. I needed to buy Imogene just a little more time.

So I let him kiss me. It was soft, full of passion and reverence. Exactly the type of kiss I fell for all those years ago.

The one that masked the monster hidden beneath.

When I forced myself to moan, Nick deepened the exchange, his hold on me tightening before he tore away and rested his forehead against mine, his heavy breaths filling the room.

"You have no idea how badly I want to feel you after so long. How badly I want to bury myself deep inside you.

How badly I want to kneel before you and worship at your altar."

He ran his hand along the curve of my body, hiking up the skirt of my dress. When his fingers skated along the inside of my thigh, ghosting against my center, I whimpered, legs shaking.

Abruptly, he pulled back, surprising me.

"But we have all the time in the world. And I need to get you fed. Make sure you have enough energy. Then we'll come back here for some...dessert."

I glanced at the clock, unsure how long it had been since I saw Imogene speed away on her bike. It felt like enough time had passed, but I couldn't be sure.

And with my daughter's life at stake, I needed to be sure.

"But you know how much I enjoy dessert, darling." I smoothed my hand down his shirt, continuing past his belt and brushing his erection. When I palmed his crotch, he inhaled a sharp breath, pupils dilating.

Hoisting myself onto my toes, I curved toward him, lips skimming his. "It seems you do, as well. So why don't we have some dessert now? Then again after dinner? If you ask me, there's no such thing as too much dessert."

Pressing my lips to his, I made quick work of his belt and lowered his zipper. I resisted the urge to gag as I freed his erection and stroked him, making him harden even more.

He groaned, deepening the kiss. Sensing his growing need, I brought the kiss to an end, sultry eyes trained on his as I gradually dropped to my knees, my stomach roiling. But that was overpowered by the immense satisfaction I felt when I saw the scars around his groin, knowing I was the cause of them.

Parting my lips, I was about to take him into my mouth when he gripped my bicep and yanked me back to my feet. Panic shot through me, pulse racing, breaths increasing.

Eyes on fire, he leaned toward me, jaw clenched, his hold becoming tighter, more punishing.

"Is there a reason you want to suck my dick right now when you couldn't stand the sight of me a week ago?"

"I..." I shook my head, floundering for an answer. *Any* answer. I knew there was a fine line between subscribing to Nick's version of reality and seeming overly eager. "I realized I was wrong about you. About us. About everything. You were right. We're meant to be together. I want to be with you. Only you."

He grabbed the knife and held it up to my neck, spittle forming in the corners of his mouth. "You're lying. Why are you lying?"

"I'm not. I—"

"*Yes, you are!*" he roared, blade digging into my skin. "I know when you're lying, Julia. And you're lying right now! Tell me why!"

He glared at me as I remained mute, wanting to buy Imogene as much time as possible.

As if able to read my mind, realization flashed in his eyes. "What have you done?"

Keeping a tight hold around my bicep, he yanked me down the hallway and to Imogene's room.

He didn't even bother knocking, throwing the door open to find the room empty, the water running in the bathroom.

Venom in his eyes, he dragged me toward the closed door. "Am I going to find her bathroom empty, too? That water's been running an awfully long time. Has it not?"

"She has her period. Believe me. A hot bath is sometimes the only thing that helps really bad cramps."

"We'll see about that."

Dizziness washed over me as he reached for the doorknob, my gaze ping-ponging between him and the dresser drawer where I told Imogene to leave a gun. I could get it. I just had to be quick.

When Nick opened the door, a wall of steam billowed out. I used the momentary distraction to my advantage, yanking the drawer open and grabbing the gun.

Finger on the trigger, I aimed, about to fire when Nick turned and knocked the weapon from my hands, a bullet hitting the floor-length mirror, shattering it.

I didn't have time to react before he wrapped his hand around my throat, pinning me against the wall. "This was part of your plan all along, wasn't it?" he seethed, lip curling, nostrils flaring. "You didn't mean a word of what you said. It was all an act."

I parted my lips, struggling to breathe. I could have tried to deflect the situation. Beg for mercy. He always seemed to get off on that.

But I was done playing Nick's twisted games.

If I was going to die, I was going to do it on my terms.

"Of course it was," I strained to say, eyes unwavering, not a hint of hesitation or fear within.

Nick blinked, obviously taken aback by my sudden change in demeanor from the meek, subservient wife to the powerful, fearless woman I'd become.

"Do you really think I'd want to be with you, you fucking sociopath? That I'd want that disgusting excuse for a penis anywhere near me?"

Face reddening, he tightened his hold on my throat, making it nearly impossible to breathe, every muscle in his body vibrating with a fury I'd never seen from him before.

And I'd seen him plenty angry.

Teeth clenched, he brought the blade up to the low neckline of my dress, slowly dragging it down the material, tearing it.

"Well, since you don't want my 'disgusting excuse for a penis' anywhere near you, perhaps you'd prefer my knife." His grip on my neck loosened for a split second.

But that was all the time I needed for some of my self-defense training to kick in.

With as much force as I could muster, I landed an open palm to his nose, a crack echoing as blood spilled from his nostrils. His knife falling to the floor, he brought a hand up to his face. I took advantage of his moment of weakness and punched his stomach a couple times. He bent forward and groaned in agony. Placing my hands on his shoulders, I delivered a powerful knee to his groin before spinning from him.

I didn't look anywhere other than at the gun on the floor, the distance seeming like miles instead of mere feet, my legs feeling weighed down. When I finally reached it, the cold metal felt like sweet relief. Just as I was about to turn and fire, Nick tackled me to the floor, stealing the gun from me.

Using his body to pin me down, he lifted my arms over my head, binding my wrists together in one of his hands. I squirmed against him, fighting to free myself, but his strength overpowered mine.

It always did.

"It's useless to resist, my love," he said, dragging the gun along my frame as he forced my legs apart with his knees. "You knew this was how it was going to end with us."

I swallowed down my sobs, not wanting to let him see my fear. But as the cold metal trailed up my thighs, it was impossible, my body shaking harder with each passing minute.

"From the moment we met, you knew this was inevitable." He ran his tongue along my neck, teeth clamping onto my earlobe, his bite harsh and punishing, causing me to release a scream. "Or perhaps I should say from the moment you let someone else *fuck* you, you knew this was inevitable. It was so simple, Julia. All you had to do was adhere to the vows we made. Fulfill your promise to love, cherish, and *honor* me." He pushed my thighs farther apart, using his weight to keep me glued to the floor, despite my attempts to wriggle free.

"Is that what you did?" I hissed as I fought against him, refusing to give in without a fight. "*Honor* me by raping all those women."

"How many times do I have to tell you?" he seethed, crazed. Wild. Manic. "I—"

"I know. You *freed* them," I mocked.

"Exactly, Julia. I freed them from the cage life had trapped them in." He brought the gun up to my temple. "Just like I'm finally going to free myself from the cage *you've* trapped me in."

"You don't have to do this," I trembled.

"I don't have a choice. We promised each other." He pressed a chaste kiss to my neck. "'Till death do us part.' And you know I never break my promises. Goodbye, my love."

"Nick... Please...," I begged one last time before a gunshot echoed in the room.

Then everything went still.

CHAPTER THIRTY-TWO

Lachlan

I'd never driven as fast as I did when I left my house and sped the few miles to Julia's place, knuckles white from tightly gripping the steering wheel. I barely had the car in park before I leapt out, leaving the keys in the ignition, and darted up the driveway.

With shaky hands, I attempted to enter the code into the keypad lock, frustrated at having to do so three times before it finally clicked. Once it did, I slowly opened the door, not sure what I'd walk in on. All I knew was that Julia purposefully put herself in harm's way so Imogene could escape.

Just like any devoted, loving mother would.

I would have done the same for Imogene. It didn't matter we weren't related by blood. She was still mine. So was Julia. And I wouldn't allow anybody to take her from me.

Keeping Nikko's gun aimed in front of me, I tested the weight in my hands. At least it was the same type I bought after the home invasion. The same kind I used whenever I went to the range with some of my teammates.

They claimed it was a good way to blow off steam.

That wasn't the case for me, though. Instead, I practiced in the event I ever found myself in the same situation I'd been in with Piper.

Now I was.

And I'd be damned if the outcome would be the same this time around.

Doing my best to remain as silent as possible, I crept farther into the house, grateful for all the time I'd spent here over the past few months, if for no other reason than I was able to effortlessly navigate the space without needing to turn on a light. I glanced around, nothing seeming out of place. If it weren't for all the blinds and curtains being drawn, something Julia never did, preferring to bathe her house in light, I wouldn't have thought anything was amiss.

Until a gunshot reverberated through the silence, my heart skyrocketing into my throat. I darted through the house, desperately searching for the source. When I didn't find anything on the lower level, I rushed up the stairs, taking them three at a time, Julia's sobs coming from Imogene's room growing louder with every step.

Breathing labored, I peeked inside, doing my best not to alert anyone to my presence, my gaze falling on Nick restraining Julia on the floor. It took everything in me to not rush into the room when the sick fuck used the barrel of the gun to lift the skirt of her dress, then pressed it between her thighs.

I raised my own weapon, fighting to keep it steady as I carefully tiptoed closer, my anger becoming stronger as I listened to him tell Julia this was how it was supposed to end between them. How he was doing this because she didn't honor him after he was sent to prison, despite his failure to honor her during the time they were actually married.

This wasn't a man who would listen to reason. Who could be rationalized with.

He was like a dog who'd been raised to fight, maim... kill. There was no rehabilitating an animal like that. Not when they'd been conditioned to do one thing, and one thing only.

Just like there was no rehabilitating Nick. He'd never change.

And just like violent dogs needed to be put down in the interest of public safety, so did Nick.

My hands trembled as I lined up my shot, pushing down the uneasiness this scenario evoked. I told myself it was different this time. I had a clear head. And I was a much better shot than I was five years ago when I'd never even held a gun before.

That still didn't make this any easier, especially considering Nick's body covered Julia's. Any shot I made came with the risk of also harming her...

But I had to do something.

When Nick pressed the gun against Julia's temple, I didn't hesitate.

Didn't blink.

Didn't falter.

I couldn't.

Not this time.

Not with so much at stake.

I squeezed the trigger and fired.

CHAPTER THIRTY-THREE

Julia

W as this what it felt like to die?

I always imagined this sort of transcendental experience as your soul left your body, everything unburdened and weightless, all your troubles gone.

My meemaw often said she believed dying was like going home. And not the going home to heaven I'd heard so often during church and Sunday school. Meemaw said it was like finally being where you belonged.

Like finally being at peace.

But as the gunshot echoed, all other sounds muffled and distorted, I didn't feel at peace. Didn't feel unburdened. Didn't feel...ethereal.

Instead, a weight crushed me, making it difficult to breathe.

Then, through my confusion, I heard a voice. But it wasn't Nick's sinister drawl.

It was deeper. More pained. But more loving at the same time.

And it had an Australian accent that still managed to make my heart skip a beat, even now.

Suddenly, the weight suffocating me disappeared. I sucked in a welcome breath, a pair of arms wrapping around me, warm and familiar.

"Thank God," Lachlan murmured, dragging me onto his lap as he showered me with kisses. "Thank fucking God."

"Pretty sure some people would consider that blasphemous," I choked out.

"I don't give a damn. Not after..." He trailed off, pulling back, scanning my frame. "Did... Did he hurt you?"

I squeezed my eyes shut, unsure how to answer that question. Nick may not have caused any lasting scars. But I feared the trauma would stay with me a long time.

"It doesn't matter. He can't hurt me anymore. He—"

A moan cut through, both of us snapping our eyes toward where Nick lay a few feet away, blood pouring out of his shoulder and onto the carpet.

"Julia..." He exhaled a shaky breath, hand covered in blood as he attempted to stop the flow, to no avail. "Help me," he begged, voice strained.

"Help you?" I sobbed, pushing out of Lachlan's hold and standing, starting toward Nick. "Why would I help you after everything you've done to me?"

"Julia, no..." Lachlan scrambled to his feet and grabbed my hand, trying to prevent me from taking another step.

I shot my gaze to his, silently telling him I had to do this. That I needed closure. That I needed to free myself from the chains Nick had shackled around me years ago.

Once and for all.

He nodded in understanding, dropping his hold on me.

"All the times you hurt me," I continued, eyes not leaving Nick's as his skin paled more with every passing second. "All the nights I had to force myself to stay awake because I was petrified of what you would do to me in my sleep."

I lowered myself to my knees as sirens wailed in the distance.

And just like that morning Ethan came over to convince us Daxton Shea was behind all of this just to throw us off his scent, I knew they were headed this way.

Knew I had a decision to make.

I could sit here and watch Nick suffer, knowing the second the first responders arrived, they'd have an ethical obligation to do everything in their power to save his life. If they were successful, he'd return to prison and be charged with all the new crimes he'd committed this past week. Hopefully the murder charge would stick this time and he'd get the needle in the arm he deserved.

But that could take years.

Years I'd be forced to live in fear for my life. For Lachlan's life. For Imogene's life.

I couldn't put myself through that again.

I *wouldn't* put myself through that again.

My ears pounded, pulse increasing as adrenaline coursed through my veins. I didn't see anything else. Didn't hear anything else. All I saw was the knife.

Nick claimed he didn't have a choice.

Well, neither did I.

I grabbed the knife from the floor and pressed the blade against his chest. His eyes flung wide, terror swirling within.

"Julia, this isn't you," he attempted to argue, his voice barely more than a whisper, the sirens close. "You're too kind. Too gentle. Too loving." He struggled to draw in a breath deep enough to fill his lungs. "You're not a killer."

"This is what *you* did to me, you sick fuck!" I exclaimed, hands trembling as tears streamed down my cheeks. "This is what *you* turned me into. It's not fun when the shoe's on the other foot, is it?" I tightened my grip on the knife, attempting to summon the strength to do what needed to be done.

It should have been easy.

Hell, Nick made it sound easy, like taking a life was as effortless as making a cup of coffee.

But could I live with his blood on my hands?

"Julia..."

"This is the only way," I choked out, meeting Lachlan's gaze. "If I don't do this, if he doesn't die..." I trailed off, bile rising in my throat.

"It won't ever end," he finished.

I used my shoulder to wipe away my tears. "I can't live like this anymore. It has to end."

"It does." He nodded, understanding crossing his expression as he stepped forward, kneeling beside me.

He covered my hands with his on the handle of the knife. "When we started this, I swore to you that no matter the obstacles we faced—"

"We'd face them together," I finished softly.

He nodded. "Together."

I shifted my attention to Nick, finding satisfaction at the terror in his eyes.

"Like you said," I began, my voice cold, not sounding like my own.

Red and blue lights flashed outside the window, but I didn't stop. Didn't retreat. Instead, I leaned toward him, not allowing him to look anywhere else but at me.

"This was always how it was going to end with us. Till death do us part, Nick."

I glanced at Lachlan, giving him a slight nod. He tightened his grip, our combined strength forcing the blade into Nick's heart, blood staining his shirt and our hands. His anguished cries filled the room, the sound harrowing. Then it stopped, his body going limp, the life draining from his eyes.

"You first, you fucking bastard."

Needing to make sure he couldn't come back from this, I twisted the knife, my muscles shaking with the adrenaline filling me just as footsteps thundered down the hallway, coming to a stop in the doorway.

I whipped my head up as Agent Curran took in Nick's lifeless body, Lachlan and me still clutching the knife lodged in his chest.

Then he skated his gaze over my frame — my dress ripped down to my waist, blood covering my chest where Nick had fallen on me after Lachlan shot him.

When he finally lifted his eyes to mine, he swallowed hard, nothing but respect and understanding covering his expression.

"You did what you had to do," he stated.

All I could do was nod as relief filled me, my body collapsing into Lachlan's arms as I drew in what felt like my first breath in years.

I rushed through the crowded hospital corridors, Lachlan barely able to keep up as I ignored all his warnings to slow down. I couldn't. Not until I saw my baby girl with my own eyes. It didn't matter how many times he had assured me she was okay. That Nikko had brought her here as a precaution and hadn't left her side.

Until she was back in my arms, I wouldn't be certain of anything.

It had already taken me longer to get here than I would have liked. After answering Agent Curran's questions, then needing to wash Nick's blood from my body, hours had passed since I'd last seen my daughter.

And right now, I needed my daughter.

Needed to surround myself with her love.

When I neared a room guarded by a pair of cops, I knew I was close. The second they saw us, they stepped aside, allowing us to enter.

"Imogene," I exhaled, overwhelmed with emotion as I took in my daughter sitting in the hospital bed.

She tore her gaze to mine, pushing out a trembling breath. "Mama..."

I rushed to her, crushing her body to mine.

"You're okay," she cried against my chest.

"I'm okay," I assured her, savoring in my daughter's familiar scent.

I didn't think I'd ever smell her again. Didn't think I'd ever feel her in my arms again. Didn't think I'd ever bask in her love again.

But we survived. Again.

Just like we did all those years ago.

She lifted her concerned eyes to mine. "And...*him*?"

"He's gone. He can't hurt anyone ever again."

"Gone?"

At the sound of the familiar voice, I looked over my shoulder, noticing Londyn and Wes hovering with Nikko and Naomi. I didn't even bother to ask what they were doing here when they had a baby in the NICU. If I were in Londyn's shoes, I'd want to know what happened, too, especially considering the hell Nick once put her through.

She stepped toward me, expression pleading. "Is he back in prison or—"

"He's dead. Saw him get bagged up myself."

She closed her eyes, as if thanking God for answering her prayers. I returned my attention to Imogene as she released a sob. But not out of pain or heartache.

Out of relief.

I wrapped my arms around her once more, soothing her tears as she allowed herself to cry over everything she'd endured the past several days. I stole a glance at Lachlan, the two of us sharing an unspoken understanding.

We didn't want Imogene to know the details of what happened. At least not now.

"It's over, baby." I smoothed a hand down her hair. "We're free."

She held me tighter. "I really like the sound of that."

CHAPTER THIRTY-FOUR

Julia

A warmth filled me as I sat at the island in Lachlan's kitchen Tuesday morning while Imogene and Lachlan made cookies...at Imogene's insistence.

Most men in his shoes probably would have said they were too busy, especially considering he was scheduled to pitch tonight.

But Lachlan didn't.

He happily volunteered to spend time with Imogene, the sound of their laughter warming my heart, especially now that she was finally back home where she belonged.

Imogene's cardiologist wanted to keep her in the hospital overnight for observation, just to be on the safe side. While I initially insisted on staying with her, Lachlan ordered me to go home and sleep, offering to stay with Imogene.

And he didn't leave her side all night.

Just like a real father.

And that was when it hit me.

Imogene may not have been his biological child, but over the past few months, Lachlan had become like a father to her. Had become family. Our family may have been a bit unconventional, but that didn't matter. All that did was the love we shared.

And there was no doubt in my mind. Lachlan's love was true. His unwavering support in the final minutes of Nick's life solidified that.

"Can we go to the game tonight?" Imogene asked as she stuffed a cookie into her mouth, eyes hopeful.

I could tell she was itching for life to get back to normal.

While her doctors cleared her to return to school and resume normal activity, I chose to keep her home one more day, selfishly wanting a little more time with her.

Time I'd hoped to have yesterday.

Instead, Lachlan's house was filled with well-wishers and friends from Imogene's school, all who were grateful and relieved she was safe...including Roman, who'd been an absolute wreck since she went missing. From the second he got here yesterday afternoon, he'd barely taken his eyes off her, as if fearing she might disappear again.

I knew that feeling all too well.

But now we were safe. No harm would come to Imogene or me because of Nick again.

It didn't mean we could forget everything. The mind

was a funny thing. I knew from experience sometimes the psychological trauma was more harmful than physical wounds. But we'd get through it.

Together.

"Of course, sweetie. Lachlan's pitching. It's finally time we went to a game."

He met my gaze from across the island as I sipped on my coffee. "I couldn't agree more."

He was about to return his attention to the batter when the doorbell rang.

"Expecting anyone?" I asked Imogene, considering the flood of visitors from yesterday afternoon, her room filled with flowers, chocolates, stuffed animals.

"It's morning. Everyone's in school."

"I'll go check," Nikko offered, standing from the couch and making his way toward the front door.

Now that Nick no longer posed a threat, he'd debated heading back to Hawaii yesterday, then decided to stay for the playoffs. At least that was what he said. But I think he wanted answers.

Hell, we all did.

We'd hoped to hear something yesterday, especially after they raided Ethan's apartment and found hundreds of journals, along with dozens of keepsake boxes, containing evidence of his stalking, rapes, and murders.

Just like the ones Nick kept.

While we were all anxious to learn what happened, Agent Curran informed us it could take weeks or even months to sort through everything they'd uncovered. Even longer to figure out his connection to Nick, considering the two people who knew the truth were now dead.

I found solace in that, though. As much as I *did* want answers, the man who tormented me for so long was dead, as was the man who killed both Lachlan's girlfriend and sister.

"I apologize for the interruption..."

At the sound of the familiar voice, I looked toward the foyer as Agent Curran walked in behind Nikko, a petite, older woman with platinum hair beside him. "I was hoping to have a few minutes of your time."

"Mrs. Shea," Lachlan greeted, brows scrunched. "What—"

"Good morning, Mr. Hale," she said evenly. "I hope you don't mind that I asked to tag along. I just shared all this with Agent Curran, who was going to brief you about it. But I felt compelled to be here. Share it with you myself." She met my eyes. "Not have you learn the truth from a third party. Although, I must admit, I feel like a third party." She laughed slightly, then drew in a shaky breath. "Nonetheless, I felt obligated."

My curiosity was certainly piqued, especially since Dax had been released from custody once Agent Curran learned of Ethan's involvement. The last person I expected to see here was his mother.

"Come on in." Lachlan wiped his hands on a dish towel, leading Lucy Shea and Agent Curran toward the couch in the living area. I gave Imogene a look. She scooted around the island and clasped my hand as we followed, sitting on either side of Lachlan.

Lucy glanced in Imogene's direction. "Is it okay if she—"

"It's fine. I'm not going to shield Imogene from the truth. After what she went through, she deserves to know."

Lucy nodded, squaring her shoulders.

"Go ahead, Mrs. Shea," Agent Curran encouraged, his expression soft and comforting.

She inhaled a deep breath, closing her eyes before she returned her gaze to mine.

"I first met Domenic Jaskulski when I was a senior in high school. In case you're not familiar with my family—"

"I know all about the Ellis family," I told her with a smile. I was pretty sure most of the country did.

Her family had deep roots in the South, their money coming from cotton and oil. To them, appearance was everything. On the outside, they were the perfect family. But I knew from experience just how deceiving appearances could be.

"Of course." She gave me a sweet smile. "Well, when I was in high school, I struggled a bit with my studies." She fidgeted with the skirt of her designer suit. "I suppose you could say I was more interested in boys than reading Shakespeare. Growing up in the family I did was quite... isolating. My father was rarely home, preferring to spend his time in the Manhattan penthouse he kept for a revolving door of mistresses. And my mother was only interested in me when there was some formal event requiring us to attend as a family. Otherwise, she barely acknowledged me. So I guess I found attention elsewhere, even if it wasn't the kind of attention I wanted."

"And did Nick give you that kind of attention?" I asked, sensing this was where the story was going.

"Actually, no." A nostalgic smile tugged on her lips. "He was the first person in my life who didn't look at me and see my daddy's money. He saw a person. He *treated* me like a person."

While I wanted to remind her of the monster my ex-husband was, there was something familiar about the way she spoke of Nick. I remembered feeling the same when our paths crossed in college.

"How did you know Nick?"

"My parents wanted me to go to Brown. They'd both attended there. As did their parents. And so on, and so on. Unfortunately, no amount of bribe money would convince the administration to admit me with my grades, not unless they saw a drastic change. So my mother hired a tutor from a college down the road in Savannah, where I grew up."

"And that was Nick."

She nodded. "He was only fifteen at the time. I thought he was another high school student. I didn't believe her when she told me he was in college. And not just for his bachelor's, which he'd already earned two of, but that he was currently pursuing his master's. The absolute last thing I wanted was to spend my summer studying while the rest of my friends were at the beach. But as Nick began helping me..." She shook her head.

"He had a way of explaining the material that made it so...interesting. I couldn't help but be mesmerized by his raw intelligence. We had lively discussions and debates, which was drastically different than the grunts and unintelligent conversations I was used to with the jocks I tended to date, even if they did come from 'good breeding', as my mother put it.

"Over the course of the summer, you could say we became pretty good friends." She paused, biting on her lower lip. "Then we became more than friends."

"More than friends?"

"I know how it appears. I was eighteen. He was fifteen. And a very...inexperienced fifteen at that. But I liked the idea of being able to teach him something in return. He could recite quotes from great works of literature, yet couldn't tell you what it was like to kiss a girl. So I gave him that. Showed him..." She trailed off, glancing at Imogene, obviously unsure if this were appropriate.

I remember being Imogene's age. This was probably tame compared to the things she overheard in the hallways at school.

"It's okay," I assured her, smiling.

"Well, I showed him how to kiss. How to touch a girl. And I like to think I showed him how to love, too. As twisted as it sounds, considering the person he eventually became, I *liked* being with him. He was different from all the other boys who made me feel like I had to spread my legs in order for them to want to spend time with me. Nick was...grateful, I suppose. Gentle. Treated me with respect.

It wasn't just about the sex with him, although we certainly did enjoy having sex, especially once he got over the newness of it and started to experiment a little more. With him, it was more about showing me his appreciation. Like I said before, he saw me. For a teenage girl who thought the only way to not be invisible was to sleep with every guy who showed an interest, it was a welcome change."

I glanced at Lachlan, his expression even as he listened to Lucy's story.

"What did your parents think of this arrangement?" he asked.

Her smile fell. "They didn't know about it right away. They weren't exactly involved all that much in my life. So when I requested to continue my tutoring sessions during the school year, too, they didn't bat an eye, especially when they saw an improvement in my grades."

He arched a brow. "But they did find out eventually?"

She nodded. "My parents threw a lavish party for my high school graduation. And it wasn't a typical high school graduation where you grilled some burgers and hot dogs. This was just another excuse for them to play host to powerful people. Billionaires. Politicians. Religious leaders. It was the who's who of the world's power players. And considering it was thrown for me, I was expected to be there, especially since my mother was also using it as a sort of an engaged to be engaged party."

"Engaged to be engaged?" Imogene asked.

"My mother wanted me to marry Alton Shea. And

since he was going to Brown, it just made sense. It didn't matter that I wasn't attracted to him, and vice versa."

"But you're married now," Imogene argued.

"In my world, sweetie, marriage isn't about love. It's about bringing two powerful families together to make them even stronger. To further concentrate this country's wealth so fewer people have the most, while even more people have little."

"That's fucked up," Imogene stated, then cringed, looking my way.

I gave her a reassuring smile. After everything she'd been through, she was due a few swears. We all were.

"Yes, it is quite 'fucked up'," Lucy chuckled. "Alton and I never agreed with it. Which was probably why we didn't object to being forced to marry. We genuinely like each other as people, even if there will never be romantic notions between us. We've done a great deal of good in the world because of our mutual respect for one another."

"What happened at this party?" Lachlan asked in an effort to steer the conversation back on topic.

She returned her attention to us. "I wasn't feeling well. Thought it was just some stomach bug."

"But it wasn't a stomach bug, was it?" I asked, already knowing the answer.

"No," she replied gravely. "I excused myself for a moment to lay down. Less than an hour later, I was holding a baby boy in my arms while my graduation party continued downstairs without me."

Imogene's brows furrowed. "You didn't know you were pregnant?"

"I know it sounds crazy. My cycle had never been all that regular, or even that heavy." She cringed slightly as she looked Lachlan's way. "Sorry."

He waved her off.

"I did have some spotting, like is sometimes typical in pregnancy. I simply mistook it for my time of the month. While I'd gained a few pounds, it wasn't enough for me to think I was pregnant. I just thought it was stress eating due to finals and waiting on college acceptance letters. And I blamed all the contractions I'd experienced on eating something that didn't agree with me."

"What happened to the baby?" I asked.

"When I'd been gone from the party a little longer than my mother would have liked, she came looking for me. To say she was absolutely horrified when she walked in on me holding a baby, the umbilical cord still attached, would have been an understatement.

"I was so scared. Here I was, eighteen, about to go away to college, and I'd just given birth to a baby when I didn't even realize I was pregnant. So I told her everything. How I'd fallen in love with Nick. With his mind, his compassion. But she didn't want to hear it, especially since he'd only recently turned sixteen, which was the age of consent. It didn't take a genius to do the math. To realize I'd slept with him when he was underage, at least in the eyes of the law, regardless of the fact that he already held two degrees. It would cause a huge scandal. A black mark on our family we'd never recover from. So she did damage control."

She swallowed hard, her voice beginning to tremble. "Before I knew what was happening, a woman claiming to be from some adoption agency walked through the door, pulling the baby off my breast as I tried to nurse him."

"And this baby wasn't Dax?" I asked, even though I already knew it wasn't. The math didn't add up.

She slowly shook her head. "No. In the short time I was able to hold him in my arms, I called him Domenic, after his father. But after he was adopted, I learned he was renamed."

"To what?" Lachlan asked, the tension in the room growing.

"Ethan." She smiled sadly. "Ethan Shore."

CHAPTER THIRTY-FIVE

Lachlan

"So *Ethan* is Nick's son? Not Dax?" I asked, struggling to put the pieces together.

Lucy nodded. "They both are. Born four years apart."

"The incident report..." I glanced at Agent Curran before looking back at Lucy. "During Ethan's 'investigation,'" I said, using air quotes, "he found a complaint you made about an assault that occurred when you both attended Brown. It had Nick's signature all over it. Nine months later, Dax was born. Is—"

"Yes. Daxton is also Nick's son. But while Domenic... Ethan was born out of something beautiful, Dax was not."

"What happened?" I asked. "Other than the obvious."

"After my graduation party, my parents pretty much forced me to stay in the house all summer, not allowing me off the property unless there was some engagement that required a happy, perfect family." She rolled her eyes. "Keep in mind, this was over thirty years ago. Long before cell phones, text messages, and email."

Imogene's jaw dropped at the mere thought of life without all the modern conveniences.

"So it wasn't like Nick and I could just follow each other on social media and stay in touch. There was no such thing. So I went away to Brown, thinking I'd never see him again."

"But he enrolled there, as well," Julia stated.

"In the PhD program for Humanities. So when I was walking through campus one day and saw him, I almost didn't believe it. It left me...stunned."

"Did he recognize you?" I asked.

"He did." She drew in a breath. "But I pretended he meant nothing to me. That I simply used him so he'd convince my parents my tutoring sessions were going well." Her chin quivered as she swept away the tears flowing down her cheeks. "I don't know why I lied to him. Maybe because every time I saw him, I also saw the baby I had ripped from me. It hurt."

"Was he aware of the baby?" Julia asked.

Lucy lowered her eyes, subtly shaking her head. "So I did everything to avoid him. To make him want to stay as far away from me as possible. Even joining in on the ridiculing he got from other students on campus.

"I could see how much it hurt him. He even approached me one day, begged me to look him in the eyes and swear that what we had wasn't real. That the love I once claimed to have for him wasn't real. It took everything I had to deny him. To walk away and declare I didn't feel anything for him.

"I saw what it did to him. How it transformed him into a different person. Yet I didn't care.

"Then one day, during the spring semester of my senior year, I was in the library with a fellow student working on a research paper. As we looked through the stacks of books, I noticed Nick watching me from a distance. I don't know why I did it. It was so immature. But I wanted to prove I was over him. That I never had feelings for him. So I pulled my classmate toward one of the private microfiche rooms, making sure to keep the door open just slightly, and we, well... You know."

"Did Nick see?" Julia asked.

"He did. The entire time, I kept my eyes locked on his. The hurt in his expression..." She shook her head, voice catching. "It was heartbreaking." She grabbed a tissue from the box on the coffee table and dabbed at her eyes, collecting herself before continuing her story.

"That night, I agreed to go with some friends to Open Mic at a coffee shop around the corner from campus."

"Let me guess," I said with a sympathetic smile. "Nick was there."

She nodded. "Halfway through the night, I couldn't take being in the same place as him, so I headed back to my apartment on campus."

"And the next thing you knew, you woke up with blood between your legs," I stated.

"Actually, I remember the whole thing."

I furrowed my brows. "But—"

"I said in my statement that I felt dizzy at Open Mic, then didn't remember anything after that because I didn't want to name Nick. If I did, everything would come out and he'd learn the truth. That I'd given birth to our child."

"Then why make a statement at all? Why lie?"

"I guess I hoped maybe if I made some sort of statement, he'd realize what he did was wrong and wouldn't do it again." She blinked back tears. "I never could have imagined he'd take my version of events and turn it into a how-to manual for assaulting women under the guise of 'freeing them', as he claimed."

Julia reached across the coffee table, grasping her hand and squeezing. "It's not your fault. I know how you feel. I spent the past seven years blaming myself for not doing more to stop Nick from harming all those women. Now I know. He would have carried out these acts regardless of anything we may or may not have done to stop him."

She smiled, nodding. "Thank you."

A moment of silence passed as we all processed Lucy's story. While I now had a clearer picture of Nick, I couldn't help but be curious about Ethan. Based on what I knew of Dax and Imogene, simply because they shared DNA with Nick didn't automatically make them serial killers.

So what went wrong with Ethan?

"How about Ethan? What do we know of his upbringing? How did he find out about Nick, and vice versa?"

"Just days after he was born, he was adopted by a

middle-class couple through a Christian agency," Agent Curran piped up. "Lauren and Michael Shore. According to what we were able to dig up on him through his school records, he was a bit...troubled. He would act out. Like his biological father, he was extremely intelligent to the point the schools didn't know what to do with him.

"But while he was exceedingly smart, he had trouble socializing. He would often sit and watch people interact, taking copious notes so he could practice, sometimes jotting down entire conversations and reciting them from memory. When Ethan was about seven, the difficulty of raising a brilliant child tore the couple apart and they divorced. But Lauren never gave up on him. She always wanted the best for him. Unfortunately, she died of cancer when Ethan was fourteen, after which he was sent to live with an aunt who was pretty much only interested in taking him in because of a trust fund put in place by an anonymous donor."

I arched a brow at Lucy. "I'm guessing that anonymous donor was you?"

She nodded. "I may not have had a choice in giving him up, but I could make sure he was provided for. So, after Dax was born and with Alton's encouragement, I hired a private investigator to track him down, not thinking anything would come of it. To my surprise, he found Ethan. I sent a letter to Lauren, telling her I didn't want anything. That I wasn't trying to come between her and her son. Because he *was* her son. Then I informed her I'd set up a trust fund with annual payments to help with his expenses until he reached twenty-five, at which point he'd receive a final distribution of $20 million."

"That explains how he was able to afford such a nice apartment," I muttered.

"As well as blackmailing Walker," Agent Curran stated, adding another missing piece to the puzzle.

"Did you find him?" Nikko asked.

Curran nodded. "In the garage of a body shop a mile from his house, car motor running. He was dead on arrival."

"Suicide or..."

"Made to look like one. But it wasn't."

"Did Ethan ever learn the truth about you and Nick?" I asked, turning my attention back to Lucy.

"Eventually." She ran her hands along her skirt. "From what Agent Curran was able to figure out, he struggled to adjust after his mother died. He was bullied. Called a freak. And that was by his aunt. The kids at school were even worse. There's also evidence to indicate physical and sexual abuse." She swallowed hard.

"If my memory serves, Ethan was probably around eighteen or so at the time, since Daxton was about fourteen. It was Memorial Day...Fourth of July... One of those summer holidays, so my parents were over, enjoying the weather. While we lounged by the pool, Ethan showed up. He barely had a chance to utter a single syllable before my mother sent him away, threatening to pursue legal action if he didn't leave immediately, even though it wasn't her house. It didn't matter. One look at the young man and everyone knew the truth. He looked so much like Dax. And Domenic... Nick."

"Your parents didn't know the truth about Dax?"

She shook her head.

"And Alton?"

"He knew. It was actually his idea to elope. He was one of the few people who knew the truth about everything."

"And it didn't bother him?"

"Like I said, our marriage has never been one of love. More of mutual respect and appreciation. And it was because of that mutual respect and appreciation that he happily raised Dax as his own. His DNA may not run through Dax, but he raised him. His influence is seen in the way Dax has grown into a compassionate and charitable individual."

She met my gaze, offering me a smile. "That's what makes someone a parent. Not blood, DNA, eye or hair color. It's the way you try to mold them into being a decent human being."

Julia squeezed my hand. I looked at her before stealing a glance at Imogene, hoping I was a positive influence on her. Having her in my life certainly made me question things a bit more. Made me temper my anger on the mound when mere months ago, I would have mouthed off after a shitty call. Now, every decision I made was done with Imogene in mind. With not wanting her to see me in a bad light.

"But if your mother sent Ethan away, how did he learn about Nick?" Julia asked. "And you?"

"I told him." She shrugged. "After he was all but thrown off my property, my heart ached for the poor boy. Not to mention, Dax certainly had questions about why someone who looked eerily like him would show up, asking about his birth mother. So I tracked him down and told him everything. And he admitted he'd discovered the letters I'd exchanged with his mother, which was how he found me. He thanked me for being honest, then asked if he could occasionally call me so he wouldn't feel so alone. I agreed. We didn't get together often, but when we did..."

She sucked in a shuttering breath. "I never imagined he could've been doing something like this. He seemed so... sweet." Her expression fell. "Then again, so did Nick."

"Do you know when or how he first made contact with Nick?" Julia asked.

"We're trying to figure that out as we speak," Agent Curran offered. "Looking through all the volunteer records from the prison outreach ministry, we determined Ethan visited Nick using a false identity Walker helped him obtain two months prior to Autumn Quinn's death. We believe he first targeted Autumn because of her connection to Dax." He stole a glance at Lucy. "That, in his mind, Dax was living the life that was ripped from him, so he wanted to take something from him, too. But he realized he liked the power he felt when he held someone's life in his hands. Something he had in common with Nick. So he continued to visit Nick every Wednesday."

"And during those visits...," I began, arching a brow.

"There's no knowing for certain what they discussed until we go through each and every one of the notebooks we found in Ethan's apartment, which number in the hundreds. We have reason to believe they discussed Ethan's...activities and planned his next attack, including selecting the perfect target. When guards went through Nick's cell after his escape, they found photos of all the women Ethan had murdered, as well as photos of Julia throughout the years that I believe Ethan took to capture the moment she received each 'gift'."

Another brief silence passed as we processed the sad, convoluted tale. A part of me wanted to feel bad for Nick. For Ethan. But any trauma they suffered didn't excuse their behavior.

"Well, I'll let you get on with your day," Lucy said in a chipper voice, slowly standing. I jumped to my feet, as well, helping her. "And you need to rest up for the game tonight." She gave me a pointed look.

"Of course, ma'am. I'm looking forward to getting back out on the mound now that all this business is behind us."

"Speaking of which..." She turned toward Imogene as she and Julia approached. "Agent Curran told me you're the reason he was able to get to Katherine McCurdy in time to save her life. That you left a 'trail of breadcrumbs'."

She nodded. "I just did what I thought was right."

I wrapped my arm around Julia's shoulders, beaming down at Imogene, proud at how brave she was to have put others first, even when her own life was on the line.

Just like her mother.

"How would you like to throw out the first pitch at tonight's game?" Lucy asked.

Imogene's eyes widened, jaw dropping. "Are you serious? Like, out on the field and everything?"

Lucy chuckled, her blue eyes brightening. "Yes."

Imogene immediately flung her arms around Lucy, hugging her tightly. "This is the coolest thing ever!"

"I'm glad you think so." She pulled her closer, then glanced toward Julia. "And if it's okay with your mom, maybe you can meet your brother, too. If it's too much, too soon, I completely understand. I just thought—"

"Of course." Julia extended her hand toward Lucy, who grabbed it with her free one, keeping the other wrapped around Imogene. "I'd really like that."

CHAPTER THIRTY-SIX

Julia

I'd never realized how loud a baseball game could get until this moment. It was mind-boggling to think Lachlan was able to concentrate with this level of noise coming from the stands.

And the game hadn't even started yet.

Since we'd arrived at the ballpark earlier this afternoon, Imogene had been on cloud nine. Lachlan introduced us to all the players, each happily posing for a photo with Imogene and signing the baseball she'd brought with her. He even spent some time with her to help her practice pitching.

After this, she probably wouldn't sleep for days, her excitement at an all-time high, despite the events of the past several days. This was exactly what she needed. What we all needed. A return to life as normal.

Or as normal as could be when you were dating a professional baseball player.

Six months ago, if you would have told me this would be my life, I'd have laughed. And not over the fact I was dating a celebrity or someone much younger. But that I was dating at all. That I'd finally taken a risk and gotten over my fears.

Just goes to show how much life could change when you least expected it.

And I certainly never expected Lachlan Hale.

"You ready?" Dax asked Imogene, looking down at her with all the admiration one would expect from a big brother.

At first, I was unsure how Imogene would feel about it.

Or how Dax would.

But there was no awkwardness. It was as if they'd known each other their entire lives.

That was Imogene, though. She had a natural ability to charm everyone.

"I'm ready."

"Good." He gave her shoulder a squeeze. "Give 'em the heater, then we'll watch the game from the owner's box. How does that sound?"

She beamed, bouncing in her shoes. "Sounds like the best day ever."

Dax chuckled, then winked at Imogene, walking away to talk to a few reporters while we remained on the side-lines as they announced the players for the visiting team, quite a few of their fans filling the ballpark.

But when they started the introductions for the hometown team, the stadium went wild, especially when they announced the starting pitcher — Lachlan Hale.

My heart swelled with pride and something so much bigger than love as he ran past me, giving me a sly wink on his way out to the first-base line. Taking off his hat, he waved at the tens of thousands of fans chanting his name, many of them wearing his jersey.

I'd seen him play before. Hell, I'd even come to a game in order to tell him I chose him. That I wanted to take a risk.

But being on the field during a playoff game, hearing the fans go wild for him... It was surreal.

After the raucous cheering finally died down, they brought out a singer to perform the *National Anthem*. With each verse, I felt Imogene's nerves increase, knowing it was almost time for her to throw out the first pitch. When it was over, Lachlan jogged toward us, a brilliant smile on his face.

I thought the sight of him in a suit was enough to make me want to rip off my clothes.

But seeing him in his uniform up close?

My imagination was on overdrive with all the fantasies the sight conjured.

"Ready, pipsqueak?" Lachlan asked, holding up a brand new ball, his long fingers gripping it as if they were born to do just that.

I suppose they were.

"Absolutely." Imogene beamed as he placed the ball into her glove.

Taking my hand, he led me out onto the field, Imogene on his other side as the announcer's voice echoed in the stadium.

"Ladies and gentlemen, please join me in welcoming Imogene Prescott. For those who don't know, Imogene is very special to Atlanta's own Lachlan Hale. She disappeared Friday night, prompting a city-wide search. Thanks to her quick thinking and bravery, she managed to save not just her life, but also her mother's and another woman's. We're honored to have her here to throw out the first pitch."

I glanced around the stadium as fans cheered for my little girl, some even holding up signs that said *Welcome Home, Imogene.* It showed how much this city cared. Sure, there was crime, and it could often feel impersonal living somewhere with such a huge population. But when push came to shove, the people of this city pulled together.

"You can move up a bit if you want," Lachlan said to Imogene as she walked up to the mound.

"You don't think I can make it from here?" she huffed, placing her hand on her hip, giving him an annoyed glare.

I couldn't help but laugh at the attitude. She was definitely my daughter.

"Is it because I'm a girl? You think I'm worried about breaking a nail, Hale?" she taunted.

The catcher, who Lachlan introduced as Josh Greene, laughed as he crouched behind home plate, pulling his mask down over his face. "My money's on the little fireball, Hale!" he called out.

"Have at it, kid." When Lachlan pressed a kiss to Imogene's head, I could have sworn I heard a collective "aww" from the stands.

Approaching me, he rested his hand on my lower back, watching with pride as Imogene positioned herself on the mound, just like Lachlan had shown her. I held my breath as she wound back, then threw a wicked fastball right across the plate, the stadium going wild. Even the ump called it a strike.

"Still think I should have stepped a little closer to the plate?" Imogene mocked as she sauntered toward us, a cockiness in her stride.

"What can I say?" He wrapped his arms around her, hugging her tightly. "You constantly surprise me." Placing one last kiss on her head, he released his hold on her.

I lifted my eyes to his. "Have a good game, Hale."

"I plan on it." He brushed a soft kiss to my cheek.

Grabbing Imogene's hand, I started walking off the field and toward the escort waiting to take us up to the owner's box.

"Julia?"

I paused, glancing over my shoulder.

When Lachlan strode toward me, I dropped Imogene's hand, facing him. Cupping my cheeks, he covered my mouth with his, our tongues dancing in a perfect kiss. I reached for his hat, removing it. As I curved into him, cheers and whistles thundered around us, people chanting Lachlan's name.

"I've been waiting my entire life to do something like that," he murmured against my lips when he brought the kiss to an end.

"What? Kiss a girl?"

"No. Make out under the lights of a baseball field. Sorry to say, it's a first for me."

I placed his hat back on his head. "For me, too."

"Good. I may not have been your first boyfriend, your first fuck, or your first love. But going forward, I want to have the rest of your firsts."

"They're yours."

"Mine," he groaned, brushing his lips against mine.

"Yours."

But before he could deepen the exchange again, I pushed him away, biting my bottom lip in an attempt to reel in my smile. "Now, go win the division."

"For you, love, I plan to win it all."

CHAPTER THIRTY-SEVEN

Lachlan

The fragrant, Hawaiian air wrapped around me as I stood on the shores of the beach mere yards from *Eme*'s restaurant, the rising sun just starting to bathe everything in light.

There was once a time when my only chance of witnessing the sunrise was if I hadn't yet gone to bed the night before.

Now, I often found myself getting up before the sun, at least whenever I was on Oahu, simply because it made me feel closer to Piper.

And Claire.

Since they both loved to surf, both loved the waves first thing in the morning.

So when it was time to finally give my sister the

farewell she deserved, there was no question in my mind that it needed to be a sunrise paddle-out.

I glanced to my right, meeting Dax's eyes that were filled with emotion over the idea of saying goodbye to Claire. It was something I'd struggled with since I learned of her death.

But now that I knew the truth, now that I finally had the closure I'd been searching for, it was time.

They say that the truth could sometimes be a burden. But it could also set you free.

For me, this truth had set me free. From my guilt. From my regret. From my shame.

Now, I could live again.

And love again.

"You okay?" I asked Dax as *Eme* made her way around the small gathering of close friends and family, placing a lei over everyone's head.

He nodded, giving *Eme* an appreciative smile as she placed the flowers around his neck. "I'm okay."

"Do you know how to paddle that?" I gestured to the board in his hands. "And balance?"

He laughed slightly. "Claire taught me. Thought she was going to break up with me because of how uncoordinated I was when I first attempted to get on a board." He swallowed hard, voice trembling. "But she didn't give up on me. She never gave up on anyone."

"No, she didn't." I held his gaze, an unspoken understanding filling the air. Then I grabbed one of Claire's boards I'd chosen to take out in the ocean one last time and made my way toward the water's edge.

"How are you holding up?" Julia asked, running her hand down my arm.

Back in July, I never thought I'd feel anything but anger when thinking of my sister and how her life had been stolen from her too soon.

How *she* had been stolen from *me* too soon.

But I'd learned to let go of my anger.

All because Julia made me realize I deserved to be happy.

I was still here. Still alive. And I wasn't going to waste the chance I had at living a full life.

A chance Piper never got.

A chance Claire never got.

A chance dozens of women never got.

"I'm...good."

She brushed her lips against mine. "Good."

I helped Nikko push the outrigger into the shallows, Claire's board under my other arm. Once he climbed into the boat, I helped Imogene and Julia into it, as well. Content they were safe and secure, I hopped onto the board, my stomach flush with the wood, and used my arms to paddle out past the breaking waves.

Reaching a calm spot in the ocean, I pushed myself up to sitting, my legs dangling on either side of the board. A few dozen people on boards and in canoes joined me, the sun casting the perfect light around us.

Once we were all assembled in a circle, I extended my

hand to Dax on one side of me, Julia on the other, everyone doing the same so we became one, linked together because of a shared love for my sister.

"Claire Kailani Hale had a thirst for life that you couldn't help but be drawn to," I began, glancing around the small circle. "If she was passionate about something, you became passionate about it, too, just because her passion was so damn contagious."

When I sensed Imogene's eyes dart to mine, I glanced her way. "Keep a tab for me. I'll pay up once we're back on dry land. Okay?"

She nodded, polite laughter rippling through our circle.

"But the one thing Claire was most passionate about was her family. Her *ohana*. All of you. And because of this, her spirit will continue to live on in each of us, even if her body is no longer with us."

I briefly closed my eyes, everyone observing a moment of silence for my sister. For the life she lived. The gift she gave us by simply allowing us to spend time in her presence.

"Now we'll go around the circle to allow any of you to say something. Doesn't have to be deep and meaningful. Anything you'd like to share."

I glanced at Nikko, nodding for him to begin.

Over the next several minutes, everyone shared a memory or anecdote about Claire. Some brought laughter. Others conjured sorrow. But through it all, there were tears of joy. Regardless of the incredible loss we all suffered, each of our lives was better for having known Claire, even for a short period of time.

"You okay to say something?" I asked Dax when it was his turn. "You don't have to."

"I want to. Want people to know the side of Claire I knew."

I nodded, allowing him a moment to collect his thoughts.

"When I first met Claire, I couldn't stand her." He chuckled through his tears. "I know. I know," he added quickly. "We're supposed to be sharing our happy memories of Claire. But, as crazy as it sounds, that *is* a happy memory. My happiest, really. Despite the fact I once found her irritating, obnoxious, and just too damn happy..."

He glanced at Imogene, her brow raised. "Keep a tab for me, too, Mo."

"You got it," she said with a sympathetic smile.

He focused his attention straight ahead once more. "Despite all that, she still weaseled her way into my heart, where she'd remained for the past year." He blinked back tears, emotion overtaking him. "Where she *still* remains."

He paused, swallowing, peering into the distance.

"In the short time I was lucky enough to know and love Claire Kailani Hale, she taught me many things, but three will always stay with me.

"One, always take your shoes off before entering someone's house."

Everyone nodded in agreement, since it was considered rude on the islands to wear shoes in the house.

"Two, never trust an animal without arms and legs, because then it's just a glorified animal penis, and you can never trust a penis."

The group roared with laughter, the sound mixing with the waves as the sun inched its way past the horizon. I'd lost count of the number of times I'd heard her say those exact words to me, especially whenever she encountered a snake, which was practically a daily occurrence during our youth in Australia.

When the laughter died down, Dax drew in a deep breath, his expression turning more serene.

"And three, if you go an entire day without telling at least one person in your life that you love them, it's a day wasted."

The light atmosphere shifted, becoming more somber. More meaningful.

"I'm sorry to say I often failed to follow this rule. Because, despite the way I felt about her, I never told her I loved her. And that..." He bit his lower lip to stop his chin from quivering. "That is my biggest regret. One I plan to rectify every day going forward, starting now.

"Claire, you were the biggest pain in my ass. But you were the greatest love of my life. And I have no doubt you're giving St. Peter a run for his money right now. Possibly even forcing him to consider a new profession."

Another wave of polite laughter rippled through, everyone wiping their cheeks.

Then Dax cleared his throat. "I love you, Claire. Be at peace."

"Be at peace," I repeated, breaking the link in our circle to take the canister from Nikko. I slowly poured what was left of my sister into the ocean, allowing her to become one with the earth.

Then I lifted my lei over my head and placed it on the surface, everyone following suit, before I turned my board around, paddling toward the cresting waves, where I caught one last wave in honor of Claire.

My sister might be gone, but her legacy would always live on in the lives she touched...

Including my own.

CHAPTER THIRTY-EIGHT

Julia

Six Months Later

"This is the last of them," Naomi announced, dropping another box onto the floor.

I glanced around the kitchen, the place a bit of a disaster after I went through all of Lachlan's kitchenware, deciding what to keep and what to replace with mine.

So far, I was keeping a lot of mine.

After everything went down with Nick, I never wanted to step foot into my old house again.

Neither did Imogene.

She already had enough nightmares, although they were slowly fading as time went on. But I wasn't going to do anything to add to them. Staying in that house most certainly would have done that.

So Lachlan hired movers to box up our belongings, and I put it all in storage for the time being while I figured out the next step. Lachlan suggested the next step should have been making our temporary living arrangement permanent, but I wasn't quite ready to admit he was right about that just yet.

Instead, I began a half-assed hunt for the perfect house where Imogene and I could start over yet again.

But no matter the upscale appliances or long list of amenities, I always seemed to find something wrong with each property. And with each, Lachlan renewed his offer for us to move in with him. Said he liked having me here. Imogene, too. Liked cooking us breakfast before taking Imogene to school and driving me to the office.

Although there was no office for me to go to anymore.

While I was initially reluctant to sell the company I'd built from scratch, the more I thought about it, the more I realized I was hanging onto it because of some twisted idea in my mind that if I sold it, I'd be a failure.

Plus, every time I walked through those doors, looked at the desk Rina once sat at before she left Atlanta for a fresh start, saw the logo on all the official mail I received, I was reminded of Nick. I didn't want that for me anymore. Didn't want to be miserable.

So, after months of negotiations, I sold The Mad Batter and was free to start the next chapter in my life... Provided it didn't include opening up a new bakery within fifty miles of any current Mad Batter location for the next three years.

But I had no plans to do that. At least not anytime soon. Instead, I was going to enjoy simply being a mom. Doing all the things I couldn't do for years because I was too busy building my baking empire. Now I was able to be there for my daughter for the little time I had left with her before she went off to college.

"Oh, my god! Look at this!"

At the sound of Naomi's voice, I looked her way, furrowing my brow. "What is it?"

She held up a bunch of crumpled napkins, faded writing on it. "Your *Forty, Fabulous, and Free* list."

"Where did you find that?" I grabbed it out of her hand and hoisted myself onto one of the barstools.

As I sifted through the napkins, memories of that fateful week in Hawaii returned. Who would have thought a jellyfish sting could have led to all of this?

"It was in here." She set my wooden tea box on the island, then scooted around to sit beside me. "I opened it to fill it with some tea. Low and behold, I stumbled across this."

"'Have sex in a bar bathroom,'" I read, remembering being horrified at the mere thought of doing anything indecent in public.

Little did I know that less than twenty-four hours after making this list, I'd allow a twenty-seven-year-old to go down on me at an overlook where anyone could see. It wasn't a bar bathroom, but the lesson learned was the same.

That it was okay to let loose.

To live.

To do something unexpected.

"I was probably drunk when I suggested that. Bar bathrooms are gross. Unless it's an upscale bar." She flashed a smile. "Next year, I'll make sure to include 'Have sex in a ritzy bar bathroom'."

I rolled my eyes. "There won't be any more lists."

"Good." She squeezed my bicep, then returned her gaze to the napkins, both of us reading through all the things I wanted to accomplish this year. Or that she *thought* I should accomplish.

"I'm pretty sure you did this one." She pointed to another item toward the bottom of the cocktail napkin.

"'Go out as a mutton dressed like a lamb.'" I smiled. "I certainly did."

I remembered being so self-conscious about the dress I chose for that first date with Lachlan. About not having the perfect body. About having curves, a few wrinkles, and boobs that were less than perky, at least in my mind.

But he didn't care about any of that.

He made me feel desired.

Appreciated.

Loved.

Even before he said those three words to me.

"And this?" She pointed at the next napkin. "Did you finally accomplish this?"

I swallowed hard past the emotion building in my throat, swiping a lone tear from my eye. "Yes. It took longer than I thought..." I lifted my eyes to hers, "but I've finally forgiven myself. Or maybe I've finally realized I didn't *need* to forgive myself."

Naomi squeezed my hand, giving me a sincere smile. "I believe it's the latter."

She held my gaze for a protracted beat. Then we continued our walk down memory lane, both of us laughing and shedding a few tears as we revisited the list I made on the eve of my fortieth birthday, hoping it would be exactly what I needed to move on with my life.

"Here's one," she said with a conniving grin. "'Buy a vibrator and use it.'"

I threw my head back and laughed. "And if I remember correctly, it couldn't be just any vibrator. It was supposed to be the Mercedes-Benz, Maserati, Lamborghini, and Rolls Royce of vibrators combined into one."

"Exactly. Ever get one?" She arched a brow, expecting me to say I had.

Instead, I shook my head.

Her jaw dropped. "You *still* don't have a decent vibrator?"

"I haven't found the need to get one. Lachlan is like a machine. And he never runs out of batteries. Pretty sure that man can give me an orgasm ten times more powerful than even the most badass of vibrators."

"Oh, my god, Mom! Gross!"

I darted my gaze toward the foyer, eyes widening when they fell on Lachlan and Imogene standing there.

My daughter looked horrified to have overheard me talking about my boyfriend's sexual prowess.

Lachlan, on the other hand, looked quite pleased with himself.

And he should have been.

Every word was true.

The man *was* a machine.

"I know you guys have sex, just... Can you please go five minutes without reminding me of the fact!" She spun on her heels, darting up the stairs and to her room, probably to FaceTime Roman, as she always did when she got home from school or soccer practice.

"I love you, Imogene!" I called after her.

"Love you, too. But I still don't want to hear you talking vibrators and orgasms. Just... Ew!" Her door slammed.

We all erupted in laughter, the sound carrying through the living area.

"Talking about vibrators now?" Lachlan turned his eyes toward mine, slowly walking up to me and leaning in for a kiss.

"It's girl talk." I winked, then pulled back. "How did she do?"

"Great." He beamed, heading toward the refrigerator and grabbing a bottle of water. "I have no doubt she'll pass with flying colors once she turns sixteen."

I drew in a deep breath. "I'm not sure I'm ready for her to drive."

"She's a smart girl with a good head on her shoulders," he assured me. "Plus, I told her the only car I'm going to let her drive is the Mustang."

I raised a brow. "And that's helpful how?"

"Easy." He shrugged. "It's a stick. No texting and driving." He gave me a brilliant smile, then glanced at all the boxes.

"What's all this?"

"Just going through all the stuff I had in storage. Deciding what to keep and what to get rid of."

He narrowed his gaze. "Does this mean you've finally ended your house hunting?"

"Sadly, there's just nothing on the market that suits my needs," I said sarcastically as I stood, sauntering up to him. "As many times as I've told my agent I need something that comes with a hot, professional ball player, she's yet to find a single one." I placed my hands on his chest and lifted myself onto my toes. "So I think I'll stay here."

"It's about time you came to your senses, you stubborn arse."

I brushed my lips against his. "And I thought you loved my stubborn *arse*."

He cupped my backside, giving it a squeeze. "You know I do." He pressed his mouth more firmly against mine.

"On that note..." Naomi stood from her barstool. "I'll leave you two lovebirds to celebrate officially being roomies." She paused. "And each other's stubborn *arses*."

"Thanks, Naomi," Lachlan said, dropping his hold on me to give her a kiss on the cheek.

When he stepped back, she turned and wrapped her arms around me, hugging me tightly. "I'm so happy for you, Jules. You deserve all the happiness in the world. Never forget that."

"You won't let me."

"Damn straight." She gave me one last squeeze, then retreated from Lachlan's house.

My house.

"I think this calls for a celebratory bottle," Lachlan announced, making his way toward the wine cabinet.

"I couldn't agree more."

"Why don't you go sit out on the patio? I'll be right behind you."

"Sounds good."

I turned from him, about to head outside, but paused, swiping the *Forty, Fabulous, and Free* list off the island. I wasn't sure why. As grateful as I was to no longer be the woman I was when we concocted this list, it still filled me with a sense of nostalgia to look back on the early days of my relationship with Lachlan.

Once outside, I made myself comfortable on the patio couch, the setting sun casting a subtle, pink glow over the massive back yard.

But instead of only a baseball diamond and batting cages, there was now a half-size soccer pitch he'd installed so Imogene could practice whenever she wanted.

"Here you go," Lachlan said, handing me the wine bottle as he sat beside me.

I arched a brow. "No glass?"

"It'll be like old times." He winked.

"Like old times," I repeated, taking a sip. When I swallowed, I darted my eyes to the bottle, laughing at the familiar label of the Opus One Cab Sav.

Just like we drank that first night together when I thought he was simply a brooding asshole.

Or beast.

"What's this?" He grabbed the napkins off the coffee table. Immediately recognizing them, he sucked in a breath, darting his gaze toward mine. "You kept them?"

"Seemed like a good idea at the time. And I'm glad I did. Now I can see how far I've come in the past year."

"Technically, ten months."

"Close enough."

I took another sip from the bottle before handing it to him so he could enjoy the amazing wine. It should have been a crime for us to drink it like this when he had perfectly good glasses in the kitchen.

But even if he offered, I wouldn't drink this wine out of a glass.

I doubted I'd ever drink it from a glass again.

"Okay then..." Standing, he strode over to the wet bar on the opposite side of the patio and grabbed a few napkins and a pen before returning to the couch. "What should be on this year's list?" He looked at me expectantly, pen poised above the first napkin.

"I think I'm done with lists."

"Come on, love." He winked. "Humor me."

I pinched my lips into a tight line, not immediately agreeing. But it was so hard to tell him no when he peered at me like that. So flirty. So full of life.

So mine.

"What kinds of things do *you* think I should put on it?" I asked with a sigh, relaxing back into the couch.

He tapped the pen against his lips, deep in thought. Then his expression brightened. "Got one."

He hovered over the coffee table, jotting something down before sliding the napkin toward me.

I leaned forward, eyes skating over the words at the same time as he read them.

"'Have crazy sex with an irresistible, younger man.'"

My laughter echoed in the peaceful evening air. "Irresistible? You think quite highly of yourself, don't you, Mr. Hale?"

"Even you have to admit you found me to be quite charming when we first met."

"Charming?" I shot him a look of mock disbelief. "No. I found you quite the opposite. But like a rare, inoperable tumor, you grew on me." Smiling, I took a sip from the bottle. "Regardless of my initial opinion of you, I think we can successfully mark that as complete. Although I'd like the crazy sex with a so-called irresistible younger man to continue, even if I've already accomplished it."

His pupils dilated, mouth forming into a devilish smirk that made my pulse kick up. "I have a feeling that can be arranged." He curved toward me, capturing my lips in a kiss, warmth spreading through me.

It didn't matter how many times this man kissed me. Each one still felt like the first.

Still gave me that same sense of wonder. Of excitement.

Of hope for my future.

"What else?" he asked, pulling back. "Perhaps something a bit more...adventurous?"

"I can do adventurous."

"Good." He grabbed the pen and scribbled something.

"'Get to home base on home base,'" I read over his shoulder, heat washing over my face at the memory of doing just that when we went to Hawaii during Imogene's winter break. We'd gone out to his Little League fields where we got caught in another torrential downpour.

And just like the first time, we couldn't keep our hands off each other.

"Are all of these going to be about sex?" I pouted. "I'm getting the impression that's all you think about."

"With you around, do you blame me?" He waggled his brows. "But fine. I'll come up with something that has absolutely nothing to do with sex."

He pinched his lips together, seemingly deep in thought. Then he grabbed the napkin, hiding it as he wrote. When he was finished, he handed it to me.

"'Say yes'?" I scrunched my brows. "What do you—"

Before I could finish my question, he scooted off the couch, dropping to one knee in front of me and grabbing my hand. I gasped, heart hammering in my chest, shock rendering me mute.

"I didn't get you a ring. It killed me not to. But considering your somewhat...difficult relationship with receiving jewelry, I didn't want this moment to be tainted with those memories. If you say yes...and I really bloody hope you do...and you decide you want a ring, I will happily buy you the ring of your dreams.

"But even if you choose to not wear one, please know that I won't love you any less. I won't want to be with you any less. I won't be any less devoted to you." He licked his lips, running his thumb along my knuckles.

All I could do was stare, speechless. This was completely unexpected.

Then again, everything about Lachlan had been completely unexpected.

"The day I met you, I was in a really dark place. But then you had to go and step on a jellyfish. Since then, my life has been forever changed. For the first time in years, I felt this strange thing called happiness. And the more I got to know you, the more I realized that my heart was no longer mine. It was yours. And I want it to always be yours, love.

"Now, I can't promise things will always be easy. They haven't been all that easy so far."

"They certainly haven't," I agreed, using my free hand to swipe at my tears, the sight of Lachlan kneeling before me causing more emotion to fill me than I thought possible.

This was what I always imagined a proposal should feel like.

Like you were so full of love you thought you'd burst.

"In case you haven't figured it out by now, we're both ridiculously stubborn," Lachlan reminded me with a subtle laugh.

"We certainly are."

Then he tightened his grip on my hand, his expression turning serious. Determined.

"But there's no one I'd rather get frustrated with, then make love to. No one I'd rather have drive me absolutely bloody crazy, then drive me wild." He swallowed hard. "And there's no one on this planet I'd rather love than you."

My chin trembled, more tears flowing down my cheeks.

And the best part was there was not a hint of deception within his heartfelt words. He didn't say them in order to manipulate me into behaving a certain way. Instead, he said them because he couldn't go another minute without telling me how he felt about me.

"So please, Julia Blaire Prescott," he continued, his voice trembling with emotion, "will you do me the honor of marrying me?"

"You really want to marry me even though I have a few wrinkles?" I choked out a laugh, needing to do something to break the tension. "Even though within, like, five years, my boobs might start to sag?"

"I don't care about that. I quite like your boobs. Like to

bury my face in them. Shall I tell you how I feel about your pussy? Because I find that quite delectable, as well."

I barked out a laugh, wiping away my tears. "This is either the worst or best proposal in the history of proposals."

"I'd like to think it's the best. Because it's real." His expression turned sincere. "Nothing more. Nothing less."

"Nothing less," I repeated softly.

"So, what do you say? Should we renegotiate our original agreement for a longer term?"

"How long did you have in mind?" I asked coyly.

"How does forever sound?"

"Like not nearly long enough to be married to you." I cupped his cheek, bringing his lips toward mine. "But it's a start."

"Yes, it is."

CHAPTER THIRTY-NINE

Imogene

Fifteen Years Later

"Congratulations, sweetie."

Mama, Lachlan, and Dax tipped their champagne glasses toward me. I clinked mine with theirs before we all took a sip.

"I told you not to make a big deal out of today," I admonished them.

But I should have known they wouldn't listen.

It didn't matter how old I got or how many degrees I had under my belt. They'd always be my family.

As such, they'd always spoil me.

Granted, Lachlan may not have been my biological

father. But since he came into our lives, that was precisely the role he filled, even before he and my mom said "I do" at the exact spot on the beach where she stepped on a jellyfish and he came to her rescue.

"It's not every day your favorite daughter graduates with her doctorate in physical therapy," Mama said flippantly.

"I'm your *only* daughter."

"But you're still my favorite." She clutched my hand from beside me at our table in the upscale Atlanta restaurant.

"And you're still mine," I replied with a heartfelt smile, grateful for everything she had done for me. And not just through college and grad school. But since the day I was born.

All the sacrifices she made.

All the trauma she suffered.

I was just grateful that was behind us. That she survived.

That *we* survived.

And since that fateful day I thought I'd never see her again, there had been no more suffering. No more trauma.

Instead, the past fifteen years had been...happy.

That wasn't to say we didn't deal with psychological effects from what my sociopath of a sperm donor had put us through. But we got through it... Together.

Thankfully, with the passing of years, the public's interest in our connection to the man who was labeled one of the most intriguing serial killers in history had diminished to the point where Domenic Jaskulski was barely a footnote in the history of our lives.

Where he belonged.

"So what's next?" Lachlan asked, leaning back in his chair, smiling at several diners who recognized him.

Even though he'd retired a few years ago and now worked as a commentator for one of the networks, people in Atlanta still loved him. It was why it was so hard for him to finally throw in the towel and retire. He wanted to go out on a high note. And he certainly did.

After his fifth World Series ring, he decided it was time. Now, he and Mama split their time between Atlanta and Hawaii, where Mama opened a small bakery on the North Shore of Oahu.

This time, she had no intention of expanding. She didn't need fame or notoriety to be happy.

She'd found her happily ever after.

Now it was time for me to find mine.

"Are you still undecided about which offer to accept?" Mama asked, slicing into her salmon. "I know you've received quite a few from teams here in the Southeast."

"Including mine," Dax reminded me with a soft smile. "And not because you're my sister. When management made you the offer to join the team as a therapist after you completed your residency with us, I told you it's because you're talented. And have an incredible bedside manner. That goes a long way when dealing with injuries."

I smiled, basking in my brother's words. Ever since I learned who he was and the connection we shared, we'd formed an immediate bond I didn't think possible between two strangers. Of course, as a teenager, sometimes he irritated me, especially whenever he learned I had a date and would just so happen to stop by at the precise time my date was to pick me up. Between him and Lachlan, it was a miracle any guys wanted to date me at all.

But as much as I claimed it was embarrassing, I liked that these two men put in the effort. That they had no problem telling my date that I meant the world to them. That if anyone ever treated me as if I were less than the incredible woman I was, there would be consequences.

Our family may have been disjointed. A strange mix of people from all walks of life and experiences. But I wouldn't have gotten to this point without their unwavering support.

"Actually...," I began, running my hands down my dress, "I *have* made a decision."

I smiled nervously. I'd been putting off telling them, knowing what it would mean. That I was finally leaving the only place I'd ever called home.

That I'd be spreading my wings and leaving the nest.

Something most women had already done by the time they were my age. But I hadn't, opting to remain close by. Granted, I hadn't lived with them since I moved into the dorm my freshman year at Emory, even though it wasn't that far from my own house. But this wasn't just about having my own apartment in the same city.

I was no longer going to be in the same city. Hell, in the same state.

"You have?" Mama asked, tilting her head.

"Yes. San Diego."

The table fell silent.

"I know it's far away," I continued, "but they made me a great offer. And there's a lot of opportunity for me to advance. After living out here all my life... I don't know..." I shrugged, smiling. "I thought a change of scenery might be nice. Don't get me wrong," I added quickly. "You all know how much I love you. How much I appreciate everything you've done. But now that I'm done with school and ready to embark on the next chapter of my life..." I smiled, briefly averting my gaze, "my first chapter, really...a part of me wants to do that without any...reminders. A clean slate, so to speak."

Mama, Lachlan, and Dax stared at me, no one saying anything for several moments. I feared they'd react this way. That they'd want to keep me close by simply because of the past.

To my surprise, Mama reached across the table and grabbed my hand in hers.

"If anyone can understand wanting a fresh start, it's me. If this is what you want, you know I'll support you. You have a good head on your shoulders. And have worked too hard to settle for something less than what you want. I'm proud of you, sweetie."

I met her gaze. "Thanks, Mama."

She nodded, squeezing my hand.

"Well..." Lachlan cleared his throat. "I suppose now would be a good time to give you this." He reached into the inner pocket of his suit jacket, then slid a small box toward me.

"What is it?" I furrowed my brow. "I told you. No presents. I—"

"Just open it, pipsqueak." He winked, using the nickname he called me all those years ago.

The nickname he still occasionally called me.

"Whatever, Hale." I rolled my eyes, grabbing the box. Most people would think it contained jewelry. A bracelet or earrings.

But I knew it didn't.

Our family didn't give jewelry as gifts.

It was an unspoken rule. One we'd adhered to for the past fifteen years.

I made quick work of the white bow, then tore at the red wrapping before lifting the lid, my eyes falling on the contents.

"A...key?" I lifted it from the box.

"Not just any key. The key that starts a certain car in the garage you have an affinity for."

My eyes widened. "The Mustang?!"

With a smile, he slowly nodded. "It's yours now. Just be good to her."

Unable to contain my excitement, I leapt off my chair and rushed toward him, wrapping my arms around his neck. "This is the coolest thing ever."

"You deserve it, sweetie. I love you."

I closed my eyes. "I love you, too...Dad."

The salty air blew around me as I navigated the Mustang along the street, turning into the parking lot of my complex. After pulling it into my assigned garage, I killed the ignition, then grabbed my bags, a bounce in my step as I made my way toward my townhome, the sun warm on my face.

If there was any doubt in my mind about moving so far away from the only home I'd ever known, they were immediately dashed the second I arrived in San Diego a week ago. Sun. Sand. Surfers.

I'd officially arrived in heaven.

And after my first day at my new job as a physical therapist for the team here in San Diego, it confirmed what I felt in my heart the second I left my interview all those months ago.

This was where I belonged.

"Hey."

I snapped my eyes up at the deep voice as I walked along the row of garages, heading toward my unit.

"Hello." I smiled at the man I'd seen in passing over the past week, then continued on my way.

"I'm Mateo."

I stopped, turning to face him.

"I live in 27B." He nodded at the unit. "Next to you."

I raked my gaze over him. Tall. Muscular. Dark hair that was slightly disheveled. Scruff on his jaw. A Spanish accent that made my toes curl.

I'd really hoped he wouldn't say he lived remotely close to me.

But right next to me? Sharing a wall with me?

Our *bedrooms* sharing a wall?

And him looking like that?

If there were ever a time for me to pray to God for strength, it was now.

"I... I'm Imogene," I finally managed to say.

He stepped toward me, the breeze kicking up his scent. A mixture of earth, ocean, and something...masculine. He extended his hand, and I allowed him to wrap his fingers around mine. I wasn't short like my mama. But this man's hands were massive compared to mine.

It made me wonder what else was massive.

"It's nice to meet you, Imogene. I'm assuming you're new to San Diego?"

"What makes you say that?" I asked, attempting to push down my growing inappropriate thoughts.

"Your accent."

"By that rationale, I could say the same about you," I replied with a smirk.

He smiled, running a hand through his hair.

It made me want to run a hand through his hair, too.

"I've been here ten years. Originally from just outside

Madrid." He crossed his arms in front of his chest, his biceps stretching the arms of his shirt.

Lord, grant me strength.

"Yet you still have an accent," I retorted. "One could make the same argument for me."

"True." He slowly inched toward me. My pulse kicked up, breathing becoming uneven. "Then I noticed the plates on your car. Georgia."

"You've seen me in my car?"

"A beautiful girl driving a vintage Mustang Shelby Cobra?" He laughed under his breath. "Damn straight I've noticed." He gradually skated his eyes over my frame. "I've absolutely noticed."

I couldn't help the blush building on my cheeks. A part of me wanted to invite him back to my place, put an end to the dry spell I'd experienced lately.

But he was my neighbor. And I really liked this complex. It only took me twenty minutes to get to the ballpark and was a block from the beach. Plus, there was a bike path nearby where I could run in the morning without worrying about traffic. The last thing I wanted was to get involved with a neighbor.

I should at least live here a month or two before complicating my life more than it needed to be.

"Well…" I cleared my throat, stepping back. "It was nice to meet you, Mateo. I'm sure I'll see you around."

His pupils dilated. "I hope so, Imogene."

I gave him a sweet smile, then turned, continuing

toward the stairs. All the while, I swayed my hips a little more than normal, sensing the heat of his stare on me until I disappeared up the steps and along the balcony.

Picking up a few packages that had been left on my doorstep, I pulled my keys out of my bag and let myself into my townhome, kicking the door closed behind me. I dropped everything onto the dining table, then grabbed a knife to open the boxes.

As expected, they contained a bunch of stuff I'd ordered only a few days ago, yet had completely forgotten about. More things I needed to make this place a home. Frames for photos. Curtains. Even some kitchen gadgets that seemed like a good idea at the time.

Further proof it wasn't advisable to drink and online shop.

As I reached the final box, I paused, scrunching my brows at the familiar logo of Mama's bakery on Oahu. She hadn't said she was sending me anything. Maybe she wanted to surprise me with some of her macadamia nut cookies I couldn't get enough of.

I tore open the box, pulling out a smaller one that had the Hawaiian art on it she used to package the cookie gift sets she sold for people to take home as souvenirs.

As I lifted the lid, my mouth watered over the prospect of digging into some of these cookies.

But there were no cookies.

No tasty treats.

No sugary concoctions.

Instead, my eyes fell on a silver necklace with a heart-shaped charm.

I hitched a breath, dropping the box as if it held some sort of contagious disease, the necklace falling onto the kitchen floor beside it.

The End.

Thank you so much for reading Obsession! I hope you enjoyed your the final chapter of Lachlan and Julia's story! If you want one last taste of this amazing couple, sign up for my newsletter to get a bonus scene of their wedding day!

https://www.tkleighauthor.com/temptation-mailing-list

As you probably guessed, I have more tricks up my sleeve... Imogene's up next, so look for her story coming sometime in 2023 - THE SAINT TRILOGY.

He claims he's no hero. That he didn't come to my aid because of some altruistic desire to help. Instead, he did so because he wants something in return... *Me.*

Pre-order CRUEL SAINT today.
https://www.tkleighauthor.com/cruel-saint

I appreciate your help in spreading the word about my books. Please leave a review on your favorite book site.

cruel SAINT

The first time I saw him was during my morning run.
Later that day, I received the first gift.

The second time I saw him was at the coffee shop.
Later that day, I received the second gift.

And the third time I saw him was after leaving the gym.
Later that day, I was nearly abducted by a masked man and
killed.

I would have been if *he* hadn't intervened.

He claims he's no hero.
That he didn't come to my aid because of some altruistic
desire to help.
Instead, he did so because he wants something in return...

He wants me.

And what Gideon Saint wants, Gideon Saint gets.

Pre-order Imogene's story today.
https://www.tkleighauthor.com/cruel-saint

PLAYLIST

Fire - Barns Courtney
Your Hand Is Safe in Mine - Blush
Hold Me, Thrill Me, Kiss Me - She & Him
Show Me Where it Hurts - Skylar Grey
In the Air Tonight - Judith Hill
Wish We Had More Time - Alice Boman
The Silence - Manchester Orchestra
Don't Let Me Go - Cigarettes After Sex
Can You Hold Me - NF & Britt Nicole
Your Own Funeral - The Striped Bandits
The Beast - Old Caltone
Pull Me Under - Baseline Drift & Deadly Avenger
Need You Tonight - Welshly Arms
Uninvited - BELLSAINT
My Body Is A Cage - Peter Gabriel
Joke's On You - Charlotte Lawrence

Soft Dark Nothing - Lily Kershaw
Fall Into Me - Forest Blakk
More Than the Day Before - Cody Fry

ACKNOWLEDGMENTS

I did it! LOL. Finishing a book, especially the final installment in a series, is always a little bittersweet for me. I started working on this series last May. It was a bit slow-going, since I was in the middle of a cross-country move, so any intense work on this series didn't really take place until September once the kiddo was in school. Regardless, I've spent the past year of my life with these characters. Hell, more than a year, considering a lot of you were first introduced to Julia, Nick, and Imogene in the Possession Duet, which I published back in 2020.

I've always wanted to write something like this. While I've definitely written my fair share of romantic suspense, I've yet to really do anything where I was able to dive into the psyche of serial killers. It was nice to revisit a lot of the things I learned during my undergrad years when I studied criminology (which is actually what my undergraduate degree is in, funny enough.)

And as you probably saw in my note at the end of the book, there will be more books like this coming your way soon, so stay tuned for more information on Imogene's story!

But before I can move on to what's next, I wanted to take a minute to thank everyone who's played an integral part in my author journey.

First and foremost, a huge thanks to my husband, Stan, and daughter, Harper Leigh. I couldn't do this without their support.

To my wonderful PA and alpha reader, Melissa Crump — You're the best. I'd be lost without you.

To my fantastic beta readers — Lin, Sylvia, Stacy, and Vicky — thanks for reading and offering your feedback on this story. If people come at me with pitchforks because of the ending, I'm sending them your way. LOL.

To my amazing editor — Kim Young. Thank you so much for all the care you put into my manuscripts. I so appreciate you!

To my girl, A.D. Justice. This author business would suck without you in it. Thanks for being my partner in crime. My sister from another mister. My bestie.

To my admin team - Melissa, Vicky, Lea, Joelle. Thanks for keeping my reader group and Facebook page running. Love you ladies!

To my review team. Thanks for always taking the time to read and review my work. I'm so glad you took a trip to the dark side with me.

To my reader group. Thanks for being patient with my

lack of presence lately so I could get this story to you all. I'll be stopping by a lot more now. Promise.

And last but not least, a big thank you to YOU! My incredible readers. Whether you've just recently discovered me or have been along since the days of Mr. Burnham, I'm so grateful you took a chance on my stories.

I can't wait to share my next book with all of you. Thanks for your support!

Love & Peace,

~ T.K.

ABOUT THE AUTHOR

T.K. Leigh is a *USA Today* Bestselling author of romance ranging from fun and flirty to sexy and suspenseful.

Originally from New England, she now resides just outside of Raleigh with her husband, beautiful daughter, rescued special needs dog, and three cats. When she's not writing, she can be found training for her next marathon or chasing her daughter around the house.

facebook.com/tkleighauthor

instagram.com/tkleigh

tiktok.com/@tkleigh

bookbub.com/authors/t-k-leigh

pinterest.com/tkleighauthor